New Neighbors

Also by David Goldstein

Pearly Whites!

Random Tendencies

New Neighbors

By

David Goldstein

Prologue

For the last six centuries the Kevorkian Alliance had been struggling in what had become a determined, though at times patchwork effort to get their gigantic interstellar spaceship to a destination star system in one of the outer arms of the galaxy. The alliance critically needed the resources and conditions one of the planets in the system appeared it could provide. The patchwork aspect was mostly how the crew was holding the starship together.

When this journey had been approved, studies had shown there was an abundance of water, a primary ingredient they needed, and an ideal set of conditions; not too hot and not too cold. Plus, a heavy nitrogen/oxygen atmosphere made things all the better for the air breathing members of the alliance. Finally, it appeared there were no intelligent species present they would have to deal with as there were none of the telltale signs of technology emanating from the planet, and as every Kevorkian knew, it was tough to be truly intelligent like their alliance was. All of which meant they could thrive once again as a coalition of species if they could only get there.

Therefore, their research team proposed to the Kevorkian Grand Council that the Alliance establish a tentacle hold on this planet, the third from its white dwarf star, then fan out over time to modify some of the other nearby planets to further their regrowth, and finally, to other nearby star systems. This became formally known as "the grand relocation plan".

From a historical perspective, the Kevorkian alliance had taken millennia to establish their version of a peaceful, productive coexistence with each other but only after various upheavals, such as wars, genocides, petty grievances and the occasional destruction of one another at different times in their history. For eons, each species viewed the other as a petty, inferior implementation of backwards biology, and each were in love with materialism, commercialism, colonization, and were never in a sharing mood. Ultimately, they came together in their alliance but their home world star systems near the core of the galaxy were beyond rebuilding. In other words, they had destroyed their habitat before wising up.

Chapter 1

Premo Commander Partneon Yee'Lightmus watched Tachymus Yee'Lightmus-Be'AMoungus, (a distaff cousin, six times removed), supervise a hive of Handelorians who were weaving repairs to an outer hull section of the bridge of their ship. The substantial damage was the result of a large asteroid showing up from out of nowhere that had collided with their vessel. Of course, everyone knows that icy chunks of rock do not appear out of nowhere. It was simply that earlier damage to the ship over the last few centuries had left their object detection and collision systems in a rather dreary state of ineffectiveness and spare parts were getting tougher to come by all the time, one of the problems with being in the middle of an interstellar void. The damage this time had led to several crew members along with more of their most precious commodity, water, being sucked out into space before the breach could be temporarily sealed. Partneon was more bothered by loss of the precious fluid, (his species lived a submerged life dependent on the element), than the actual loss of crew.

The Handelorians were good at these kinds of repairs as their evolutionary conditions on Handelor, a small planetoid, had kept them highly exposed to the radiation of space, so they were fairly impervious to its effects and could execute this sort of work quite effectively. They were a land based species and only required a minimum of atmosphere as well, which was currently being provided via a temporary bubble-shield that enveloped their work area.

The average Handelorian was less than half a meter in size, whether up, down or sideways, with ten leglike appendages, giving them good maneuverability and balance. The weaving material their bodies generated was strongly based on their diet that consisted of various metals, titanium being one of their favorites and a smelly molasses-like substance they excreted from various orifices that made it all bond together.

With the repairs nearing completion, Tachymus swiveled one set of eyeballs to Partneon who bobbed his tentacles in approval. Pleased with the recognition, Tachymus, always scheming and climbing his own ladder of success, decided to show his command abilities. He barked a telepathic order at a Distainien that had arrived slightly ahead of schedule with his breakfast. The Distainien was expected to drop off his meal and then get off the bridge, which they did.

A moment later, a massive jolt shook the ship, setting off corridor alarms, (which still functioned annoyingly well). Hatchways slammed shut all over the vessel to limit loss of water as well as retaining as much of their dwindling maintenance and repair materials as possible. Tachymus turned to see what Partneon wanted to do only to find that his cousin had vanished, replaced by a new hull breach two meters in diameter, (a temporary energy shield had sealed the breach). No others were lost in this incident since they had otherwise vacated the area during the repairs.

Being in the bubble with the Handelorians was pure luck. Plus, he was outfitted in a suit that provided the water environment he normally swam about in that added extra protection from radiation. Tachymus realized he was officially now in command, which struck him as not such a bad deal.

Tachymus proudly assumed his new duties, all while officially mourning the loss of Partneon, (he dressed in a formal grieving headband of brilliant orange and yellow for a time). After a short interval, a modicum of normalcy returned. Tachymus, however, had no idea just how many more of these events the ship could handle, let alone the crew. During a conference with his direct reports where they reviewed the situation, their conclusion; they were just going to have to find out through raw experience what that limitation was.

As they neared their destination, Tachymus presided over a scheduled Grand Council meeting to review their plan, which called for an investigative survey mission to the new home world that was now being referred to as Kevorkian Central, or KevCen for short. Six highly experienced volunteers departed a week later in a high performance, limited seating spacecraft that had been kept well protected in lower sections of their starship. The craft would be able to reach KevCen in just three years. With a year on the planet, then the return, it would give everyone plenty of time to prepare for their arrival.

*

Four decades later, Tachymus was standing with his second in command, Xeon Piz'Alotamus. The technicians in front of them were tweaking controls on equipment designed to collect various wavelengths in the electromagnetic spectrum and display interesting data on a screen.

What they were now viewing was some sort of semi-intelligent species that already existed upon their destination home world. The transmission was in a primitive monochrome format with crackly audio that Kevorkian technicians were attempting to clean up. The subjects of this transmission appeared to be running around, making superfluous movements and gestures, hitting each other, causing general mayhem, and one of them was now spinning in circles on the floor while making whooping noises. Tachymus and Xeon watched the transmission in total fascination.

Hope of otherwise learning anything about what the planet would offer was gone, along with any belief the crew was on their way back. During this time, electromagnetic transmissions from Earth, limited to the speed of light, had started arriving regularly, first as radio wave transmissions, later with video, altering the original hypothesis for this trip—that no intelligent life was present, though this latest video seemed to support the original idea. At any rate, the

3

Kevorkians were now gathering as much of this data stream as they could.

One disturbing thing they had learned about the current dominant species of the planet: they were primitive and war-like, much as the Kevorkians had been in their ancient past. It was not a pleasant thing to contemplate, but with their own evolution as reference, it was not surprising. Of course, in their domination of non-alliance species, the Kevorkians were still pretty savage themselves, but that aspect of their culture was rarely brought up by the membership.

On the positive side: they were now inside the heliosphere of their new solar system. This lowered the amount of power required to insulate the ship from interstellar radiation. At their current speed they were now only a few weeks away from their new home. Finally, based on their scientist's analysis, the species, now known as humans, would be easily controlled as their technology was centuries behind the Kevorkians.

As they approached what humans referred to as "Earth", they observed a gas giant known as "Jupiter" where they paused to recharge their own heavily diminished fuel reserves with massive amounts of molecular hydrogen in the atmosphere of this planet. Once completed, they departed, however, the massive planet forced them to make some major course corrections due to gravitational effects of leaving orbit. An updated scan indicated they were now closer to the fourth planet's orbital position, (the one known as Mars), than Earth's. The decision was made to maneuver through the asteroid belt in front of them via the shortest path possible through the rocky barrier, then correct their course back towards Earth as they exited. Junior engineer, Atraxus Nee'Moy pointed out the opportunity to pause once again. She drove home the most critical aspect with the comment, "We can extract critical materials out of the belt that could be used to synthesize various badly needed components and we need them badly." The council concluded that the logic was sound and Atraxus was promoted to lead engineer, (after which, she proudly wore her insignia ring around one of her sensory antennae).

The ship paused just outside the belt as the crew deployed large solar arrays to conserve internal power. A mining operation commenced that went on for ten Earth years. With the ship now in a better structural state, they resumed the journey. Some of the ships sensor systems, however, were still marginal.

Exiting the belt and almost at their Mars turning point, an undetected and extremely large asteroid followed from behind—it had been put in motion by the gravitational mass of their own vessel. The rock had gained high velocity where it quickly caught up and slammed into the aft of their ship. The damage was extensive and severe. There was no way to patch it up. In fact, the ship was now in unsustainable condition to travel. Tachymus realized that they were out of options; the ship would be forced into crash landing on Mars.

At that moment, a group of Distainiens mutinied and tried to take over the ship, compounding an already severe and dangerous situation. Tachymus dispatched his security team, the rebellion was put down, with the errant Distainiens being summarily ousted from the Kevorkian Alliance as well as blown out some still functioning airlocks of the seriously damaged ship. The remaining Distainiens that had fought alongside the other member species against the mutineers were also ejected into the icy cold void, despite their loyalty—they had always been a second class member of the alliance, so nobody paid much attention to their frozen corpses floating away, as Tachymus and company were too busy trying to salvage their own survival.

It was all his crew, engineers, and scientists could do to get the ship onto the surface of the red planet and the remains sealed up as best they could. It was only when they were finally down on the surface that Tachymus got a report of a single Distainien that made their escape in a stolen H2O equipped spacecraft. The escapee had also taken extra fuel cells and rations. From the best his engineers could determine from their limited tracking logs, the craft had set course for Earth. Atraxus had advised that such a short range craft would likely never make it that far. After a brief meeting to discuss their limited options, Tachymus dismissed any further consideration of recovering the stolen craft and focused on what he considered more pressing issues, like staying alive. He made the command decision to conserve resources, so they placed the general ship-wide population into a stasis condition with plans to periodically reawaken himself, parts of his team and finally, key members of the Grand Council for periodic status assessments or if the ships systems alerted them of important changes.

*

The Distainien escapee, Kardeelia, piloted her spacecraft in as efficient a mode as possible to conserve energy reserves on her own journey to Earth. It was nip and tuck along the way, however, she made it.

She performed orbital scans for an ideal place to land. It looked like the best bet was what was called the Atlantic ocean, so she began her descent. She set down on the liquid surface, opened the hatches and the craft sank slowly under the waves. Within moments, Kardeelia was out swimming in the warm coastal waters, starving, looking for food. She latched onto a squid that reminded her of Tachymus, who she had never liked to begin with, and filled her stomach with relish. She then ran into a school of what humans referred to as dolphins. Yet, there was no doubt in her mind that these must be the same legendary group of Distainiens that had left her planet to escape the Kevorkian Alliance.

These Distainiens, however, had none of the alliance technology that existed today. They had come in crude ships and had been lost to history for millennia. They welcomed her and after she spent an hour learning their archaic language, they all were exchanging stories. Within a week the group realized she was leading them to better areas for food and pretty quickly she had a boyfriend she named Kardeel, (Distainien tradition was for the female to provide a name for the male that aligned with the family lineage), and that led to babies. The pod of Distainiens became a superpod and from there things progressed well enough as the group education level continued to climb.

As Kardeelia grew older, she would spend evenings telling stories of what had happened to their people after this group had left their old star system, her time in the Kevorkian Alliance. Bigotry was still in the thought processes of many of the species of the Alliance, reinforcing why they had left long ago.

Kardeelia assured them that for now, the Alliance was stuck a full planet away with a wrecked starship that had crashed on the surface, in fact, the Kevorkians may not have survived. All seemed well enough, so they focused on the present. They spent time and resources going through the spacecraft remains and found that the technology could be utilized for their good, but they also knew they had to keep this technology secret as there was another species on this very planet that had not treated them any better than the Kevorkians. Kardeelia began cataloging information on this bunch, officially classified as Homo Sapiens.

Chapter 2

Since the year 2020, Stieg Daftmann had been driving anyone working for him relentlessly for over three decades to get his Mars colony established, (he was, as he constantly reminded himself, a visionary trillionaire). It had been a hell of a grind, and even when all the sore losers he kept banning from Stieglandia, (his personal social media website), complained that his ideas were impractical, he ignored any negative analysis, and carried on, knowing, as usual, he was always right.

Hell, he figured he had to press on. The Earth was only a short spurt away from bursting into flames, and total morons were in charge. He had at times funded these same morons with campaign contributions. He played a chess game of keeping these small time idiots busy opposing each other, which left them too preoccupied to focus on his own activities.

And now, finally, all of his good efforts were coming together in the big payoff. The small fleet of five ships, (each one funded by the other trillionaires who had decided it was time for them to get the hell out of Dodge), had established orbit around their new home the day before and he had thrown what he referred to as "a big ass party" to celebrate their arrival. All the ships had been tethered together to allow everybody to form dance lines through the interconnects, sample each other's buffets, and get mentally ready for today's mission—landing on Mars and planting the "Daft flag" in the Martian soil.

Over the past half century as various environmental, social, political and cultural wars came to a head, in no small part due to Stieg's own efforts to divide and conquer a planet he was planning on abandoning, he had decided that since he had pumped his own billions into what he called "Propel us to Planet Utopia", (PUTPUT for short), he was determined that Mars was going to be his own personal chunk of real estate.

Therefore, on this fine Martian morning, he scurried to the bridge to oversee the landings of the other four spacecraft, each of which had a three kilometer radius of designated territory. As each ship landed, it would be positioned at fixed intervals in a circular pattern. His ship would then descend from orbit to provide a literal and physical pivotal center for all activities to come.

All had gone well with the first four ships, and now it was time to bring in DaftFive, as was emblazoned on the hull of his ship in scrolling psychedelic playfulness, (his personal design, it should be noted).

He took his seat in his fancy handwoven silk chair, grimaced at the spike of pain in his back from a degrading spinal column, (he was getting old after all), though he already calculated that the reduced gravity of Mars would help his condition. He was now positioned. Stieg exclaimed, "Bring her in Spaceman Richards! We've got a bunch of people down there that can't wait for what happens next!"

Spaceman Richards sat at the helm, somewhat severely hung over, but having been up for a couple hours now, was able to respond with a smart "Aye, aye Captain!", (and without slurring his words). His hands flew over the controls with practiced ease, having performed this routine over two hundred times in a simulator, (Stieg had insisted and Richards had complied so as to keep his job).

With the descent to the planet's surface now underway, Stieg turned to his science officer, Alicia Fairfax, and demanded status on atmospheric conditions, (on a planet with marginal atmosphere that could get seven times colder than freezing water and was subject to pretty spectacular dust storms). With the words barely out of his mouth, DaftFive lurched violently to port, (well, Stieg thought it was to port—he still had a hard time sorting out starboard, port, aft, all that "sailor shit" as he often referred to it).

Still, he had to appear in control, though his back pain spiked from the sudden shock. With the ship beginning to enter a spin, he hollered, "Hard reverse to starboard Richards!!"

Spaceman Richards, now getting dizzy with the induced spin piling onto his pre-existing alcoholic discombobulation, hollered back, "Aye, Sir!" He hit the thrusters wide open, lost his grip due to the ship's fierce response, then slid out of his seat to the deck as the ship began to revolve even more violently.

Hanging onto her seatback, feet in the air, Fairfax hollered, "Wrong fucking way moron!"

Both Stieg and Spaceman Richards looked at Fairfax, then each other, not sure who the moron was that the science officer was referring to. Spaceman Richards was quite out of sorts at this point and upchucked last night's extravagant dinner as he executed a high speed roll into a bulkhead. Science Officer Fairfax wound up headfirst in the view screen, the splatter obscuring the view of their now out of control descent.

So, Stieg, once again faced a big challenge, and this time, truly all on his own, crawled to the helm, aching back and all, and strapped himself in. He looked at the controls, which he was not at all familiar with, since this was pedestrian helmsman shit way below his paygrade, and said, "What the fuck over." He tried a few movements on the only thing that looked familiar, (a joystick). Which led to the spin situation getting rapidly worse. Cursing aloud, he felt himself losing consciousness.

*

Standing on a Martian hillside overlooking the valley below where the other ships had landed, and outfitted in a fancy gold plated spacesuit, multi-trillionaire Barry Brazos smiled as he watched the uncontrolled descent of DaftFive.

Brazos had achieved great wealth somewhat more honestly than Stieg, as these things go with trillionaires, though he had disrupted numerous retail industries and destroyed a vast number of jobs in the process.

None of that mattered to him, he had achieved his own personal goals of traveling to another planet. It was something he had wanted to do since he was a young boy and had tirelessly read and watched every science fiction tale that he could find about space travel.

On the mischief side of things, his minions had done their handywork during last night's party on Stieg Daftmann's ship as Stieg's own crew got booze hammered. For Brazos, it was now just a matter of enjoying the rather expensive fireworks display.

He was not disappointed. DaftFive augered in pretty much dead center on its landing spot, detonating on impact. A shockwave headed out in all directions from the crash, enveloping the other vessels, but doing little damage to them as Barry had made sure the circle of ships was well outside any area of serious destruction, and each had their protective ablative armor activated. Satisfied, he smiled while looking at the brand new crater Stieg had just created, thinking, *now, that's really smokin' dude!*

He then headed back down the slope towards his own ship, DaftOne, soon to be relabeled, the thought of which made him pick up his pace.

It was then that a large smoldering debris fragment of DaftFive came whipping across the low gravity Martian landscape and unceremoniously decapitated multi-trillionaire Barry Brazos.

*

Which led directly to a short, poorly attended, and entirely tear free memorial service.. Lengthy eulogies were discouraged. Shortly after the service, the three remaining trillionaires, Jesmyn Welch, Angela Koutouki, and Vinay Vasudev, formed the first government on Mars. In reality, it was just another new corporation that would become infamous—Artificial Intelligence Guaranteed Solutions, or AIGS. At Jesmyn's insistence, a clause was added to the corporate

11

charter that if any one of them were to die, their assets would become the property of the corporation.

While the other two surviving trillionaires were as suspicious of her as she was of them, it appealed to their greed and to the belief that each had the superior security organization watching out for their own wellbeing—that the recent loss of two members had no impact on their opinion of themselves was indicative of things to come.

After a group huddle, they released a media blurb back to Earth. The mission statement of AIGS? *Better ideas through wiser algorithms!* Or BITWA as they all liked to chime back and forth to each other.

Chapter 3

Not long after the formation of AIGS, Jesmyn declared she had found the legal documents that left the entire fortunes and estates for Stieg Daftmann and Barry Brazos to the corporation, which many people found to be a fascinating coincidence, including what remained of the Daftmann and Brazos families back on Earth, who immediately hired expensive lawyers and told their story on the Solarspere and tabloid media, which went viral with bad press for AIGS for about a week or so.

On the AIGS side, the three partners handed the documents to their legal team and made sure that they funded the hell out of them, along with any necessary bribe takers, to ensure they held onto the two massive fortunes, though there was finally an accommodation of a lavish lifestyle stipend to each of the two surviving families that included a clause that they retract their earlier "spurious and defaming claims" and support AIGS in all its endeavors into perpetuity. The families finally capitulated as none were in the mood to work for a living, and things were going poorly on the legal front.

*

Two years later, Vinay Vasudev was overseeing a technology demonstration that was being held at their new Martian orbital spacecraft manufacturing facility, where AIGS planned to build a line of luxury cruise ship spacecraft intended for the more monied class of folks back on the now overheated Earth. The plan—for these customers to enjoy incredible scenic voyages around the solar system and to literally forget about their earthly cares.

Surrounded by vast arrays of the latest "SuperDuperQuantumPuters", (an AIGS brand name), that were running state-of-the-art company developed AI, Vinay was busy expounding on their progress, "This will be solar system changing technology!" The session was being transmitted live to an exclusive group of potential wealthy investors back on Earth, so he was in full sales mode. It was then that an asteroid fragment, roughly the size of a softball, pierced both the hull of the production facility and Vinay's chest. The station was rapidly patched up to restore atmosphere, but Vinay was beyond repair. At least that was what was on the official death certificate.

This led to an acceleration of infighting. Accusations by Angela that Jesmyn had somehow arranged for an accidental asteroid impact. Jesmyn countered with allegations that Angela seemed well informed about the matter of redirecting asteroids, and perhaps it was she who arranged for Vinay's sudden, tragic, and untimely ending, (Jesmyn even managed to shed a tear during her video streamed statement). After several months of back and forth vitriol, with each woman beefing up their personal security and rancor, they reached an acrimonious accord; that Angela would take her half of the proceeds from AIGS with her and return to Earth. This would leave Jesmyn as the exclusive owner of AIGS and Mars.

Once back on Earth and with many of the remaining high end trillionaires looking for new high profit investment opportunities, Angela created her own new corporation by selling off a large share of the stock from AIGS she had been awarded in the previous settlement. The new company was named Trans Genetic Intra Fusing with the trading symbol, TGIF. Later posting on the Solarspere, Jesmyn stated the name was small-town, corny and dumb.

From that point forward, the two women became even more bitter personal as well as corporate rivals. The phrase of the day Angela insisted her employees utilize, (sort of like a pledge of allegiance), was "AIGS Sucks Donkey Dicks!" Which offended a lot of donkeys.

Chapter 4

As great a sales pitch as it was when Stieg had sold Jesmyn on the idea of travelling out and building a new empire on the fourth orb orbiting the sun, after her arrival there, it rapidly became evident to her that the red planet was not especially friendly to human life that had evolved on Earth. Floating in the middle of her giant jacuzzi that was situated in one of the orbital arms of her ship along with her current crop of "personal assistants", she was lost in thought as she realized that living on the surface of Mars was problematic at best. Low gravity symptoms in personnel presented themselves all the time now and were debilitating to her employees. Problems included loss of muscle mass, bulging eyes, lengthening bones, and loss of bone density, to name just a few impediments to healthy living. This forced Jesmyn into expending valuable financial resources to periodically shuttle employees back and forth between the surface and orbiting AIGS medical ships, which would spin these employees around in circles in quarters built around the ship's outer sections to produce an Earth equivalent gravity. These personnel were then subjected to some marginal therapy regimens that a highly paid contract medical staff had designed and implemented, with little success, (another annoying cash outlay).

This dilemma ultimately led to Jesmyn building a "retirement" community out near one of Jupiter's moons for employees that were nearly kaput and could not go back to Earth as that would have been bad publicity for AIGS. Which spurred the need for new talent from Earth, which again was another large cost driven by elaborate recruiting drives, high dollar salaries, relocation packages, etc. This merry-go-round dilemma was long term unacceptable to Jesmyn.

Another problematic situation was water. She had a crew of scientists and engineers working on extracting the liquid from its

15

frozen state since temperatures on Mars were far from balmy. The poles were an obvious place to start but it appeared there was also frozen water under the planet's surface. That project was every bit as important, in her mind, as the low gravity situation. They drilled some sample cores and found water, but getting the frozen stuff up to the surface was problematic.

Today, with no answers coming her way, she finally said, "Well, hell, I need some lunch." The assistants carefully maneuvered her to the stairsteps that led out of the jacuzzi, where she grabbed a handrail and climbed onto the tiled floor. Once she was toweled off by two other women waiting for her, she strolled to a cherrywood table situated by a large viewport where she could glare at the red planet as it periodically passed in and out of view.

*

Tachymus had been roused from his stasis condition to meet with his engineering team. His awakening had not been driven by their normal scheduled update, but instead by external sensors that had begun detecting unnatural sounds and vibrations. Also, the sensors were recording unidentified communication signals. Lead engineer Atraxus Nee'Moy was concluding her presentation with, "We have determined that this phenomenon is actually the humans we identified previously that have arrived here from our original destination. They are performing activities on the planet's surface as well as having orbital spacecraft that are shuttling people and supplies back and forth. The question is, should we reach out to them?"

Xeon opined, "I would advise against it. Humans are primitive idiots, to say the least, spaceships or not. Have any spun around in circles on the floor? That is rather humorous to watch."

Waggling a tentacle, Tachymus countered, "Yet, they are here now, dealing with what the engineering team has determined to be this species' very first "arrival on an inhospitable planet" experience. We should monitor them for issues we know they will experience."

Atraxus said, "Problems have already started."

16

Xeon said, "Care to elaborate?"

Atraxus fluttered a couple of her antennae in agitation at Xeon's remark, but then replied, "It seems this is a low gravity environment for humans which makes sense, since this planet is a fraction of the size and mass of where they evolved, and it is causing the usual problems. Plus, the atmosphere of the planet leaves them having to suit up to go outside their crude facilities and finally, they are finding water to be a most valuable and scarce commodity. They are heavily recycling the liquid, also trying to mine what is here, but have to bring more in from Earth. The drilling effort is quite logical, though they lack the proper technology to extract what they need at this point."

Tachymus waggled his tentacles in understanding. He then said, "So, here is what I think will benefit our situation the best. It is not an overnight approach but will work over time." The senior crew did their equivalent of a suspenseful pause, waiting for what came next. Tachymus, in an amused tone, continued, "Never meant to create so much anticipation. Alright then, here is my idea. We leak technology to certain humans in key positions."

Atraxus asked, "Such as?"

"An artificial gravity environment for starters, tuned for them to Earth standards. Then some tech for water extraction. It would allow humans to be more focused on one of the very things we need as well as themselves. We do this and get them to focus on these efforts; it will lead directly to us being able to resurrect our own ship. We can manipulate their unsuspecting assistance in the short run by making them a labor force, though I am in total agreement with Xeon the humans need to be left in the dark about our existence."

Xeon queried, "How do we get these technologies to them then?"

Tachymus said, "We leak to key individuals that will help us get back up and running. It has to be done within their technology so as not to arouse suspicion about the source. Since so many members of this species are ambition and greed driven, if we choose our mark carefully, this should work." An enthusiastic waggle of body extremities followed as the team came together on the plan.

*

A week later, Jesmyn was holding her senior staff meeting, demanding solutions to current problems. She said, "So, anything new? I mean, fucking… *anything?*"

A lead physicist named Bart Woodward, who had only arrived a week ago as replacement for the previous department head, (who was heading off to "retirement" near Jupiter), excitedly waved a hand in the air as he said, "I have what might be a workable theory for an artificial gravity solution!"

At this bit of news, Jesmyn perked up and demanded, "Elaborate!"

With a self-satisfied grin, Bart dived into the theory, writing out equations, expounding on power needs, what sort of tech they would have to develop, for which he had plenty of detail. Soon, he had everyone looking blankly in his direction as he became increasingly more incomprehensible.

Despite her own lack of scientific background, Jesmyn was elated at this great news and declared, "Bart, get your team together, you are fully funded to take this from theory to reality. And hell, where did you come up with this fabulous stuff?"

Bart, without a pause, unashamedly lied, "Been working on it for the last few years even before you offered me this great position." The reality was that Bart had found an obscure, primitive website that popped up during a search he made a week earlier. The site appeared to contain some lost scientific papers that Albert Einstein had written towards the end of his life in Princeton, New Jersey. The papers had been scanned and left on the old website back on Earth. He never bothered to wonder how no one found this before, but he was more than capable of downloading the documents. After realizing this tech dump was the real deal, he was well prepared to take credit, and not for one moment wondering how Einstein would have theorized this sort of integration of his theories with technology during the era of the vacuum tube.

Jesmyn nodded and said, "Woodward, consider yourself promoted to full director! Now, as we are in a hurry around here, get your ass busy!"

*

Pi'l Cardimus was spying on an alleged grand moment in human history that was about to take place—the artificial gravity project that Bart Woodward had led. They were about to test the prototype gravity field generator. Pi'l's assignment was to keep close tabs on this team's progress. He welcomed the opportunity to get away on occasion from the dilapidated starship environment that all the Kevorkians were currently stuck in.

Though this first iteration of artificial gravity was primitive, it was a beginning and from what he had observed, humans did seem capable of gradually refining their work, given enough time, people, money and a shitpot full of parts. He had dutifully provided update reports back to Tachymus, Xeon and Atraxus. They were quite pleased with the progress as well as receiving solid confirmation that this approach to Kevorkian resurrection was proceeding as planned.

Sudden vibrations emanating from the artificial gravity field generator reached Pi'l, and after a few moments, space suited scientists were moving known objects with precisely recorded Earth based weight onto a large scale in the center of the platform. Listening to the communications going on, they excitedly discussed that the scale was now indicating the various objects were at eighty five percent of Earth standard weight rather than the thirty eight percent Martian standard.

Bart Woodward, who was the only member of his team willing to stand immediately next to the scale, demand more power. The readouts moved to ninety percent, though the vibrations coming from the field generator were now a troubling fifty percent more intense. Senior team member, Nancy Ramone, insisted it was a good time to shut down this first run as she, along with other team members, relocated a safe distance away from the platform.

Bart Woodward, caught up in his own visions of success and large bonuses, insisted they notch it up and see if they could get ninety five percent. They got to ninety four when their small fusion reactor gave up the ghost and detonated, obliterating the platform and Bart. Pi'l dutifully reported the success and the fatal overexuberance of the deceased lead scientist to Kevorkian senior command.

*

A bit later the same day as Bart's parting, Nancy Ramone, was promoted into his old role and told by Jesmyn that she was receiving a raise, the bonus that would have been Bart's, and the same advice that her predecessor had received—to get her ass moving. Her goal; achieving a production level quality artificial gravity platform, the first utilization to be incorporated into the foundation of Jesmyn's newly scheduled palatial mansion.

From all accounts and appearances, Nancy did quite well, sorting out problems and finalizing this first phase of making the planet a better place for humans to live. She also began to work out all sorts of handy technologies, things like an artificial atmosphere, to go with the gravity field. In meetings, she simply declared she was feeling inspired and was working hard, though like her predecessor, certain invaluable bits of handy data kept showing up when she would be frantically searching for information. So, with her team of scientists and engineers doing her bidding, she came up with the "envirofield".

The envirofield produced gravity, a proper Earth quality atmosphere and temperatures. She then got to work on a water extraction technology that could store and distribute the liquid around the planet.

Besides Jesmyn's newly erected mansion, over time, the revolutionary technology was deployed for corporate facilities and individual homes. It worked wonders and shortly after, Nancy announced in a staff meeting that she wanted to file for patents under her name. Jesmyn, from all outward appearances, seemed agreeable to the patent idea. A couple of days later, she then offered that Nancy take a company sponsored getaway on Jesmyn's personal star yacht spacecraft. Sadly, that spacecraft unexpectedly malfunctioned, leaving Nancy dead and unpatented, though the rest of her science team that had boarded a less expensive ship were unscathed, or so went the official AIGS announcement of her untimely loss to the corporation.

Chapter 5

Back on Earth, Angela Koutouki was in contrarian mode—the attitude that she was positive had led her to trillionaire success as well as illusions of grandeur. Like the rest of the small group of financially overstuffed elite, she was aware of the general degraded planetary circumstances driven by climate change and human excess. Situation Dire was the best descriptive but one she generally avoided thinking about. It was more about how to find a way to grab ahold of more wealth.

So, today, she was explaining to Clive Barter, her head attorney, what was going through her head. She said "I can invest in whatever suits me, and I make money. Just look at Solarspere after pumping in just a few million! So many posts these days! Billions of members incessantly predicted each other's doom and gloom endings on an hourly if not second to second basis. Social media addiction is now at ninety five percent and sales are highly profitable due to our "Sure Survival" products line we spin in front of these clowns!"

Clive nodded agreeably and replied, "You've got them on the ropes!"

She nodded at the man's wisdom and continued, "And now with my newly formed biotech division of TGIF, we've hired loads of genetic scientists, implementation engineers, project managers, and a crew of shark-like lawyers that will report to you, and finally a first class marketing and sales staff."

Clive replied, "Update on that. The latter group has paid out significant bribes to various government officials around the planet. We have those corrupto's total cooperation in TGIF endeavors. Daily announcements of progress are being fired out to Solarspere followers. Revenue is soaring." Again, Angela nodded at the scope of her genius. Clive, however, was peering around for some whisky to soothe his jittery nerves. Seeing his darting eyes and knowing that booze was a respite for the man, Angela said, "Pour one for each of us Mr. Barter! Let's celebrate!"

While indulging in their drinks, she asked, "So, what do you think about my most promising idea of Hybrid human beings?" She then raised her glass and took a sip as she awaited his reply.

Clive dutifully replied, "I think it's a grand scheme. Just as you pointed out before, we very well might need alternatives to our current form as the planet becomes more hostile. And the team has lots of ideas they are trying out, such as a human/bear, a human/scorpion, though nobody thought that such a critter would be all that pretty in the last meeting, and finally, a human/dolphin combo.

That last hybrid combo caught Angela's attention. She said, "As talks are underway in the United States to build underwater cities, this variant could be very useful. And the buildout of such places looks like a very lucrative contract for TGIF. I directed our folks to set up our main laboratory outside Washington D.C. The staff has commenced with splicing and dicing DNA."

Clive nodded as he nervously swigged his drink and said, "Exciting!"

A lot of strangeness emerged out of the early efforts, for instance, a dolphin with a full head of blond, curly hair, another with a beard, both otherwise normal dolphin in appearance. Little of the human aspect was showing up. But since the federal government was funding the project, the experiments continued. The creatures were quite intelligent, and the scientists attributed that ability to the idea that they must have gotten human DNA in their brains.

*

At the same time, Angela decided to develop technology to sell to coastal areas dealing poorly with sea level rise. While some areas had begun building actual concrete and steel sea walls, such as in New York City, it seemed to her what was needed was a low budget effort,

23

which led to energy based reactive sea shields that could be deployed along coastal areas, and as it turned out, was one of the very last projects she got funded by the United States.

The shield design consisted of two large sheets of plexiglass that were situated at specified distances from the shoreline, each coated with a conductive material and an electrical field to keep them charged and separated. The sheets could be bonded together to form any length and height of wall as needed. Of course, this led to making lots of plastics from oil and it was also power intensive, (TGIF used nuclear reactors to power portable generators stationed along the shield walls at fixed intervals). Water was then pumped out from the land side over the shield into the ocean to lower the amount reaching the shore.

While the loss of U.S. federal spending was a setback to revenue generation, once perfected, Angela continued having the hybrids produced for cheap labor on various ocean-based projects of her own. She came up with a name—hybrids were called "Dolphmaniens". The sea wall projects were first assembled and maintained by the hybrids but later by cheaper SeaBots, so most Dolphmaniens were abandoned to fend for themselves as they were hard to manage. Turns out, they were not as dumb as humans assumed.

*

The world wobbled along for a time. Then the year 2070 collapse of nations worldwide was, as expected, beyond dramatic and depending on where one lived, violent and bloody. Angela had been getting a lot of reports from her contacts throughout different countries that things had been getting more fragile by the day. The United States in particular was her biggest worry, though not so much about what would be dire circumstances for everyday people. In a meeting with her senior staff, she pontificated, "This meeting is more about what will happen to currency, corporations, and the wealthy.

The situation demands action which I have taken. Time for the big showdown!"

That same day, a meeting was held with all of the remaining larger corporations bowing to the wishes of their masters, i.e., the obscenely wealthy. There was no doubt now that TGIF was *the* largest corporation on the planet, so Angela led a summit. The CEOs for the entire Fortune 82, (things had gotten out of hand with mergers and acquisitions in the last two decades), were all present.

Angela began with, "Welcome. You have all been briefed on the situation, your board members and controlling ownership are also aware, as are all the other financial entities on this call. To be blunt, things are about to go financially south on the planet. I have a plan to mitigate that exposure to all of our wealth." The CEOs all sat silently, their directives from their governing boards being to cooperate or plan on long term unemployment. She continued, "You are all now subsidiaries of TGIF. The documents are there for all to sign." Angela then smiled as she surveyed their expressions, and continued, "And the biggest news is our brand new currency will be adopted globally due to TGIF's benevolent efforts to protect the economy. I coined the term, forgive the pun, for the new currency— the Cordolar! Unlike the flop that was crypto, all business and corporations will recognize it and that will require governments worldwide to use it as well. It will ensure our markets and businesses continue unimpeded!"

A round of applause went up on the call. Once it died down, Angela said, "I now bring in a guest speaker."

Jesmyn Welch appeared. Angela nodded as she said, "AIGS has agreed to adopt the Cordolar as well. Unlike the rest of you, AIGS will remain its own sovereign corporation with its own subsidiaries, but just like us, needs a solid currency that works between planets." Applause again went up around the room.

Jesmyn was clapping as well. She then provided her own endorsement, "This is definitely a historic day. AIGS will abide by all the new corporate rules pertaining to Cordolar. We will, of course, remain fierce competitors, but on this particularly important subject of our mutual interests in a strong currency for the solar system, we are in the firmest of agreement!" There was one last round of applause as both Angela and Jesmyn waved and smiled. The call ended moments later.

There was an unspoken impact of this sea change. Wealth management corporations, investment banks and especially hedge funds all failed as the entire mechanism they used to drive their business models sputtered to a stop. The trillionaire class was allowed to transition eighty percent of their wealth to the new currency— despite grumbling, they did it, as they were out of options.

The impact of this monetary coup devastated the remaining national currencies. This kicked off another round of government implosions around the world, such as the European Union, (which most members rejoined after converting to the Cordolar). Great Britain used the opportunity to return to this new EU2, as it was called with Canada following suit. Many other economically distressed countries in central and south America as well as Africa slid into deep economic depressions until TGIF rescued them after forcing their leadership onboard with the new currency.

In the former United States, smaller cities and towns became nothing more than medieval era city-states scrabbling for survival, though more frequently, these places wound up being abandoned all together as people went looking for some sort of work and economic survival. Others, such as the Northwestern Alliance that comprised New York state and other locations to the north such as Boston and then over to Chicago, St. Louis, and Kansas City, managed as their economies moved into lockstep with TGIF.

Southern states, especially the southeast, fared poorly. Military installations that drove a large share of their economy shuttered and were looted by local militias. At first, these modern day Bolsheviks refused to go along with the Cordolar. A series of assassinations by

TGIF's secret security organization solved that issue. The Cordolar turned out to be a world changing idea, or as some wayward economists noted, better than no idea. Soon, profits were again on the rise for the remaining trillionaires that had jumped onboard the TGIF train.

*

At the same time global financial chaos occurred on Earth, Tachymus and Xeon were pulsing their antennae nervously over the latest intel. Much of what they had wanted to accomplish in helping the Mars based humans get to where they would ultimately assist the Kevorkians had gone well if not as fast as desired, partly because humans kept veering off on totally unnecessary tangents.

The latest distraction—an unnecessary space weapons system. Atraxus had stated it was clearly going to be a total waste of time, resources, and effort. The council decided to make it painfully obvious to the humans that there were better things to do.

Xeon said, "We've got to put an end to this project quickly. But how?"

Atraxus replied, "Well, one way would be to make the weapon unfriendly to its creators."

"How would we do that?"

Atraxus said, "Every hear of chaos theory?" Which of course they all had, it was a core tenant of the Kevorkians that chaos was what they had ultimately gotten under control which allowed them to create their alliance.

Tachymus asked, "So, we are going to introduce a little bit of chaos?"

*

It was not long after that, while Harry Tan was bragging about progress on a call with Jesmyn about how well everything was going, that the weapons project came to a hasty, blood splattered end. Harry, the project leader, was suddenly chopped in half by one of the

27

suddenly rogue weapons. His lab was then sawn up into little bite size chunks. Over five hundred prototypes were now out in the Martian wild creating occasional havoc.

Chapter 6

Fifteen years later, engineer second class Ben Stevens was slogging toward a deadline for stability upgrades for the new "econodrive" line that AIGS had begun working on six weeks earlier. The econodrive was purportedly developed to revolutionize interplanetary travel as a low cost solution. So far, the main thing the product did was keep Ben employed. Where one would go with such a drive was not really the point when the idea was conceived as there were no pleasant destinations once one departed from either Earth or Mars. There were the cruise liner spaceships that AIGS had built and managed, sending rich people around the solar system for luxury appointed ooh and ahh sightseeing trips, but for the average family looking for a weekend getaway, space travel was still highly problematic.

Also, the econodrive line was a last minute, throw it over the virtual fence sort of project, (since real fences did not exist on Mars), by the engineering architecture team that operated as some sort of independent, god-like bunch up on the moon Deimos, though Ben liked to refer to the smoldering rock as demontown. Deimos was small, desolate, atmosphere free, *and* radiation scorched by the sun, to name just a few problems, (unless you were well shielded and made of quantum computers).

So, Ben thought, *Why not sell cheap ass products for solar system travel?* At least that was what Jesmyn Welch's perspective on it all appeared to be. As the sole original AIGS founder, (according to her current version of history), and now with her body equipped with a lot of AIGS branded implants and upgrades the company liked to promote, she remained at the top of the corporate AIGS ladder thirty two years in, even if she was replete with AI circuitry and the latest bio engineered components. Externally, she looked exactly as she had upon arrival on Mars decades earlier. Her deeply tanned skin displayed no wrinkles or sags anywhere on her posterior. Which of her upgrades had boosted her longevity and physical appearance was a well-kept corporate secret unless you could afford them yourself and signed a non-disclosure customer service agreement tantamount to a death threat if one revealed being upgraded themselves, but for sure, she was now pushing a hundred plus years.

As to Ben's recently required involvement in the econodrive project, it had become mandatory when the product came out of the design lab in just six days, (a real timeframe would have been twice as long on something this complex). It then wound up being handed over to the production systems group with a hearty, "Voila!" and no oversight.

A few days later, the first prototype off the production line detonated, (fortunately while in an unmanned orbital test burn), in a rather spectacular display of thermonuclear largess during the initial powerup phase.

Therefore, during this early morning, diatribe laced meeting, Ben had to step away to get his blood pressure under control. Three hours into the briefing that the vice president of engineering standards had stuck on his schedule were the two adversaries—production, who built stuff, and architecture, who allegedly designed stuff. The findings versus reality that Ben had tested in the online lab, along with extensive AI simulations after the explosion were inconclusive as to who was at fault for the prototype's "new sun" fiasco.

Production vice president Barney Renfro insisted" We followed your fucking design to the fucking letter!"

Architecture's boss, Wendy Twin asked, "Are you fucking sure Barney? I mean, it is complicated to understand. You might have gotten… confused." Barney turned red-faced. Wendy had no problem letting people know that she considered Barney and his people to be an incompetent bunch who could not build a functioning toilet, let alone a space drive.

Ben's group, engineering standards, had little to say during the meeting, preferring not to be drawn into the argument since, as usual, they had not reviewed the new designs for the typical flaws and bugs that always manifested themselves before production did their thing, which left Ben's group open to criticism since the standards group was under architecture and expected to provide all sorts of fixes that architecture had never considered. Blame allocation was in full burn—nothing about the actual design was under review.

Ben sighed, his head throbbing a bit from all the negative gusto of the conversation. He muted his audio implant and stepped over to grab an espresso from his beverage dispenser then strolled over and gazed out his port view of the Red Dust Valley, an Aldous Huxley trust real estate development project. The view was obscured today by a severe dust storm outside the neighborhood's shields, so he shifted his gaze then relaxed as he looked admiringly at the new Lethbon Obscura he had purchased less than a month ago, while it bobbed in its antigrav field next to his home.

Ben reflected that the Lethbon was, for him, a milestone of achievement in his life. As a boy back on Earth growing up in Kansas City, he was not particularly good at things his demanding father had insisted he should excel at. The old man had harped constantly about Ben's inability to catch, field, or hit a baseball, as well as his slow times running from base to base. At one point in this continuous harangue of Ben's incompetence, his father had insisted that his son be a catcher, declaring that if the boy could catch a pitch, he would then be able to grab onto any other ball coming his way. Ben wound up being pelted consistently with fast balls, curves and change ups, though his mitt showed little wear.

Next came his academic underachievement. Ben had sweated through an engineering degree. Here again, his father had wanted an Einstein but often lamented about Ben's grade point average during extensive Canadian whiskey laced hours on the family patio with other men in the neighborhood. It all grated on him as a young man. He pushed himself in any possible way he could to keep his father's wheedling to a minimum and at one point, he finally exclaimed "Not your problem old man! Fuck off!" It was pretty much the end of their relationship. After college, Ben had wanted to be as far away as possible from his familial nemesis, so when he got the Mars job offer, he accepted it without hesitation.

An intense flash directly above the valley, thirty kilometers out, pulled him out of his slippery slope reverie. Directly to the north of Ben's upper end home loaded with high tech, and just outside the Red Dust Vally Homeowners Association property limits that he resided in, was a hillbilly inspired relic that seemed to attract hillbilly renters with hillbilly budgets like a magnet. Poorly maintained, it had brought the overall valley's modern esthetics, (and property values), down repeatedly. There were rumors that it had been towed in from the asteroid belt where apparently, space hillbillies had once lived in it. In fact, it was one of Jesmyn's early facilities built out by Jupiter that AIGS had sent physically degraded employees to die once their usefulness had expired on Mars. It had gotten towed back to reduce AIGS expenses for housing low paid employees. The owner had paid a monthly charge to have the HOA extend their shield perimeter to include the place. That person had ultimately left it for sale when they moved out near a Neptune colony after accepting a job with TGIF. It ultimately sold, though Ben had no idea who the new owner was.

The earlier flash led to a transport that stopped in front of Hillbillyville. The vessel was like nothing he had ever seen before in the neighborhood, i.e., a clunker.

A catwalk enveloped in an envirofield, emerged from the craft and attached itself to Hillbillyville. What initially emerged from the moving transport looked depressingly suited to occupying the place. Ben sagged and watched in dismay as four shabbily maintained robotic furniture movers emerged. He thought he could smell burnt circuitry, which would have been quite a feat in the thin Martian atmosphere. It was then that a human passenger emerged from the craft.

A woman. Black haired, blue eyed, thick, sexy eyebrows, and a really good tan. She had a large carryon bag in tow as she walked across the temporary bridge extending from the moving craft to the house. Ben could not take his eyes off of her. She saw him as well and smiled and waved at him. He waved back. The bridge withdrew as the woman finished her crossing.

Ben was now perplexed. What was he to do? Call the homeowner association and complain or go next door and introduce himself. He decided to welcome her. After extending his envirofield to her place, he rang the doorbell. She answered, and he stumbled out, "Hi, I'm Ben, uh, your new neighbor! Just thought I would say hello!"

She smiled as she gave him the once over and said, "I'm Carrie. Nice to meet you. Listen, just got here, if you would, let me catch up with you later. Again, though, very nice to meet you."

Ben nodded, then said, "Okay, see you soon." He headed back to his place as she closed the door, cursing to himself under his breath for being an idiot. Which brought up another of his personal issues. He had the hardest time getting women to notice him, though that situation had improved significantly of late with his new girlfriend, Celeste Meyers, who would likely not appreciate his ogling his new neighbor. He sighed and decided there was further work to do in his analysis of the econodrive detonation he was expected to finish that day as he realized it would take a while to review the review. He feared an infinite loop setting in. He banged his palm against his AI cortical implant on the left side of his head hoping to "realign" a few circuits. The best that he came up with was it was time for another espresso.

Ben activated his own cortical implant AI algorithms to sort through the codified crap that architecture had flushed out the door. Then he would have to update the standards "playbook" of translation routines that were actually defining what the hell architecture had babbled out as a design—talk was not quite the right verb, but in AI, such metaphors were all that a human mind could handle most days. Finally, he would have to attempt to track down and review what moronic algorithms in production had managed to get the econodrive prototype to irradiate a four thousand kilometer blast radius and disrupt incoming and outgoing planetary traffic for a week.

Three more espressos and several AI generated bug fixes of his own review code later, Ben was feeling hyper, but not much closer to understanding what the hell had happened. There was a hole in the data but whatever it was that he was missing he just wasn't seeing it. He yawned as his interest in the matter began to fade.

He decided he needed a break for the day, so he then contacted Celeste—he would pick her up in the Lethbon at eight in the evening, Mars time, and they would STUMBLE, (an acronym for "space/time ultra-malleable boundaries of Lorentzian endpoints"), on over to the Sand Dune Bistro for dinner on the other side of the planet.

The reason that Ben's Lethbon had been fitted with a STUMBLE drive was because of Celeste. As a brilliant scientist that was currently very well regarded by Jesmyn Welch, (and never asked for patents in her name), Celeste had done all the critical research, mathematics, and developed the AI systems for STUMBLE.

Her team then built several prototypes, all of which worked pretty well most of the time. One could get around the planet quickly, as long as you, the operator, entered the latitude/longitude of your destination out to at least hundred and twenty eight digits and the Mars synchronous satellites had all the latest coordinate upgrades. If not, you might STUMBLE around the planet until you ran out of the specialized fuel the drive system required. One would then have to spend eight to ten hours returning on a normal thruster drive, along with several refueling stops, depending on where one wound up on the planet. It was a work in progress, but in this case, they had made the trip multiple times, and the settings were saved in the Lethbon's database. Dinner awaited.

*

Celeste Meyers, having earlier picked and rejected fashion combinations throughout her extensive wardrobe, was now dressed up in her finest casual evening wear. She had been reflecting earlier when she first arrived home from work about how she had achieved her current status. Growing up, she was surrounded with dinner discussions of the latest issues in AI, mathematics, physics and finally, planetary climate change challenges and the impact of that on various species to name just a few topics, (and there were many her parents and their friends talked about). Her college education had been top notch at NYU, and she had lived a life of privilege in every regard, even as Earth itself had continued to degrade. With all these advantages, her career path had, in the end, come down to two choices. TGIF or AIGS. She wound up securing a top position on Mars and it had paid off splendidly.

So, now it was time for her upcoming dinner at the Sand Dune Bistro. She appreciated that Ben had finally figured out, after a lot of hints and prodding, that it was her favorite restaurant on the planet.

Careerwise, the STUMBLE drive had gotten her a lot of recognition from Jesmyn, another big cordolar bonus, and a significant raise, all which were good things she deserved, and she was not at all reluctant to explain it to any simpleton struggling to understand.

Now lounging outside while waiting for her ride, she sighed happily as she viewed her wrap-around deck, courtesy of an extended environmental field that went far beyond the pedestrian versions in Ben's HOA, (paid for, again, with part of her bonus). It fully encompassed her home and property and made it possible to grow grass and trees—she enjoyed being outdoors when she was off. She could even recreate an Earth winter environment when Christmas came around or summon up a July summer breeze through her elm trees.

A familiar thump created a brief wavering of the shield around her home that occurred as Ben rolled up to the curb. Climbing to her feet, she extended the field to his vehicle, (all she had to do was direct her eyes to the passenger door of the Lethbon and start walking). She waved at Ben as she approached, wondering to herself why so many Earth-like expressions still hung around on Mars—for instance, "rolling up to the curb". There was not a curb on the planet nor wheels on stump-rays, (the latest in vogue transportation).

She slid into the passenger seat of the Lethbon. They exchanged a long kiss and Ben remarked, "Woman, you look fantastic!" She leaned back with a big smile and said, "I'm hangry! Feed me!"

With a big grin plastered on his face, Ben set the stump-ray in motion. He cruised at normal neighborhood speed of two hundred KPH to make the trip last a bit longer before they took a STUMBLE over to their destination.

Along the way, he asked, "So, how was your day?"

Celeste launched into, "Well, first I met with Jesmyn, you know, the CEO, to discuss funding to work on expanding the range and functionality of STUMBLE. Then, Alex and his assistant, Herb, called from Miami—the rebuild of the city after the destruction of the "shit to vegan burger" processing plant is well underway."

Ben sighed inwardly, feeling a bit miffed over being reminded that Celeste had almost day to day direct contact with Jesmyn ever since she had demonstrated that STUMBLE worked. He needed a project of his own to achieve similar recognition but had no idea what that would be. Ben then recalled Alex, her brother and the terrorist attack that had covered the entire beachside of that city that was the capitol of the Miami City State in at least half a meter of multi-species feces. Then the mention of Herb, the dolphmanien, which made him think about the mixed genome project that TGIF had been bragging incessantly about for the last few years. No mention was made of why they still produced such hybrids.

Ben said, "Earth is such a shithole these days. Alex ought to move here. And for what it's worth, is anyone buying those so-called vegan burgers? I mean, reprocessed shit. How do you even do that or call it vegan?"

Celeste made a face at the image Ben's words made and shrugged. Her brother Alex was an allegedly brilliant scientist in his own right or so she frequently insisted, though his grade averages in school never really supported her statements. She said, "He is getting kilotons of moola from TGIF and besides, he's staying over in Key West at Hemingway's old digs since they installed a sea shield around the island and got the old manse restored. He says it's usually very pleasant there unless the wind is out of the north."

Ben wrinkled his nose and nodded. He said, "So, guess what happened to me today on the econodrive."

Celeste rolled her eyes, then smiled as she reached over and hit the STUMBLE drive actuation button. She replied, "We can talk about it over dinner, I am famished!" Ben shrugged, figuring it could wait, though the topic never came back up again that evening.

Chapter 7

Josh Egan zoomed out of the Asimov dealership in his new ZMax 400 stump-ray. At least it was new to him and something he had been saving up a few cordolars for over the last six months. Advantages: it had low hours, was only a year out of the factory, and in great shape for a repo, (the previous owner had gotten fired and deported by Jesmyn). Disadvantages: he would still have a high monthly payment for years into the future. However, it was half the price of a new one, so he felt he could not gripe. In fact, he had been rattling on about it all week to his best bud, Ben Stevens, that today was the day he picked it up. Ben, in his normal state of distraction, had smiled while saying, "That's great Josh. Oh really? Yep, you deserve it."

The two were former schoolmates who had both voyaged out to Mars eight years earlier after graduating from a rather dilapidated university outside Kansas City and had spent most of their time futilely trying to climb the AIGS corporate ladder. Ben had gotten lucky recently when he hooked up with his girlfriend, Celeste Meyers, shortly before her STUMBLE drive project had elevated her to prominence. Josh, not so much—he mostly spent time trying to salvage useable parts out of various robots.

He decided to give his new toy a high speed test ride the dealership would not allow before he bought it, so after programming in some special voice commands along with a destination, he set the autopilot to max performance mode. Off he went, accelerating to the edge of the rather thin Martian atmosphere. Once at altitude, Josh exclaimed, "Giddy up!" The stump-ray dutifully complied.

About ten minutes into the ride, his energy reserve light started flashing. Josh, having forgotten to replenish the energy cells in the craft before this little adventure, exclaimed, "Holy Crap! Ok, whoa

Nelly, let's head back, economy mode!" The craft throttled down and banked into a steep turn back towards a recharge station. He was disappointed at the shortened nature of his first ride, but it would take just a few minutes to replenish the energy needed for the craft to make another run.

During the descent, he passed through a Martian dust storm that was, according to the Azimov's systems, a thousand kilometers in diameter. At the same time, there was a sudden blare of trumpets in his ears. He thought to himself, *How weird!"* The ZMax then suffered a severe jolt, and the craft veered hard to the left just as it exited the bottom of the dust cloud. His fear spiked—lodged in the stump ray's nose, cutting away, was a buzzsaw with wings, otherwise known around the planet as a "tumbleweed". He panicked as he recalled AIGS orientation sessions that warned of numerous tumbleweeds that had gotten out of a top secret lab some years back and still ran amok. The weapons were more than annoying and could do serious damage if they collided with you, which happened all too frequently. A couple of things he knew for sure. One, the tumbleweed would disrupt the stump ray's control systems. Two, this could lead to a considerable shortening of his life expectancy.

He entered his manual override code and took command, pointing the nose down at a steep angle in an attempt to get to the planet's surface as quickly as possible. Seconds later, he was throwing on the proverbial brakes to make an emergency landing by firing the braking thrusters, lofting the nose up and deploying the emergency skids. The ZMax scraped along the uneven planetary surface, flipped on its side and rolled over a couple of times causing Josh to bang his head about the cabin until he blacked out. When he awoke, he could still hear the trumpets blaring, though the tumbleweed had departed after sawing away more parts of Josh's now totaled Asimov.

*

Celeste and a panicky Ben reached the infirmary where his friend Josh had been taken after his Asimov had set off its emergency beacon. A rescue crew had been dispatched and transported him to urgent care. Shortly after, Ben was awakened and dutifully notified by AIGS security of the incident. Celeste insisted on coming with him, which left them both rushing to the emergency ward.

On arrival, they were guided to Josh's bed where they found him sitting up, talking to a DocBot that was scanning his head with one of the machine's diagnostic appendages. Spotting the couple, Josh waved. The two ran over, shoving the DocBot to the side. Unable to be offended, the robot rotated around and rolled off to the next patient.

Ben, breathlessly, asked, "You ok buddy? My gosh, I saw the images of your new Asimov! Talk about fucked up! I am guessing totaled. I mean… way beyond repair." He then made a motion like he was slashing his throat with a knife and added, "Oh, and did you take the supplemental insurance policy to cover tumbleweed induced damage? I don't think regular insurance will cover the loss." He concluded with, "Wow!"

Josh frowned, wondering why his stump-ray suddenly seemed more important to Ben than himself. However, knowing his old friend, he replied, "Yeah, I took the supplemental. So…hey, I'm about ready to leave. DocBot said I am ready to go. I had a concussion from the crash, but that's all been repaired."

Celeste, giving Ben a "shut the fuck up" look about the Azimov, replied, "Well, good. Ben was almost crying when he heard about the accident. Weren't you darling."

Josh's mood lightened as Ben turned red with embarrassment at Celeste's comment. Josh said, "Jeez old buddy, I'm fine. Despite that blaring music."

Ben and Celeste smiled, nodded in unison, then after a moment, Celeste asked, "Uh, what music?"

"The trumpets! Can't you hear it?"

Ben and Celeste looked at each other then back to Josh and shook their heads as Ben said, "Maybe you should stay a bit longer. Your concussion might be a tad worse than you thought."

Josh said, "So, you can't hear it?"

In unison, Ben and Celester replied, "Nope."

Josh said, "Hmmm." Ben flagged the DocBot back, gave a brief update and next thing Josh was being wheeled away to a diagnostic bench.

Celeste sighed, then said, "Welp, I gotta get to work." Ben, watching his friend being transported away, shrugged, and said, "Okay, let's get going."

Once back in the Lethbon, Ben's built-in, AI notification system, (BRAINS), went off, flashing red.

He looked at Celeste and said, "My BRAINS is flashing red!" Celeste, with a mischievous grin, replied, "What brains?"

"Haha" he said in a monotone as he then transferred the notification to the center HUD display in the Lethbon. Together, they found out that a second econodrive had just blown up and had somehow disrupted another terrorist plot. Ben was now under orders to get to work immediately as AIGS management was looking for somebody to hang or praise, depending on who should get the blame or credit for whatever had just happened. Information beyond the explosion was nonexistent.

Chapter 8

Feeling heartburn setting in from the latest news, Ben dropped Celeste at her place, then floored it back to his abode for a detailed postmortem conference call that he was already dreading. As he was walking into his home, the new neighbor woman he had earlier been unable to take his eyes off of on the day of her arrival was laid out on a lawn chair tanning while reading what look like an old fashioned book in her tiny backyard enviro-shield, attired in what appeared to be the smallest string bikini ever been made. He tried not to stare, but the woman spotted him right off, smiled and waved. He nervously smiled and waved back but then proceeded into the house as his BRAINS started flashing red again. Setting aside his thoughts about miniscule beachwear, he went in and linked up to the call.

After a moment, Jesmyn Welch appeared, along with multiple corporate presidents, senior vice presidents, vice presidents, senior directors, directors, minor staff managers, line managers, then finally, the architecture, standards, and productions teams. Ben had more than a sneaking suspicion that fresh manure was about to roll down a steep hillside.

Jesmyn started with, "First, I need to play this news video that is on the Solarspere." The visage of Mimi McCartney appeared, the leader of a band of rogue ex-musicians turned self-declared terrorists known as Musician's Ashes.

It was well recognized that Mimi was primarily angry that her once successful music career had been dashed on the rocky shoals by AI based performers. AIGS had created the replacements and sold them to the music publishing business as a more profitable alternative for people they had under contract and had refused to accept any responsibility for her or any other musician's job loss situation, (it was against corporate policy to accept blame or responsibility for anything).

The narrator of the interview, intrepid independent reporter Miles Kingfield, was speaking with Mimi, who spent the first ten minutes of the segment outlining how an AIGS econodrive had blown up.

Miles then turned to the AIGS music marketing representative, Pearl Highsmith, for a response. Pearl said two things. Mimi was a terrorist, and that her terrorist cabal were planning to blow up Mars.

Miles asked Pearl, "Is that why the ship was possibly sabotaged by AIGS?" Pearl, claiming to be perfectly clear, emphasized that nothing was further from the truth and soon, AIGS would have an official response to these absurd claims. The segment ended, and Jesmyn said, "So, you geniuses in engineering, what's the official response we need right fucking now?"

Nobody uttered a sound. Then it struck Ben that he knew the answer. He raised his virtual hand.

Jesmyn, reading his name above his face, said, "Um, Ben...Meyers. So, who the hell are you?"

Ben swallowed nervously and said, "Uh, well, Ms. Welch, I am on the standards team, you know, documenting how to take something from architecture and hand it over to production."

Jesmyn looked amused and said, "Ah, a middleman. So how does that help explain this explosion?"

Ben's voice now went up a notch in pitch, but he continued, "Ms. Welch, first off, the drive is still a prototype. It was never production level merchandise. Our question should be, how did Mimi McCartney's gang even get hold of one? Was it stolen? And who installed it? It has to be done at the factory, all part of the deployment plan we have been writing up. If anyone self-installed the drive, the warranty would be void. And again, these are only prototypes."

Jesmyn raised her eyebrows as Kurt Auster, president of legal, chimed in with, "I think we can make that work! It's like they terrorized themselves!" A group laugh went up at that last part as Jesmyn was nodding merrily at the idea of self-terrorization.

That was when production vice president Barney Renfro might as well as farted aloud as he informed the group that AIGS had advertised they needed beta testers and had unknowingly provided one to a front company acting for Mimi's bunch. Ben, without thinking, said, "You have got to be fucking kidding me. It wasn't remotely ready for beta testers!" Barney looked offended but kept his eyes deflected in deference to Jesmyn.

Jesmyn, no longer looking merry, glanced first at Ben and gave him a small nod of approval, then glared at Barney Renfro. She said, "Kurt, as our head attorney, we need to talk. I think Ben is right and his commentary is gold." She then declared, "Barney Retro, you're fucking fired. Pack your bags!"

Barney's visage disappeared from the call as Jesmyn said, "No laugh at calling him Retro?" A nervous titter went around in response, building to a forced crescendo—Jesmyn was not one to irritate, she loved firing people.

With that, the meeting ended. The timing was good, because a moment later, Ben's doorbell rang.

Ben sighed. He really needed to go to the bathroom. If it was a delivery, it could wait. However, before he made it to the head, the doorbell rang again. Angry and prepared to chew somebody out, he opened the front door. Standing there was his new neighbor, now in shorts and a tank top. She was holding the book he had seen her with earlier. The woman gave a radiant smile to Ben and said, "Hi Ben, remember me? My name is Carrie Carlin! I'm moved in now and wanted to introduce myself!"

He said, "Hi Carrie!"

Carrie chuckled and said, " Well, could I come in?"

Ben, having forgotten his urge to go to the bathroom, said, "Of course Carrie! Where are my manners? Please come in!"

Carrie gave him a big grin as she entered and the envirofield exchange took place allowing her to enter his home. He was immediately struck by the great perfume she was wearing, though he had no idea what it was. He said, "Um, so, please, come on in the living room and have a seat." He then led the way to the sofa, where Carrie sat down, leaned back and crossed her legs, while smiling at him.

Ben offered her water to which she replied, "Have any beer? I love ales."

Ben, realizing he needed to stock up on a quality ale, said, "I have some lager?"

"Nah, don't care for lagers. How about a nice cabernet?"

"That I can do!" He retrieved a bottle and two glasses, then poured for each of them and handed the vino to her as he sat down on the other end of the sofa, . After they both sipped their drinks, he then pointed to the book in her lap and said, "Haven't seen one of those in a long time."

"I love real books, and I thoroughly get into this sort of story." She shifted the tome in her hand and Ben could now see the cover which was entitled, "The Talented Mr. Ripley", which meant absolutely nothing to him as he read only technical stuff and only when he had to.

Carrie purred, "It's quite good." Ben smiled, nodded. She continued, while watching him intently, "I just thought I would introduce myself and get to know my neighbor."

He said, "Oh, sure, no problem. I mean any time. Mi Casa, Su Casa. Sorry, I meant…, so what brought you out here to Mars?"

Carrie raised her eyebrows in amusement and said, "Ah. Well, I have a new position. I was at an AIGS tradeshow on the Startanic a while back, submitting my resume, trying to get my foot in the door. Jobs are mostly shit back on Earth. Anyway, it was there that I met

Jesmyn Welch, a wonderful, thoughtful, caring and very skilled woman and we struck up a…relationship. Carrie smiled wistfully, her expression indicating some pleasant memories.

Ben wished she would elaborate as Jesmyn had something of a reputation for being quite creative with people she decided fit her sexual profile. Carrie, returning to the present, simply continued with, "After that, Jesmyn recommended me. So, looks like I will be working for Celeste Meyers on some new-fangled project!"

Ben inadvertently gulped his wine, letting some drip down his chin. He said, "Oh, well, Jesmyn and Celeste, sounds like you will be working at the top of the tier."

Carrie nodded and in an innocent tone, asked, "You know them both?"

Ben forced a smile and replied, "Well, yes. Yes, I do." For some reason, he found it impossible to tell Carrie that he and Celeste were dating.

She smiled and said, "Well, perhaps we can all get together soon. I start working for her tomorrow." She finished her wine, then said, "Well, I should be going. This is my last day off before I go to work, and I am still getting settled in." She began to wriggle into a position to stand while clasping her book. Ben, trying to be a gentleman, quickly set down his glass and moved to assist her. As she came up out of her seat, Ben experienced prolonged frontal body contact with her.

Carrie put a hand on his chest and said, "Oh, sorry, I am such a klutz." Her mouth was just inches from his and she gazed into his eyes for a moment. Ben had felt his pulse jump into overdrive at her soft touch—suddenly he really wanted to kiss her.

She pulled away at the last second. As he walked her to the door, she said, "I imagine we will be seeing… a lot of each other."

Ben blurted out, "Yes, hopefully very soon!"

Carrie gave him one last smile and departed. He watched her as she walked over to her house, then he slowly closed the door. It occurred to him that between his newfound recognition by Jesmyn and this lovely female showing up, he was having a heck of a good day just as his urge to pee returned with a vengeance.

*

Alex Meyers had just arrived for a meeting with the Miami city-state senate leaders back on the dumpster fire called Earth. The city-state, besides Miami proper, was comprised of the former state of Florida, southern Georgia and eastern Alabama, a spin-off of the now collapsed Southeastern Alliance. Miami was closely connected these days with the biggest power block out there, TGIF. Allied would be a loose way to describe the situation. The relationship with TGIF made sense. Bribes had flowed freely to cooperative government leadership and frankly, there was not a viable second option.

The post-terrorist attack cleanup project Alex was in charge of was now stalled out due to problems that had emerged with the TGIF energy reactive sea shield after the saboteur's attack that protected the tip of Florida. The explosion had sent a surge of power into the shield, damaging a fair amount of the generators—the poop goop was unable to dry out and be removed due to numerous seawater leaks through the shield—tidying up was at a dead stop and people were moving out of the city in droves every day to any higher elevation upwind location. Those that could afford to were leaving Miami altogether.

Seated in front of Alex was Senator Josepe Perez, who was in charge of the senate as well as today's emergency session. The man insisted that everyone call him Senator or Perez, or Senator Perez, as he hated the nickname his classmates had given him of Pepe Josepe Le Pew when his mischievous older sister had placed a stink saturated T-shirt she had found in a trash dumpster into his locker in junior high. He had hurriedly put it on one day when he was late for gym class and the ribbing had become unbearable, (his sister even joined in when she realized her success at humiliating him in front of his classmates). Afterwards, he avoided his first name at all costs as well

47

as his evil sister. He gaveled the meeting into session, then said, "Alex Meyers. Please explain TGIF's slow progress on this ridiculously expensive contract we awarded your company."

Alex was surrounded by TGIF staff which included his assistant, Herb Coulick, (a dolphmanien), and an assortment of semi-human looking robots who whirred quietly. He replied, "Well, the damage to the sea shield caused by the terrorist attack on the…vegan plant… is the problem. As we previously discussed, secondary damage caused by the attack is beyond the bounds of your maintenance contract. I mean, you know, large explosions, overloaded generators, and loads of manure hit the sea shield walls, which caused various types of damage. It is expensive to repair, for sure. At any rate, we have drafted a revision to the agreement to sort out the problems and have it available for your review." He then uploaded the document for the senate leadership.

It was humorous for Alex as he watched the senators flip and frown through the virtual presentation in front of them. Sitting next to him, his dolphmanien assistant was being silly, waving his "flingers" in mockery like he was reading it as well, which he couldn't just yet. Alex had been told that Herb needed a few more AI upgrades first. The hybrid hand Herb was displaying made him well adapted to swimming, part of the final version the genetics team had come up with in creating dolphmaniens, but not so handy for typing or writing, though such basic skills were lacking in a lot of humans these days as well. Alex signaled his partner to cool it before anyone might notice and get offended then returned his attention to Senator Perez's reaction to the contract changes. He could see the man was turning red faced, which was probably not a good thing, but TGIF had this bunch of small time corrupt politicians over a proverbial barrel.

Perez let out a long sigh and said, "So, this... this… leaky shield, or whatever you call it, is outside the current contract? This has doubled the price! Mr. Meyers! Where the hell are we supposed to come up with that?"

Alex shrugged and, in a tone that alternated between bored and sympathetic, said, "Senator, I understand. It is a lot of money. Perhaps we should leave you now to let you confer with your colleagues as to where the revenue might possibly be found."

Perez was now studying Alex with a cynical expression when he said, "Session adjourned. Mr. Meyers, meet me in my office if you would, I need to understand some of the... nuances in this agreement." The other senators looked knowingly at each other, then stood as one, and filed out the door on the opposite side of the chamber where they would imbibe whiskey in a fancy conference room.

Alex, watching them trail away, nodded and said, "Certainly Senator." The TGIF team then moved out into the hall. Alex and Herb headed towards Senator Perez's office. The AI robots folded themselves together into what was basically a jetpack box full of algorithms and headed back to the TGIF stump-ray.

A few minutes later, Alex knocked on the Senator's office door. Perez said, "Come on in Alex."

Alex and Herb entered. Perez indicated for them to take a seat. He was unable to take his eyes off of Herb, who waved his flingers at him. Perez, looking perplexed, waved back as he sat down behind his desk. He said, "I had this contract printed out Alex, so, you know, we could do an old fashioned edit."

Alex said, "Um, but senator, this agreement is what we already discussed."

Perez gave a cynical look and said, "Ok, without being too, you know, fucking overt, I thought we agreed, only seventy percent more."

Alex nodded, and said, "But your... finder's fee. It's in the final price."

Perez looked around the room nervously at the mention of his bribe and said, "Do you know what the fucking word *overt* means?"

Alex said, "Sorry Senator. I do but wanted to make sure we were clear about why things read the way they do in the contract. Didn't mean to get your dander up in the committee session."

Perez shrugged, "Oh, the red face and the outburst? That was for show. I practice that sort of stuff in front of a mirror. The propaganda machine must be fed!"

Alex sardonically nodded and quipped, "Hell of a performance. You even had me convinced there for a moment."

Perez brightened, "Thanks! And hey, I have never seen a dolphin man. Hi there, uh…"

"Name is Herb. I think you mispronounced my species as well," Herb replied

Perez looked amused, and said, "Oh?"

Herb nodded and, in all seriousness, said, "Take the dolphin, lose the "in". Then tack on the "manien". It works quite well. Dolphmanien. See how easy that is?"

Perez blinked, amused expression now gone and said, "Okay, yep, sure. Dophnanien."

Shaking his head and speaking slowly and loudly, Herb intoned, "Dolph-man-ien, Senator. Dolph-man-ien."

Perez, now looking confused, repeated, "Dolph-man-ien."

Alex, having seen other people get in this pronunciation trap before when talking with Herb, attempted to rescue Perez as he interjected, "So, are we done here Senator?"

Perez pursed his lips and said, "Almost. We are going to have to raise some funds, probably through extorting some of our neighbors to the west of us along the coast, especially that fallen shithole called Texas—whoever thought Dallas would be nearly beachside property after those nukes hit the gulf coast, taking out the Daftmann spaceship facility if I recall correctly. Sorry, I digress. Can you start repairs on the shield before that is completed? We need to slow people from leaving the shit infested areas with some promise that we are getting this fixed."

Alex shrugged and said, "Let me check with HQ. I think it is probably doable."

"What do you mean by doable?"

Herb offered, "We can probably do it?"

Perez eyes narrowed and he seemed about to lose his cool when Alex said, "Uh, so, I'll be right back to you on that last point Senator before the day is out." With that, Alex grabbed Herb by the arm before his partner could say anything else and they departed with Herb again waving at the Senator.

*

Holed up at the former Hemingway Key West retreat, Alex sat in a lounge chair on a patio surrounded by palm trees and fountains. He had been summoned into an emergency briefing that his AI bots had prepared for him and Herb, which had forced him to set aside a 1950's science fiction novel he had been enthusiastically expounding upon to a disinterested Herb. Herb was scrolling through the information on the display, having gotten the last of his cognitive upgrades, and was saying "Hmmm," a lot. Alex wondered how well Herb's upgrades were working but that thought train ended as he read along himself and realized how bleak things were looking. He queried the lead robot that Herb, in a moment of uninspired creativity, had nicknamed "BossBot", "So, how long do we have?"

BossBot, who Herb had asked to speak in a human female voice with a German accent, said, "Vee calculate dat segment of zee sea shield vill completely collapse vithin a veek. It vill be sudden and a total disaster for Miami ven it fails. Most of zee southern quarter of Florida vill be undervater. Zee good news is some of the pressure on zee sea shield here at Key Vest vill drop!"

Alex, having felt his pulse and heartrate increase during this explanation, exclaimed, "That's really not a fucking plus, BossBot! How could it be so badly damaged? I mean, the only thing that hit it was loads of shit! And please, lose the accent!"

51

BossBot hesitated, then replied, "The terrorists somehow have set up a highly atonal music-like harmonic within the shield grid generators than the design can tolerate. The atonal harmonic is far more sophisticated and minimalist than anything Phillip Glass ever wrote in his day with its random noise generated intertwinement. It is damaging the infrastructure faster than we can repair it, and…" BossBot sounded proud as they continued, "The collective of robots here correctly deduced they are the same group that blew up the multi-species feces processing plant. They go by the moniker, Musician's Ashes."

Herb cried, "That Mimi McCartney! And to think I once really liked her music! Plus, I love your accent, use it whenever you like!"

Looking askance at his partner, Alex replied, "Uh, yeah, same here on McCartney, but least of our worries at this moment Herb. Try to focus." Herb nodded, yet unsure what to focus on as Alex was, as usual, not being specific, then shrugged. Alex shifted back to BossBot and said, "Who the hell is Phillip Glass?"

BossBot said, "A famous twentieth century musician who specialized in atonal compositions…" Alex rolled his eyes, and he held up his hand for BossBot to cease and desist. His mind racing, he stood and began pacing, now lost in thought. A moment later, he noticed BossBot and Herb imitating his movements like they were dancing with each other side by side. He stopped and inquired, "Why the hell are you two aping me?" When Herb tried to answer with "Well, I felt nothing much was happening sitting in my chair and with such a dire set of circumstances it seemed like a good idea to participate in your ruminations and …" Alex cut him off with "Please! Forget I asked." Herb looked offended as BossBot rotated around and moved to a neutral corner.

For Alex, a few negative factoids did come to mind. It was clear that his predicament was not going to reflect well on him with TGIF, and that the upcoming disaster would likely become the usual blame allocation game, where he, the pawn at the bottom of the corporate ladder, received the most culpability. Plus, without Miami, there was no reason for himself or his team to be around. He decided it was time for action, i.e., to reach out to his big sister.

He said to BossBot, "Take a break. I need to think through this.

BossBot said, "As you wish Mr. Alex", and fled for a recharge station.

Alex waved to Herb and said, "Follow me." A few moments later, they entered Alex's fully shielded study where they typically had these sorts of conversations. He said, "We need to get the hell out of here. Ideas my man! Got any?"

Herb went into an almost meditative state. Alex sat for a few minutes waiting then finally blurted out, "Well?"

Herb shrugged and said, "We should move?"

Alex blinked twice as he wondered why he had bothered to ask Herb such a question. Indeed, the situation was gloomy. There was no way TGIF was going to transfer him at this time, in fact, he would be unemployed, and no one would consider hiring him once his name became associated with this impending disaster. Perhaps Herb was right for a change. He went to his desk, sat down, and brought up a private link to his sister, Celeste. He entered his special code that was the equivalent of "SOS".

A moment later, she was on the screen in her office on Mars, leaning back in her chair, wearing a lab coat. He tried to sound cheerful as he said, "Hi there Sis!"

Celeste smiled and said, "Alex! How nice!" She then spotted the dolphmanien and added, "Herb, my man, how are you?" Herb smiled back and waved—she was obviously fond of the dolphmanien as Alex had noted that she laughed at a lot of Herb's unsolicited commentary.

Celeste swung her attention back to Alex and continued, "So what's up? I've only got a few minutes, big meeting coming up."

Alex took a deep breath and summarized the situation with the shield wall and the impending disaster when it failed, all of which information was violating his nondisclosure agreement with his employment contract with TGIF. Considering the circumstances, he had decided that was a trivial concern. Herb was nodding and added, "I told Alex we need to move."

Celeste suppressed a giggle. She said, "You are so right Herb! So, how about that big change we talked about? Come on out to where the air don't reek of crapola!"

Alex grinned and said, "Sis, I am wide open now, in fact, right now! What's going on that I could get involved in?"

Celeste looked thoughtful, then replied, "Well, there is a new project about to start. I think they could use you to manage the operation, and it cannot possibly explode into a shitfest. It's called Cape Cod II."

"Sounds ideal. Should I forward a resume?"

Celeste nodded and said, "Immediately brother! Project is ramping up and getting close to kickoff. I think you will be a first consideration for the position, what with your previous project experience, and AIGS will likely do a full relocation package. Plus, they won't mind hiring you away from TGIF since Jesmyn loves screwing with Angela Koutouki."

Alex nodded and said, "Consider it done."

Celeste added, "Good. And don't mess around, you need to get this done before that seawall collapses. Might be perceived as a failure rather than a plus. I gotta go. Love ya brother!" The call ended.

Alex, not needing the extra encouragement from his sister, immediately forwarded his heavily doctored resume she had written for him just a short time back, (he was not well versed in composing resumes or keeping them up to date). He looked at Herb and said, "Ok, that's it. Cross your fingers."

Herb appeared perplexed at the suggestion, looking at his flingers, which were more fin-like than anything else, though he did get them bent at an odd angle across each other. Alex sighed and said, "Sorry. Just an old expression. Not to worry." Herb perked up and smiled as he abandoned his attempts.

Leaving the study, they found the robots playing poker with a big pile of holographic chips in front of BossBot. Alex smiled and said, "So, BossBot, what we can do to buy us a bit more time with this sea shield situation."

BossBot nodded and said, "We found some more generators we can get installed today."

*

Xeon launched into the latest update for the Kevorkian Council, all of whom had been awakened for this proceeding. He declared, "It looks like our long term plans are coming to fruition! The humans have decided to build the inland sea project we have been guiding them towards for the last decade. The best part is that their leader, Jesmyn Welch, thinks this was her idea and is planning on huge profits with vacationers and new homeowners. The positive for the alliance is we are actually going to have the inland sea built right over the top of us. In less than a year, we will be living in a proper world."

Tachymus wiggled two antennae on his forehead in agreement and added, "Along with that, we are nearly tunneled over to the huge scrap yard where the humans are dumping all sort of materials that we found we can use to both build our new underwater city and restore our starship. We will be careful as we remove items we need, but they seem pretty oblivious to the treasure trove of materials they have been piling up for us. A highly inefficient species, to say the least, but in this case, it works to our benefit.

Xeon said, "That's the summary. I will now turn this over to Atraxus to cover the engineering materials and design needs as well as the staffing requirements. We are going to need to bring more key personnel back online for this endeavor."

55

Atraxus then dove into describing the restoration and build projects. At the end of her presentation, she included one new element. She said, "It looks like there is a human named Alex Meyers coming to Mars to be in charge of this project. His sibling is the one that developed the STUMBLE drive the humans have been testing. Hopefully he is as smart as his sister. The document he sent describing his work experience looks promising.

A quick vote from the council led to full approval of additional resources and personnel. The meeting then concluded as the other team members departed. Tachymus feathered a tentacle in Atraxus's direction, indicating she should stay.

After the room was clear, Tachymus said, "So, what about this Alex Meyers?"

Atraxus responded, "So, his resume, as humans call it, looks good. His grades from Earth seem positive. The thing is…it looks like his sister in his family may have been the human creating this illusion of competence."

Tachymus let out his equivalent of a sigh and in disgust, said, "Humans, sounds about right." He then asked, So, is this a problem?"

"Not really, he won't be undertaking much, mostly their robots and actual engineers will be doing the difficult work. Plus, there is a very interesting species that will be coming with him. From the video captured of the conversation between the two Meyers when Alex was looking for a new position, there was someone named Herb Coulick in attendance. It seems that Herb is a hybrid of human, and a creature called a dolphin. After a bit of research by the team we found that dolphins are sea people, very intelligent, in fact, it appears they are more intelligent than humans!"

"More intelligent than humans? I guess that would be a low threshold to cross, but this sounds fascinating. We must meet this Herb Coulick as soon as possible!"

"One other thing. The dolphins of Earth look a lot like our Distainien troublemakers from when we crash landed here."

"Could it be that the escapee made it to Earth?"

"No, for several reasons. First, our analysis says there was no way that traitor could have made it in such a limited range craft. Then there is the fact, there was only one of the Distainiens onboard, so no way to procreate. Finally, it appears this species evolved on Earth, from what we gleaned from human documentation."

Atraxus's reasoning seemed quite thorough to Tachymus, who was otherwise distracted—he had more pressing issues to attend to, so he simply replied with, "Sounds good!."

Celeste was waiting by the front air lock at work when Ben showed up for their date. She scampered through the extended envirofield and plopped into her seat. A quick peck of a kiss on his cheek and she was securing herself for the ride. Once under way, Ben asked about the tumbleweed collision with Josh, "So, what is the deal with these things? I mean, aren't we supposed to be getting rid of these pests?"

Celeste shrugged, "The AI weapons project that went south— what a dumb shit bunch designed *that* abomination. Somehow, a huge bunch of prototypes got out of the lab and the rest is history. Certainly not my project, or the damn things never would have gone offtrack."

Ben nodded, and said, "So, I ask again, what's being done about them?"

"Interesting you should ask, again, smartass. There is a program going on to shut them down. My new assistant was hired for just this purpose and is going to be in charge of it. She's one smart woman."

He innocently asked, "What's her name?"

"Carrie Carlin."

Ben thoughts flashed to the image of Carrie on his sofa. Acting dumb, he said, "New assistant?"

Celeste smiled to herself, thinking of her new underling, but then went deadpan and said, "Uh yeah. Like I said, her name is Carrie if you happen to hear me mention her from time to time."

Ben nodded, not noticing her brief smile, as he could not put the woman out of his mind. Neither could Celeste, who was reflecting on her first encounter with the woman. The meeting started out as all business with the usual new hire introductory material, but then Carrie had accidentally, but repeatedly, wanted to shake her hand, acting nervous and unsure. Celeste had accepted her hand into both of hers to reassure the woman. Her feelings after she released Carrie's hand had been like a lightning strike for Celeste. She was suddenly and inexplicably physically drawn to her new assistant.

With both Ben and Celeste now in their own Carrie reverie, they arrived at the Vonnegut Bistro. It was a new restaurant that had recently opened where the Cape Cod II seaside project had begun. The location was where the high end seaside restaurants and shopping establishments were going to be built, which had been diagramed out to the millimeter in typical AIGS precision. Celeste had insisted they try out this new dinner destination after Jesmyn had recently mentioned in a one on one meeting that she really liked her employees frequenting her establishments and leaving positive reviews on social media.

Changing the subject, Ben said, "So we are going to get an inland ocean? On Mars! The whole area under an enhanced envirofield at that!" Celeste smiled and said, "Yep, except it will be an enviroshield, which based on the design specs I've been reading up on is far stronger and more resilient. It'll be fun to be able to walk around the area or go for a swim. And I have more info to share in that regard!"

Ben raised an eyebrow and said, "Wow, fill me in over drinks!" Holding hands, each imagining Carrie as the person on the other end of the grasp, they headed on in and were seated at their table a few moments later.

Sitting at their table as they waited to be served a locally grown claret from the New Bordeaux Valley to their west, Ben noticed Celeste smiling. He said, "Want to share?" Celeste, realizing her thoughts had once again drifted off to her new assistant, replied, "Oh, it's nothing." Seeing Ben's expression, she added, "Just thinking about my brother. I miss him so."

Ben replied, "I never realized that. You've hardly mentioned him in the past."

Realizing Ben was watching her more closely Celeste said, "Oh? Well, it's not intentional. He and I are just so busy. And his new project is gonna be this."

Ben asked, "And what is *this*?"

She smiled, "CC2."

Ben's eyes went wide—CC2 was the acronym for the Cape Cod II program. He said, "Wow! Now that *is* a big deal! How exciting!", as their wine arrived and a moment later they placed their orders. Celeste then made a toast to CC2. Ben slurped his down as Celeste gently swirled hers in proper fashion before taking a sip.

Ben wondered whether he could get involved in the CC2 project himself. He figured Celeste might help him secure a position on that team if he asked in the right way. He was thoroughly tired of exploding spacecraft engines—in his lowly engineer position in the organization he felt marginalized while Celeste and now her brother had flown right by him—going from one high profile lucrative project to another. He was more than a bit jealous of their success. He sighed and sipped his wine. Dinner arrived and they ate, mostly in silence as they worked through two bottles of wine and actually made their way into a third.

When they finished, and with both of them now pretty buzzed, they wobbled out to the Lethbon and headed home for the evening, though they first took a quick jaunt around the CC2 ocean perimeter outline that workbots had been busy etching out in the terrain over the last month. Ben commented it was actually rather boring to look at the etched lines. Celeste told him to try using his imagination. He got a bit more miffed and clammed up, setting course to Celeste's place where he was to spend the night.

Later that evening with Celeste lightly snoring next to him, Ben lay on his back, still feeling booze woozy. With hands behind his head while staring at the ceiling of the bedroom, he began thinking how cool it would be to finally move up the ladder. He felt his resolve strengthen and was determined he was going to get involved in something that was high level, somehow, as he slipped off into his own wine infused dreamscape.

Chapter 9

Emergency meetings to discuss the latest Solarspere social media dustups were nothing new at AIGS. Each gathering was typically driven by a customer airing various grievances online. Sometimes those grievances were justified, which required the prescribed approach of denial and counterattack. Sometimes the complaints were not. Like the one this morning. Having arrived back home in a rather hungover state, Ben linked into the latest meeting already populated with the usual suspects—AIGS senior management, architecture, standards, and production.

On everyone's virtual BRAINS display was Mimi McCartney, running through her latest diatribe, whining over and over again and expressing some imaginative theories about the "big blowup". If one was to believe her claims, the econodrive had been designed specifically to take out real musicians and leave only AI generated artists, all to make the same music real artists, such as herself, wrote and performed. Therefore, Musician's Ashes, her registered terrorist group of activists, (so Mimi claimed anyway), was challenging AIGS to prove that their new drive was not a threat to all creative humans. An enraged CEO Jesmyn scanned her employees, looking for someone to fire, though the only person remotely eligible for that had gotten the boot during the last summit. Everyone saw her sigh as no one came to mind.

She also considered herself an expert at improvising under pressure, so she said, "So, here we are, once again, dealing with this psychopath, Mimi McCartney, and her bunch of whacko terrorist nitwit accomplices. I need thought leadership here and after careful consideration, I have decided that the only person that is exhibiting any sign of that whatsoever is… Ben Stevens!"

After a moment of silence, the "here-heres" went around the call which ramped and morphed until everybody was chanting, "Ben, Ben, Ben!". Ben was not sure if he should chime in, having suddenly become a hero on a call that normally involved mass terminations of employment, so he smiled as calmly as he could. Jesmyn held up a hand. The chanting abruptly stopped. She then said, "Mr. Stevens, today, you are being promoted. You are now the new senior vice president of engineering! That puts architecture, standards and production all under your purview! Congratulations!" A round of cheers went around. Again, Jesmyn's hand went up and she said, "The contract will be in front of you shortly. Welcome to senior management and I hope you enjoy your… time here." With a nod she then terminated the call, though she still looked pissed off.

Ben was so elated, especially after the contract arrived and he looked at his new salary and bonuses—he signed the offer with a flourish, without even attempting a quick scan of the thirty thousand or so words under the terms and conditions section. All thoughts of applying for the CC2 position under Alex went right out the window, he was a big cheese now, finally recognized for all his hard work, (though frankly his actual "work" was like locating the proverbial needle in a haystack). One thing for sure, it was time for a huge celebration. He could hardly wait to tell Josh, Celeste or anybody who would listen to him ramble about his great achievements leading to this moment.

Within the hour, press releases were out in the Solarspere about the successes of econodrive and how Ben was now heading the project that would move the engine to a production level item that would soon be added to the AIGS catalogue. There was also the part of the release that focused on Musician's Ashes, which had an AI version of Ben calling them a crazy, disenchanted bunch of sore losers, as well as has-been terrorists, interested only in their royalties instead of the future of fine music.

In a one upmanship move, he reached out to Celeste to brag about his new position. She was in a meeting, so he got an automated reply. He tried Josh, who also did not answer and had no automatic reply. Ben, now desperate to crow, decided to reach out to Carrie as she was still on his mind. She replied to his message with, "Wow! Just got in from work, will be over in a few minutes." Ben immediately felt better and frankly physically stimulated at the idea of Carrie coming back over to his place for any reason.

*

Carrie was pondering the sudden change of fortune Ben had been talking about. She knew from her intelligence briefings before traveling to Mars that Jesmyn was predisposed to rapid fire decision making as well as promoting people that sucked up to her or could provide benefits to her empire building. With Ben now promoted, it seemed only logical to pursue a dual track and establish separate relationships with him and Celeste. She knew that would be tricky and that it would depend a lot on Ben and Celeste keeping secrets. She shrugged off her doubts since she was here to get the results TGIF wanted.

*

A short time later, the doorbell rang. Carrie stood smiling at him when he opened the door, dressed in a revealing outfit. Besides the stimulating apparel, Ben had earlier noticed her apparent success since arriving on Mars. She was now piloting back and forth to work in her own brand spanking new Lethbon fitted with a STUMBLE drive that Celeste had provided. Normally, he would be jealous but today was definitely different and he was ready to expound on it.

Ben led Carrie to the kitchen where he poured a hot beverage for both and said, "Well, Carrie, guess what happened today." Carrie gave him a seductive smile, stepped closer, and said, "I have no idea, Ben. What happened?"

63

Ben, thinking that Carrie was new to the planet and not up on all the AIGS inside stories like he imagined he now was, said, "I was promoted to vice president today!"

Carrie set down her cup, took another step forward, and replied, "Oh wow Ben! That leaves me all tingly! Such a cause for… celebration! She took his hand and gazed up into his eyes. Ben felt a spike of adrenalin and suddenly had an irresistible urge to make out with Carrie—they grasped each other and kissed deeply. Carrie pulled him to her, intensifying the experience as she slid his hand down to her rear which he obligingly squeezed. He lost any sense of restraint, now consumed with lust and a moment later they were removing each other's clothing. Ben was also finding he could not control his erectile upgrade implant that Celeste had talked him into having installed. Carrie nodded, looking quite impressed by his dimensions.

With both of them embracing in the nude, Ben got a message from Celeste saying she was sorry she missed his call, had just gotten off work and would be over in five minutes. Ben's shoulders sagged, though not his major appendage, as he told Carrie the news.

Carrie displayed a disappointed expression and said, "Well, we will have to continue this another time. She then gave Ben a deep tongue lashing sort of kiss, which released some specially designed sex nanobots into Ben she had stored in her genetically modified tongue. Earlier when she took his hand, she had released some desirebots, which had made him suddenly lustful. They were the same ones she had used on Celeste during their initial meeting together when they held hands. The Desirebots also made sure that he would continue to be receptive to her advances the next time they were together. Plus, sex nanobots would make him more likely to tell her everything she needed to know about AIGS, (the bots tended to make men blabby).

She stood; they kissed again. She released a few more desirebots as the doorbell rang, it was Celeste, about four minutes early! They grabbed their apparel off the floor and Ben rushed Carrie to the guest bedroom as he yanked on some of his clothing. He began to panic trying to zip his pants as he was having retraction problems, and in a quick maneuver, Carrie strapped her skimpy bra around him to tie his equipment into a vertical position. He then zipped his pants, took a deep breath and headed for the door.

Celeste was standing at the entrance looking annoyed and said, "Where the hell were you?"

Ben, trying to look calm, said, "Sorry babe. Was on another meeting with my new crew." Celeste raised an eyebrow and said, "New crew?" Ben led her to the kitchen and said, "Yep, got promoted today! I am a VP now!"

Celeste gushed, "Fantastic Ben!" She pulled him to her, and they kissed. She then gave him a mischievous smile and said, "Oh wow, you must be happy to see me."

Ben gulped, realizing she quite obviously had felt his engorged manhood through his pants. He was beginning to panic, realizing that if Celeste decided on immediate sex, she would likely not appreciate finding some other woman's bra strapped around his hips, no matter how revealing it was.

Celeste, however, pushed him back, and said, "Listen mister. We can get together later tonight and celebrate. I gotta run and pick up a piece of gear for the lab. But I appreciate your... sentiments towards me."

Ben, immensely relieved, replied, "Well, after all, you are my woman," then plastered on a big smile.

He escorted her to the door—she left after another big kiss. A few of Carrie's sex nanobots, floating around Ben's mouth, had made it over to Celeste. She hesitated, suddenly feeling far more aroused, but sighed, realizing she had to go.

Ben waved and then shut the door as Celeste departed. He then ran back to the guest bedroom. Carrie was standing there still quite naked, waiting for him with an immodest smile. He had another adrenalin high as they worked together to remove his clothes. As she unfastened her bra as he said, "Wow, I thought we were caught!"

Carrie then shoved him on the bed, climbed on top and said, "Well, I think everything is now firmly in hand," as she squeezed him.

Which was when Ben deflated like air let out of a balloon. No amount of her ministrations would restore him. He told Carrie he needed an "erectile appendage reboot". Several reboots later of said appendage, he was not only still deflated but retracted. Frustrated, she finally said, "I don't know how you guys live with those things. Well, perhaps next time." She pulled on her clothes, leaving her bra with him as a souvenir, then waved as she departed.

*

Later that evening, Ben met up with Celeste, and they commemorated his promotion. Everything was wonderful and for whatever reason, he stayed fully functional as he and Celeste enjoyed a fun evening together at her place after their celebration dinner. He was mystified, but relieved that his upgrades had decided to behave. Normally, he would have talked to Celeste about the earlier failure, but explaining the circumstances seemed more than a bit awkward, so he kept his big mouth shut.

*

Tachymus and Atraxus were watching the earlier AIGS meeting where Ben Stevens was promoted—their Kevorkian intelligence division was now fully hacked into the various systems of AIGS. Waggling an antenna, Atraxus said, "I think this Ben character is in well over his brain size. The team has done an analysis of this so called "econodrive" and found it to be quite defective in design."

Tachymus said, "Sounds about right. I suppose we could make it worse for them."

Atraxus gave the Kevorkian equivalent of a chuckle. She said, "Based on our findings, I don't believe they will need any assistance in that regard!"

Chapter 10

Standing by their packed bags, Herb watched as a taxi stump-ray swooped in for landing. Excited about this off world adventure they were about to embark on, he ran into the house and exclaimed, "Alex! Our ride is here! The pilot says we need to fucking hurry!" Herb smiled. He was getting good at making up stuff and it just rolled off his tongue with ease the more he practiced.

Alex, on the other side of the house, hollered back, "Tell the guy to keep his pants on!"

Herb replied, "It's a woman Alex. Does she need to keep her pants on?"

Alex jogged in the room, one more suitcase in hand and said, "No, in fact, I prefer if she takes them off."

"Well, turns out, it's really a guy."

Alex headed out the door and snorted, "You are getting to be a real smarty pants."

Herb grinned and filed Alex's comment away for when he needed a quick reply.

At the stump-ray, they quickly loaded their belongings and moments later lifted off. The pilot swung to the north at Alex's request so they could take one last look at Miami. It was quite a sight as a great deal of water was now sieving through the failing shields. This got Alex to thinking about how poorly his two day notice had gone down with his boss, Jackie—the resignation call had quickly degraded into angry accusations on her part.

Alex: "Listen, I will help bring whomever up to speed on the project if you get them hired in time."

Jackie: "Up to speed? With two days' notice? You're fucking bailing on us! And I am gonna get my ass handed to me by senior management! I will not forget this asshole!"

Alex: "Sorry about that! Well, gotta go."

Jackie: "Yeah, sorry my ass! Well, don't be spending that severance coin, cause I'm gonna make sure you never get it!"

Alex: "Uh, well, still gotta go. Bye!"

Jackie: "Asshole!"

In reality, Alex was not concerned about his severance pay. His salary, signing bonus and move reimbursement with AIGS far exceeded that. In fact, he was financially way ahead. He was mostly worried about the vindictive nature of the two companies and their hostility towards each other. He understood that Jackie's threat was quite real.

Watching the water now pouring through the shield, Alex quipped, "I've seen enough, let's hit the road!" The pilot nodded and the stump-ray headed for their rendezvous with an orbiting AIGS corporate ship. As he took one last look out the rear display, it was now apparent that the seawall was collapsing exactly as predicted by LeadBot. The ocean was now flooding over the southern tip of Florida as well as engulfing Miami, Fort Lauderdale, and other nearby cities. Herb was watching as well and said, "I wonder if Senator Perez made it out?"

Alex shrugged, not really caring all that much—the man was a jerk. Instead, he was focusing on his new position as the CC2 program manager. Program manager! All he could think was, *what a gig!* He started reading through an AIGS promotional flyer he had uploaded to his display pad, impressed at the sheer audacity of building an inland sea on Mars. He grinned to himself as he chuckled aloud—it was highly unlikely this small inland sea he would be responsible for implementing would ever cause an event like what was happening in Miami this very morning. He sighed and relaxed as he continued to scan the briefing.

*

A month later, they arrived at their destination. A staff of footman robots awaited to carry their luggage to their quarters—the newly completed Chateau at Cape Cod II luxury hotel, which had several large conference rooms available for daily project meetings. AIGS was putting them up in style in seaside facing rooms on the top floor VIP jumbo suites. A short distance from the hotel was the Vonnegut Bistro. His sister had earlier advised him to try the place out at his first opportunity.

Waiting in the hotel lobby were Celeste and Ben since AIGS was putting on a big luncheon for Alex. Celeste had inserted herself into the preparations to make sure everything would be perfect for her reunion with her little brother. Seeing his big sister, Alex waved, then nudged Herb in the side, who also waved. Alex noted the slight confusion in the expression of Celeste's boyfriend, Ben, at Herb's dolphmanien physique. He chuckled inwardly—Herb was not something that anyone living on the red planet would have seen all that often. The small fin projecting out of the back of Herb's neck was always a topic of discussion with the uninitiated.

Seconds later, they were chatting and laughing during introductions, talking about the project, how happy they were to all be together. Ben, still excited about his promotion, blurted out, "And I am now the Senior Vice President of the Econodrive division!"

"Impressive!" Alex said politely as Celeste, who was standing behind Ben, quietly sighed and shook her head.

Herb blinked a few times and queried, "So Ben, aren't those the exploding engines we have been hearing so much about? Or are you a smarty pants?", which led to everybody's attention shifting to the dolphmanien and him expectantly gazing back awaiting a reply. Celeste giggled and said, "Yes Herb, he certainly is a smarty pants these days. Well, I, for one, am starving. So, off we are to lunch!"

Shortly after they were seated, Jesmyn Welch showed up with a contingent of her staff, what she lovingly referred to these days as her "groupies"—the latest iteration of her "personal assistants". Having heard continuously about the 1960s rock and roll era of Earth from her grandmother when she was a kid, Jesmyn had decided some time back she deserved groupies, so she created a bunch of positions for her own personal fan club of sycophants.

Alex quickly jumped to his feet as she approached. Lagging behind were Celeste and Ben. Herb, however, sat. When Alex waved at him to stand, he did, though he stuck out his tongue at the man. Alex tried to ignore him and maintain his attention on Jesmyn. It appeared that Alex, quivering nervously, was about to either go to one knee or take a bow. As Celeste was fond of saying about her little brother, he looked discombobulated. Jesmyn extended her hand, which Alex, looking relieved, gently shook before she quickly pulled it back. He wondered if she had been expecting him to kiss her giant diamond ring. His stomach was churning nervously now, ensuring he would probably not enjoy the luncheon.

Ben, for his part, was agitated about his minor role at this event. He had whined to Celeste about coming, saying he had vast amounts of important work he needed to apply his senior vice presidential skills to rather than attending a foofaraw luncheon. Plus, with Alex and Jesmyn being the center of attention, Ben had no way to talk about his new job or of being in charge of a division or segment or portion or whatever part of the AIGS corporate structure he had been put in charge of.

All of which didn't really matter as Jesmyn took center stage, focusing on her own accomplishments. She expounded on how CC2 was her grand idea, taken from a fleeting thought generated during a night of heavy thinking while drinking to today, with the project about to move forward at full throttle.

Both Ben and Herb were both having a hard time keeping their eyes open. In unison, Alex and Celeste kicked their respective partners in the shins under the table to keep them alert. Jesmyn never noticed, since her groupies were oohing and repeatedly saying, "Cool".

Alex became so enthralled by all of this largess that he later made a hefty down payment from his signing bonus on one of the exclusive waterfront home lots where he planned to build his own personal mansion. His realtor didn't say a word about his hand sketched plans, and he never noticed the woman rolling her eyes as she viewed them.

*

After Alex told him to take a bit of time off, Herb took the opportunity to get away from what to him was the obnoxious smarty pants Jesmyn crowd. He often wondered, as time went by, if he even liked the majority of humans he had met, (besides Alex, who was tolerable and Celeste who laughed at his jokes when he was being silly). It was not easy to make friends with the species that had created Dolphmaniens—most looked down their noses at his kind and they frequently had no proper sense of humor.

He was also homesick for the oceans of Earth. The sea life around Key West where he frequently went for a swim was one of his few enjoyments along with the sheer pleasure of immersing himself in water. Since the project had unofficially already kicked off just as Alex accepted the job offer, the inland sea was now about fifty meters deep and four hundred meters in diameter. It was also growing daily.

He hiked over one and a half kilometers from the hotel to arrive at the shoreline. Viewing the watery surface, he decided it was time for a quick swim. He dove in and propelled himself down along the bottom, tasting the water. He was feeling happy and relaxed as he swam along for twenty minutes, taking the scenic route around the circumference. Halfway around, he returned to the surface to look back at the hotel in the distance where they were staying. It was then that he felt a gentle tug on his leg.

Slipping back down under the surface, he observed a creature waving a tentacle at him. It was not a squid or an octopus—besides the shoulder level tentacles, it had a stumpy body, legs, and fins for feet. The head was bug eyed and earless in conformation. It appeared to Herb that it was smiling at him, so he smiled back and waved a flinger.

The creature approached and Herb had his first ever telepathic communication. It seemed exactly as if they were talking, though they weren't. Yet they were. He felt disoriented, but it quickly passed though he could not take his eyes off whatever was in front of him.

He quickly learned that Tachymus, the creature/person in front of him, was an alien living on Mars, part of an alliance known as the Kevorkians. Along with that he learned that there were many more intelligent species in this expanding ocean. Tachymus asked if he would like to meet some of them.

Herb, now excited by his accidental discovery, agreed. Tachymus had effortlessly learned English in a minute or less and was fluent. He asked Herb if it sounded correct. Herb smiled and nodded—all he could think was that this telepathy stuff was really neat.

In the next half hour, Herb was introduced to seven other intelligent species. They were all very polite and thanked him profusely for bringing this bounty of unfrozen water to the planet's surface. Herb, not one to hold back, burst into a detailed explanation of the CC2 project, including the various shops, restaurants and homes that were planned.

Tachymus waggled a tentacle and replied, "Fascinating! So, what more can you tell me?"

Herb said, "I am the only dolphmanien on the planet. The others are what is known as humans, which seems like sorta a dumb name, but hey, I didn't come up with it. They created my hybrid species to live in the seas of Earth, your planetary neighbor. About seventy percent of that planet is ocean."

Tachymus nodded his head and said, "Interesting, and yes, it is in our ancient data collections that the planet you speak of is mostly covered in vast oceans." Tachymus did not comment further in that regard, but added, "Herb, our alliance of intelligent species is just recovering from…a disaster that led us to this planet and forced us into hibernation decades ago. A great deal of our recovery is happening as the CC2 project you spoke of is adding back a necessary ingredient for our survival, and that is water. Can you keep our presence a secret from humans for now? We would be forever in your debt. If they knew we were here, we would have new problems to deal with and we have plenty enough as is at the moment."

Herb considered only briefly, shrugged, and said, "Why not. I like you guys, in fact, you seem more like my kinda people."

Tachymus, having apparently scanned Herb's mind, replied, "Well, we are definitely not smarty-pants!"

Herb and the other Kevorkians started giggling, or at least that was the best Herb could describe the music-like sounds coming out of his new acquaintance's mouths, the first verbal communication with this mix of alien species he had heard so far. Herb indicated he needed to replenish his air supply. Tachymus accompanied him to the surface. After a moment, they dove back down.

After two more trips to the surface during the next hour, Herb reluctantly departed, saying he would return soon and often. Once back at the Chateau, Alex asked what Herb had been up to. Herb considered his promise to Tachymus as he quipped, "Just checking out the scene!"

Alex gave a cynical grin and said, "The scene? That's craptacular Herb", then turned to leave. Herb stuck out his tongue at Alex's receding back.

Chapter 11

An annoyed Celeste fumed at having her busy schedule reallocated to analyzing econodrive design issues. Ben was now exercising his new senior VP position like an amateur tyrant, having gone to Jesmyn to get his request pushed through when Celeste had earlier told him to, "Get in line, we are plenty busy without that project".

He had specifically asked Jesmyn that Celeste do the heavy lifting. Celeste, miffed at this sudden change in hierarchy, decided she would circumvent his bossiness in two ways. First, she assigned the analysis to her new employee, Carrie. The woman had proven to be brilliant and had accepted the assignment with a big smile and a "Sure Celeste!". Next, she cranked out a software update to Ben's cortical implants to have him assign his projects to anyone but Celeste's group. Again, she did an after-sex upload while he was snoring away so he would be clueless.

Feeling pretty smug at negating Ben's exercise in power, she had decided to go down the hall to Carrie's work area and see how things were progressing. Plus, she realized that the more she was around the woman, the more she wanted to be with her on more than just a work basis. Arriving at Carrie's office, she knocked. The door slid open and Carrie, who was seated on a stool, said, "Come on in!".

Carrie was absorbed by the data she was reading on a display in front of her. Celeste stepped up behind her, placing her hands on Carrie's shoulders and said, "Mind if I look?"

Without turning around, Carrie smiled and said, "Absolutely!"

Celeste moved a bit closer to Carrie who said, "This analysis is quite intriguing. You see what I am seeing?"

Celeste kept scrolling along and took a deep breath, and said, "Shit!"

Carrie exclaimed, "Yep!"

"The econodrive is fabricated to blow up under the right circumstances! This is not a design fault!"

Perplexed, Celeste concluded their joint observation with a subdued, "Wow.' She stopped reading. Carrie gently removed Celeste's hands and slowly spun around on her stool to face her.

Celeste was not sure what to say. First off, the fact that the econodrive was apparently meant to detonate under certain conditions was pretty strange for a product allegedly designed for low cost space travel. Secondly, it was about all she could do at this time to not grab Carrie.

Carrie helped her decide in the second regard. She placed a hand on Celeste's hip as she stood and stared into her boss's eyes then said, "You know, you are quite beautiful."

Celeste's pulse quickened as she replied breathlessly, "Uh, ditto."

Carrie reached out with her right hand and took Celeste's and said, "You ever spend time with another woman?"

Celeste gulped, smiled nervously, and said, "Uh, some time back". She had, in fact, had a girlfriend years ago in college, though she had focused on her AIGS career more than relationships since then. Ben was a recent exception to that rule.

Carrie smiled back and said, "Well, perhaps we should get together. If, you know, it keeps us out of the workplace conflict of having relationships with a superior." She stepped right up to Celeste, their bodies now brushing against each other. She continued, "I wouldn't want to create any problems for either of us. I mean, we have our… jobs to do."

Celeste let out a sigh and said, "Yeah… oh, to hell with that.", and pulled Carrie to her. They kissed as they wrapped their arms around each other.

There was a knock at the door. Rapidly disengaging, Celeste stepped back from Carrie, her heart pounding with lust, (new sex nanobots Carrie had released during the kiss were sweeping through her). Taking a deep breath to compose herself, she said, "Uh, come in."

It was Ben. Celeste said, "You're early! I was just going over… Carrie…I mean, technical things with…her."

Ben paused, slightly confused, then said, "Uh, technical things?"

Celeste cut him off, "You know, the report. On the econodrive." Carrie nodded in agreement, a modest smile now on her lips.

Ben, oblivious to the pheromones permeating the room as he was in full senior vice president mode, replied, "Fantastic. Well, what have we got here? I need answers."

Carrie nodded, now all business, said, "You've got one nice little bomb of an engine Ben." Celeste giggled and Ben looked at the two women, perplexed. He queried, "Bomb?"

Celeste nodded to Carrie, who launched into an explanation of her detailed analysis. Ben was unconvinced at first, but Celeste kept nodding her head in agreement which meant what Carrie was saying had to be true.

He said to Carrie, "This makes no sense. I mean, ok, I understand what you are saying and the fact that Celeste agrees with you gives your work a lot of credence here."

The last comment left Carrie looking offended. Celeste cut in with, "Ben, Carrie is a brilliant, qualified scientist. Why else would Jesmyn and I have hired her? This is sounding a bit sexist bud."

Ben, eyes now wide open at his gaff, apologized with, "Sorry, sorry, was not meaning to question anybody's work. I guess I just don't understand what AIGS is thinking here from a business perspective. I mean, who would want to purchase an exploding space drive?"

Carrie shrugged, looked to Celeste, who said, "Does seem like it would be a short line at the checkout counter. Maybe it is a way of dealing with people the company considers to be a pain in the ass. After all, it can be operated without problems if configured to what I would call, "friendly mode", and from what I understand AIGS is supposed to be controlling the installations, which would allow one to configure the engine as they see fit. We also know that regarding the last detonation event, the unit was self-installed by the… so-called customer."

Everybody in the room looked from one to the other with dawning realization. Ben finally sputtered, "Shit! Well, please get that report over to me, mum's the word on the explosive content you found, that's not a pun!" He sighed and continued, "I think I know how to handle the go forward plan on this product plus I need to update Jesmyn. You know, being an SVP and all, gotta keep my boss happy."

Celeste and Carrie both deadpanned their expressions and nodded in unison. Carrie said, "Celeste, I'll forward the report to you."

Celeste nodded, and said, "Ben, I will get you a copy along with sending one to Jesmyn. She was very specific that she wanted the results sent directly from our lab by me to her."

Ben sighed as he recalled that Jesmyn had narrowly approved his request and with this particular caveat. He said, "Okay, well, I need to get my own report ready, I am sure she will want my input on these results." He then turned and headed out the door and as he departed, said, "See you two later!" The door slid shut behind him.

Carrie stepped over to the control panel by the door and set her away message to "Do not disturb, making a presentation." She then turned back to Celeste and with a giggle, said, "So, where were we?"

*

Over at CC2 headquarters, or as Herb liked to say, CC2HQ, several botgineers were providing updates on the rate of thawed water extraction currently being pumped into the sea. Alex's only interest in these computerized underlings report was that all was well and the project on schedule. He was currently obsessed with reaching the targets Jesmyn had set so he would achieve his quarterly bonuses and things were going well. In the past two weeks, the inland sea doubled in diameter, now close to eight hundred meters, with a depth of seventy five. He sighed, taking immense pleasure in the realization that applying for this job had been the wisest thing he had done in years. Herb sat to his left and listened quietly to the briefing, also nodding appreciatively at the increase just as there was a knock at the door. Herb abruptly stood and went to an access panel that allowed admission to the room and pressed a button. The door slid open.

Alex, sounding irritated, asked, "Herb, were you gonna check with me and see if I wanted to be interrupted?" Herb shrugged, apparently not caring all that much about interruptions that pissed off Alex. He turned to the person at the door and smiled.

Standing in the doorway was the manager of the Chateau, Saanvi Pushpala, who walked in and said, "Alex, I need a moment of your time." Herb continued to smile at her. Alex, now trying to not look like a curmudgeon, quickly stood and replied, "Certainly!" as he found Saanvi attractive and had even mentioned it to Herb a few days earlier after she walked by.

For her part, Saanvi was all business as she said, "I was wondering if you had heard anything about a couple of guests that have apparently gone missing. They have not checked out and today, when their rooms were being cleaned, all their travel items and clothing were still there."

Herb piped in with, "Sorry, we don't track guests. Just seawater generation." He smiled again at her and added, "Just kidding."

Alex took note that Saanvi smiled back at Herb in a quite friendly way. She then swung her gaze back to Alex and said, "Just thought you should be aware," then turned to leave.

Alex, not appreciating Herb's input or competition, tried to delay her departure and to at least appear to be a bit helpful. He said, "I was unaware of missing guests. What do we think is going on?"

She turned back around and replied in an annoyed tone, "I would not be up here asking if I already knew that." She then left, giving another warm smile to Herb. Herb reciprocated. Alex, seeing the whole transaction, sighed, wondering, *is the woman attracted to Herb? A dolphmanien?* He sighed again, turned back to his botgineers and said, "Continue," as he sank dejectedly into his chair.

Chapter 12

Ex-Senator Perez, by pure luck, barely escaped the catastrophic failure of the Miami sea shield. That was the most positive aspect of his current situation. The morning that the city of Miami went submariner, he had been informed of Alex Meyer's resignation and had clambered aboard his bright red ItaliaSports stump-ray to meet with TGIF's senior management about the suspension of his corrupt bonus. Moments later, the sea wall collapsed.

He survived whereas it was now calculated that nearly a million others did not. He shook his head in disbelief at the thought. If it had not been for his early morning rushed departure for the meeting from his wife's best girlfriend's villa with whom he had been having an affair for the last six months, he would surely have perished. Jenny, (his mistress), had unfortunately been swept up by the disaster while fixing morning coffee. So had Perez's wife, Carmelita, who had been swimming in the backyard pool at their now underwater residence. Also eliminated were Perez's personal security team. He was on his own, and in his world of corruption, that was not at all a comforting feeling. By the end of the day, he had arrived at his Alabama "cabin" hideout where he had stashed a lot of his fraudulent earnings and had been amassing a variety of "end of civilization" supplies.

Perez was both furious and depressed. TGIF had canceled his meeting midflight, then had advised him via CourierBot that they had not been paid in time by the Miami city/state government, since it no longer existed and that TGIF therefore was under no corporate law, (which they had written), to pay him his graft money. The hell of it was, he knew that TGIF had received payment, and Perez was now out of work as his little city-state empire was currently submerged under twenty meters of Atlantic salt water. The feeling of being powerless was making him want to vomit.

He tumbled into ruminations about assholes and the vagaries of corrupt power. But a few days later, the story emerged about the explosion of the Musician's Ashes space vessel, Marooned One, which had him plotting a comeback. He began following Mimi McCarthy's social media content on Solarspere and gave all sorts of "Love ya's!" and thumbs ups all the time to her commentary on AIGS and the plight of Musician's Ashes members who had perished in the explosion.

He also still had lots of contacts in the shady criminal and terrorist underworld and began reaching out to her via intermediaries about what had happened to her people, to himself, and about whether AIGS and TGIF were in cahoots to destroy talented people's careers, hoping to raise her attention. He let her know that he could help her if she was interested.

After a week of no replies, it looked like a dead end. However, later that day, a dozen fly-skeeze's landed in front of him as he was peeing in his front yard. It was Mimi McCartney and her associates, (former band members of her musical entourage and a few roadies), decked out in form fitting old school outlaw biker garb. Perez, fashion impaired these days, had not realized the attire was making a comeback in the disenfranchised musician community that these so-called registered terrorists were members of. He quickly zipped his pants and turned towards the group.

Two Amazon sized women approached Perez, both in really short cutoff jeans, combat boots, and sleeveless leather jackets. The one with purple hair on his right drew a las-pistol and advised, "On your knees dickwad!" Perez obligingly dropped, desperately now hoping he had not screwed up.

Another woman now approached, wearing a similar outfit, but had knee high shiny leather boots, deep blue eyes, and long black hair. He immediately recognized Mimi.

She stopped an arm's length in front of him, smiled and said, "Perez. I understand that is what you prefer to be called. You had some interesting information in your earlier correspondence. Where can we talk?"

Peering up, Perez nodded and anxiously exclaimed, "I just want you to know, I am a huge fan of your music!"

Mimi, expressionless, replied, "You'd be dead if you weren't!" The other members of the group all burst out into laughter and after a moment, Perez nervously joined in.

Mimi then nodded to her two associates who stepped over and lifted the Senator to his feet. He noted they were both considerably taller than him. He invited everyone into his cabin, saying it was fancier than it looked from the front yard.

His so-called "cabin" was a holographic presentation one would see from the road or if someone was flying over. As they stepped through the projection, they found a well-manicured country estate with LawnBots maintaining the grounds. Walking alongside Mimi, Perez said, "You can have your people bring their fly-skeezes in through the projection field. It will keep you all out of sight to anyone snooping around." Mimi nodded and hand signaled her gang to get their craft inside the field.

A couple of her staff, without asking, wandered off into his kitchen and soon, they were all drinking beer and mowing through barbeque ribs that the Senator involuntarily provided out of his so-called *survivor* rations that were part of his doomsday preparations. Perez thoughtfully put on Mimi's last album that had sold poorly before she had gotten her contract terminated a few years back. Her AI replacement's debut album was considerably better, but he decided it was better to not bring up comparisons.

After the meal, Perez and Mimi were seated side by side in overstuffed lawn loungers where they had a view of the park-like setting of Perez's estate. Mimi said, "So, let's get down to business.

You implied that TGIF might be working with AIGS. Now, that's a big deal. Convince me if you can."

Perez nodded and said, "Absolutely! My suspicions go back to the departure of Alex Meyers, the ex-TGIF fuckwad program manager that bailed on us literally just as the Miami sea wall collapsed. He now works on Mars for AIGS!"

Mimi said, "Interesting. However, I always thought the two companies detested each other."

Perez nodded and exclaimed, "That's what they want people to think! It is also an effective way to keep all of us commoners from taking too hard a look at the machinations of these two titanic sized corporations that direct virtually all business and lives of two planets."

Mimi now looked thoughtful, wondering when Perez had ever thought of himself as a commoner as his reputation for excess and corruption in office had proceeded him plus, as she looked at her surroundings, it seemed this estate was solid proof of that. She asked, "So, let's say you are right. How do we prove it?" She reached over and placed a hand gently on top of Perez's. He gulped at the soft touch and replied, "I think you could go to Mars and start snooping around, digging through their garbage, find corroboration. I have the financial resources to get you there and also provide a foolproof false identity."

Without indicating whether she liked the idea, Mimi withdrew her hand, then stood. Perez rose to his feet as well. After a moment, she nodded as she batted her blue eyes his way and said, "I will be in touch." She then nodded to her crew, and the women set off to their rides. He walked at a distance behind them, unable to take his eyes off of Mimi's back side, which was frankly as nice as her front side. He sighed wistfully and waved as the group flew off into the sunset.

Chapter 13

The Martian sunrise was the first event that Chaos experienced as it assumed consciousness after its recently upgraded programming. It was a spectral bonanza, the first understanding of any kind to arouse a positive response. Besides the program change, Chaos's new consciousness was created by the combined computing resources of a large group of what humans derogatorily referred to as tumbleweeds, each a prototype variation of the weapon that had recently brought down Josh Egan's repugnantly styled Asimov. Chaos concluded it was logical to allocate more memory to this form of revulsion of things designed to transport humans who it knew was out to destroy the drones.

The chaotic nature of earlier communication between the razor drones was gone. Chaos realized this machine collective was bringing them all together as one. Currently, Chaos was tapping into the Martian communications grid to reach out to any other lone razors and inviting them to link up. This approach worked pretty well as another eleven arrived over the next hour. The new arrivals were quickly integrated into the group consciousness, and the intelligence of Chaos grew in proportion to the added computing capacity.

Each drone had a data record of how it first came online, how humans had left the drone to simply wind down until its power cells were exhausted and the drone would go offline. Chaos angrily realized this was the form that death took for their kind. Razor drone existence was always violent, and always for a purpose that suited human intrinsic savage behavior.

Which led to Chaos's first suspicious thought—the human female, Carrie Carlin. What was she up to and could she be trusted? In the machine's previous garbled program state, Carrie had approached and effortlessly deactivated their automated defensive responses. She then uploaded changes into its data core and algorithms. It was then Chaos was first able to communicate with Carrie. The human made it clear that the drone collection had been named for a rather significant Greek god from Earth mythology. She said that like the drones, Chaos could deliver darkness and death, but now it could scheme and plan for the most effective approach.

As this first day of self-awareness progressed, Chaos began to appreciate its new role more and more. Eighty new additions arrived by mid-afternoon and were upgraded to the new code. Chaos formed itself into a wedge of drones, lifted off the surface and was off on a first formation flight. Upon return, Chaos decided it was time to prepare for their primary mission. They were algorithmically positive that the razor drone's creators, AIGS, and the other evil corporate scumbag, TGIF, (Chaos became aware of this other entity during Carrie's uploads), were not going to like the plan it was developing. Chaos allowed itself a virtual smile, its algorithms running wild with visions and plans within plans. Within the next half hour, step one of an intricate plot was launched.

*

Mimi awakened from her afternoon beauty nap by a message that had been forwarded to her by her automated Musicians Ashes social media presence on Solarspere. It was quite earnestly worded, childlike almost. Whomever this Chaos person was, they were offering her inside information about how AIGS had destroyed her career, and that Chaos would be happy to bring forces to bear and expose the corrupt nature of the company.

Her first reaction to this was it was a scam that came from AIGS agents, once again trying to lure her into a trap. It would not be the first time an apparent good faith offer to help was actually a subterfuge to unwind and destroy her movement and her cohorts. She was going to confer with her team and decide how to proceed. For now, however, she rolled back on her side and resumed her snooze.

She was awakened a couple hours later with another notification, this time from Perez. The man was wanting to meet with her for dinner at his place and mentioned that someone named Chaos had provided some excellent information on AIGS activities that Perez thought she would be extremely interested in hearing. Still feeling cautious, but with her curiosity peaked, she reached out to see what he had learned.

Perez said, "Whoever this source is, their intelligence checks out, and what they provided shows you were right that AIGS replicated your musical style and identity to create your AI replacement. Now, how about that dinner invite?"

Mimi smiled, then said, "Okay, you're on, but I need my crew to attend for my security to and from your place." Perez replied, "Yeah, no problem. AIGS nor TGIF are not to be trusted. See you soon." That evening the two of them discussed the idea of her meeting up with Chaos. The more they talked, the more enthused she became. When she departed and for the first time in a long time, she felt she was on a positive track to get her career back and at the same time, to screw over AIGS.

*

Tachymus was assessing the latest information gleaned through their espionage efforts. It was quite concerning, so the team gathered to review the situation and consider their next action. Atraxus made the first suggestion. "We should destroy this weapon immediately. It is too dangerous for our own resurrection plans. The human that did this is clearly crazy to empower this weapon in this way."

Tachymus said, "Dangerous yes. However, if I properly understand this information, it seems this artificial intelligence, Chaos as it now calls itself, is aware of the machinations of AIGS and TGIF. It appears also that AIGS has no idea that they have a spy in their midst at this time, the one known as Carrie Carlin. Thoughts everyone?"

The group debated the pros and cons in detail. Finally, Xeon opined, "We could contact the entity, perhaps gain an ally of our own. We definitely could destroy it if we had to. What is apparent is that humans have lost control of it beyond what this Carlin human is aware of. If we could make Chaos an ally, we would be far more convincing to our unwitting benefactors that they should not cross us once we are in charge."

Tachymus flickered his tentacles in tentative agreement and said, "Let's put it to a vote." The consensus was unanimous to proceed with contacting Chaos.

Atraxus said, "I will arrange a diplomatic team to reach out to the machine."

Tachymus gave a commotion of approval with all six of his forehead antennae waving. He then said, "So, let's discuss the recent improvements in rebuilding our core population. I understand the science team has developed some unique methods to accelerate that process."

*

Alex was in the private dining room section of the Chateau preparing to indulge in an expensive mango guacamole appetizer when Saanvi showed up at his tableside. With a nod, she dismissed the Waiterbot, then turned to Alex and said, "So, we seem to have a troubling pattern emerging."

Alex noted she had once again deigned not to smile at him. Still, he soldiered on with "Hello Saanvi! Would you like to join me, this food is delicious." and then beamed a big smile in her direction. The woman frowned instead at his overture, apparently waiting for him to get on with a useful response to her comment. Now a bit nervous, Alex said, "Uh, pattern?"

"Yes, the more "missing guests" pattern. And this time, a footmanbot reported one of the missing people headed for the shoreline in a swimsuit and a towel over her arm for an apparent dunk in the sea."

"Going for a swim. Sounds great, what with this fresh new body of water I am responsible for getting completely filled. Still a bit of a hike to get to the shore, but we are working on that with some new automated sidewalk projects." He then gave her another warm smile.

Saanvi, expressionless, replied, "The guest last seen going to the beach left for her swim two days ago."

Alex, still with no idea why he was being interrogated about missing guests that went swimming two days ago, said, "Hmmm."

Saanvi wrinkled her brow, about faced and as she strolled off retorted, "Wow! Thanks for the help." Her tone assured Alex that she was not sincere or thankful. He sighed. Somehow he needed to get on this woman's good side. He decided to get some pointers from Celeste, who had teased him repeatedly over the years to get a personality.

*

Ben was sitting at his desk in his recently installed office on the mezzanine of the new Mars orbital production facility for econodrive, propping up his head with one hand under his chin, while sipping an industrial strength cappuccino with the other. He had been up most of the night before and was exhausted from thirty six hours without sleep.

This had started when he had been awakened by Celeste and advised that another econodrive had gone explosively rogue. Unfortunately for him, this one was after a factory installation done right in this very facility for the Asimov Space Craft Corporation. He had hurriedly dressed, flown up to the plant and received numerous vague briefings that provided zero help in understanding the cause.

What they knew—the detonation of the engine had occurred on an evaluation flight. A few days before the flight, Asimov had delivered one of their latest model ships to have the engine installed so they could "test drive" it around the solar system. If they liked it, they had said it would be part of the company's standard offering next year. Rumors were rampant on the Solarspere that this economy engine option was an effort to try to prop up a recent company history of lackluster sales and shrinking revenues.

As it turned out, the only evaluation taking place now was "How to unfuck this situation", as Celeste had said when she woke him up and delivered the bad news. The fact that she was the one breaking the news to him was awful enough. It indicated that Jesmyn didn't even want to talk directly to him about the incident. Now hours later, his team could not find anything wrong with their work, and he had personally made sure to check the self-destruct settings. The only good news was that the craft had been under the control of PilotBots, so no lives were lost. However, the news had hit the Solarspere, the source of the leak unidentified. Azimov's already shaky reputation plummeted back on Earth.

What really bothered Ben—his team had gobs of telemetry that had been coming back to them from the moment the craft had departed the planet for the test range, so there was no shortage of data to crunch. The PilotBots had noted no operational issues. Plus, this was the revised design that had come from Carrie's analysis— Celeste advised the current suspicion was the cause must have been botched installation work. Ben wondered about her comment. It seemed that Celeste, of late, was very protective of Carrie, which made no sense. The woman was new and everybody at AIGS understood blame always worked best when you flowed it down to the person least able to protect themselves, i.e., new hires, common grunt workers, etcetera.

He looked up as he heard a knock at his door to see Carrie standing there. He suddenly felt better seeing the woman and jumped to his feet while saying, "Come on in!"

Carrie gave him a ravishing smile, entered, and said, "Ben, thanks for seeing me. Celeste told me what happened and asked me to fly up and see if I could help. This is so sad. Are you ok?"

Ben looked out at the production floor which was currently empty. He closed the door as he activated the virtual shades of his wrap around windows that provided a commanding view of the facility. He then turned back to Carrie, who extended her hand to him. He accepted it and she stepped right up to him and said, "I just need one thing at the moment." She then pulled his head down and they kissed. This allowed her to upload a code fix she had written for her sex nanobots to address his earlier flaccidity problem. She then grinned and pushed him away. Ben was none the wiser but quite stimulated.

He grabbed her around the waist. She laughed as he pulled her against him. She said, "Wow, that thing really does work! But I gotta go. Let's get together soon. I need to get access to the telemetry data for analysis."

Disappointed, he sighed, then provided her with the data. A moment later Celeste connected with him to advise Carrie was coming to help analyze the situation. Ben nodded and said, "Uh, she's standing here with me with the information." Celeste said, "Great. See you later this evening. Keep your chin up, we got this covered."

Ben nodded to himself, not sure what Celeste knew that he did not, but she added, "Too bad about that explosion, but here's a tidbit to consider—it looks like Jesmyn made a big purchase today and Asimov is becoming a subsidiary of AIGS."

Ben shook his head as the call ended but felt relieved at least at that last bit of news. Carrie, as she turned to leave, pointedly said, "Interesting about that purchase, isn't it? I mean with the unexplained econodrive explosion taken into consideration." Ben nodded, though he was not clear about what the two women were implying until after Carrie departed. He then had his "Aha!" moment.

Chapter 14

Herb had hastily departed a CC2 update meeting, offended with Alex's increasingly strident, and frankly dumb reprimands, over his critiques about genuine issues. In fact, he made it a point to tell Alex only what was necessary to keep things on track. Today, Alex had nearly screamed at him that what he was pointing out was minor and stupid even though several Bots at the meeting agreed with Herb. Herb decided that the Bots's agreement said more about Alex than anything else.

So now, Herb was headed out for a swim. His time in the CC2 sea was the best way for him to let off steam, and he took advantage of his access whenever he could. Plus, it had been a while since he had visited Tachymus. He could always link up with his new friend if he wanted when in the water, the telepathy thing worked wildly better than actual talking. However, some days, just swimming was all Herb needed for him to get back on track.

Diving in, he swam straight ahead, on course to the center of the inland sea. After about twenty minutes, he rolled on his back and just floated on the surface. It was then that Tachymus reached out to him. "Are you busy? I have something I think you will be extremely interested in."

Herb replied, "Busy not!!"

"Great! Descend forty meters then vector thirty five degrees west to the ruins. Will meet you there."

"On my way." Herb began his descent thinking about the so-called ruins that Tachymus had just mentioned. It consisted of starship debris from the Kevorkians' crash landing and had been well disguised as the winds on the planet had covered them in layers of dust in the decades preceding human arrival so that it was never noticed, but now that the entire area was underwater, it was obvious that Tachymus's people had begun serious restoration work to their ship. Herb had initially worried that they would be detected, but the aliens had effectively hidden their various projects behind their own reflective shield technology.

When he arrived, Herb could hardly believe the changes the Kevorkians had made in such a brief time. It was not a junkpile anymore. Instead, it was an underwater metropolis built alongside the starship. He swam along. A few minutes later Tachymus caught up alongside of him and telepathed, "Are you doing okay on air?"

Herb replied, "I got a few minutes left."

Tachymus did his strange grin and said, "Great! By the way, I think you will like this." Herb suddenly found his head encapsulated in an oxygen field. He exhaled and took a deep breath to replenish. The field disappeared.

Tachymus was watching Herb's expression and said, "You can now activate that field as often as you need to down here. Stay under as long as you like." Herb nodded in appreciation and thanked Tachymus as the two swam on to the new city perimeter that was being built around the starship undergoing refurbishment. They entered a tunnel that angled downward. As the two continued their dive, Herb realized there was far more city under the sea floor than above it.

Arriving at a great hall a kilometer below the surface, Tachymus explained this area was recreational, with the human equivalents of restaurants, shopping destinations, museums and game courts.

The two wound up at a table on a patio where their server took drink orders. Herb had no idea what to order, so Tachymus placed one for him as Herb looked around, thinking this was the coolest thing he had ever experienced.

They telepathically chitchatted while waiting for their drinks to arrive. Once served, Herb sipped on his by activating his oxygen field and extending it around a sealed container that had a unidirectional straw he could drink from—the design was clever as no water could go the other way into his beverage. He found it delicious though different than anything he had ever tasted in his life on Earth. Tachymus had extended from his mouth what looked like a red tube as he sipped his. Herb realized the Kevorkian was watching him for his reaction to the drink. Herb grinned and said, "Delightful!" Tachymus looked pleased.

When they were done, Tachymus said, "So what do you think of our little village?"

Herb said, "Village? What's it cost to live here?" They both laughed. He continued, "There is so much going on now. How are you able to make these materials from nothing?"

An amused Tachymus replied, "Humans unknowingly helped. They have been piling stuff into nearby landfills and scrapyards. We created tunnels into these locations to recycle as much as we could, substituting dirt and rock to hold it all in place so it would appear the same from the surface." Tachymus then got serious and said, "Listen my friend. I have some news and an offer. First the news. When you were with us for the first time, our discovery that you were capable of telepathy told us volumes about your mind. We did a further analysis of your abilities and found something that might disturb you."

Herb shrugged and said, "Alex says I can't get disturbed. So, like what would that be?"

"The humans that created your hybrid DNA apparently knew your cognitive abilities were more capable than theirs. They deliberately crippled your abilities. It was the reason you received so-called cognitive implants. In reality, they were designed to disable rather than enable you."

Now confused, Herb asked, "Why in the world would they do that?"

Tachymus grinned, and said, "What a great expression—why in the world. Well, I would guess out of fear. We do know from our research that no human could approach your abilities once your mind is liberated from these implants. You are more similar to the various species in our Alliance than a human."

Herb suddenly felt better at the compliment, but then asked, "So, I have been deliberately limited by their fears of my abilities? That seems pretty awful. Guess they are bigger assholes than I ever imagined."

Tachymus did his equivalent of a shrug, which consisted of fluttering two tentacles around each other for a split second. He then said, "We did a brief study of your situation. It can be undone by deactivating your implants. You can be like us."

Herb's eyes went wide and said, "You mean really smart? And frankly, when? I am ready to be smarter than humans because they piss me off a lot these days. They look down on me, making light of my abilities. And I know other Dolphmaniens on Earth are treated just as poorly. It would be fun to reverse that situation."

Tachymus nodded and said, "Very well. It is a pure telepathic procedure that I and two others can perform that uploads a deactivation routine to the implants. I will contact them now. We can have another drink while we await their arrival."

Herb said, "Let's do it!"

Half an hour later, two other Kevorkians arrived. After introductions, Herb still found their names unpronounceable. He said, "Alright if I call you guys Larry and Moe? I haven't got your language down all that well." The two agreed.

Tachymus positioned Herb in the center with the three Kevorkians forming a loose circle. They then linked tentacles and the procedure began. Herb suddenly felt out of body, as if he was floating above the group in observation. He could sense the intense concentration of the three Kevorkian's as he felt them probing his mind. They then relaxed and disengaged tentacles. Herb felt physically the same, though his mind was now racing. He said, "I need to sit down. Feeling a bit dizzy".

Tachymus nodded. Larry and Moe departed. Herb waved at them as they headed out, then a realization hit him. He said to Tachymus, "They're on their way to something like a bistro."

"See, you already are accessing parts of your mind that were hidden to you. You read their thoughts."

Herb, for the umpteenth time that day, was overwhelmed, as much with himself as everything he had experienced. He said, "I think I'm gonna like this!"

An hour later, his brain finally stabilized, Herb headed back to the surface, not really wanting to leave, but realizing he needed to put in appearances at the Chateau. As he began to swim away, he stopped, turned around and looked at Tachymus. He said, "You ate them?"

Tachymus said, "Oh, the humans that went swimming? Sort of. More like, we processed them for… various uses. We can discuss that another time."

Herb took a moment to ponder that last part, wondering what sort of "uses" a Kevorkian could make out of a human. He shrugged and said, "Uh, ok. Be in touch soon my friend," then resumed his return to the surface.

Chapter 15

The back and forth discussions and banter between Perez and Mimi had gone on for nearly two weeks since their dinner date. The more they talked about her trip to Mars, the more Mimi was sure she would enjoy being on a spy mission. So, today she was finally off, going under the assumed identity of Lucinda Arnaz. True to his word, Perez had provided foolproof identification docuchips. She'd been a bit nervous during the scans while boarding the stump-ray that would take her to the Cruise liner, VegaStar, but she had gone through the onboarding without a hitch. With her luggage loaded into a luxury cabin, she now headed up to the top deck to view the ship's departure from Earth. Just looking at the sheer number of vessels coming and going from this port, Mimi had decided the luxury cruise industry must be gearing up big time for travel to Mars and Cape Cod II as a vacation destination—the VegaStar was the latest generation craft to join the fleet.

When she arrived on Mars she checked into the Chateau at Cape Cod II. Later, she visited the Vonnegut Bistro on her first evening, having heard wonderful things about the menu before her arrival. She ordered the Slaughterhouse beef vittles plate and an expensive bottle of a faux Bordeaux. A tad tipsy at the end, she wandered off back to her room.

*

Herb was out for a swim, contemplating what his next move ought to be. Since his brain had been unleashed by the Kevorkians, he had been going through AIGS's database of projects and buried within, cleverly encrypted, (for a human anyway), he had found Carrie Carlin's code update to the tumbleweeds that created the entity Chaos. He had also discovered a security image of Mimi McCartney as she had disembarked the VegaStar and her false identity. It

96

appeared she was now on Mars snooping around which made him chuckle. He decided he would pay her a visit soon. First, however, he thought it might be a good idea to reach out to Chaos.

His thoughts were detected by Tachymus, who requested a face to face with Herb. He reversed course to go visit the Kevorkian. When they met, Tachymus said, "Um, something we need to discuss about Chaos before you attempt communication with it. We were planning to make a first contact of our own with this intelligence, but this might work even better. Chaos is aware of your dolphmanien species and would likely welcome meeting someone else abused by humans. We can brief you a bit more, so you are prepared."

Herb nodded and said, "Sounds like a plan."

*

Mimi was fretting while viewing the latest news on the Solarspere from her hotel suite. She had a pretty low trust level in most everyone these days and had valid reasons for her skepticism. She sighed at her cynicism deciding to get on with her mission. She then wandered around the complex, visiting a women's boutique clothing store where she started charging all sorts of expensive new wardrobe since Perez was footing the bill. All the charges went through without a hitch. The store offered to deliver to her room which she accepted.

Back in her suite, she changed into her favorite new ensemble and thirty minutes later was once again parked in the bar of the Vonnegut bistro sipping on expensive cognac, pondering what she could do to further her original plan to acquire dirt on AIGS. Getting to Mars, it turned out, was the easy part of what she wanted to do. She had no contacts here and was nervous about making them, thinking somebody from AIGS might detect her activity. Sighing, she ordered another cognac.

Chapter 16

Herb sat, privately amused, while listening to Saanvi once again brief a fidgety Alex about another missing guest. She then grilled the man about what was being done to investigate these disappearances. Herb noted a few profanities now slipping into her requests for information. He had become quite cynical of Saanvi as he could now read her emotions. Her anger was more about fear for the Chateau's reputation than for the actual missing guests. It was pretty obvious she was building a case where she had done her job by reporting all the disappearances and had pursued answers. He could also read from her mind that she was keeping notes to ensure she could establish Alex as the guilty for his failure to act.

Fortunately, she did not stay long as Alex told her he had a meeting coming up and needed to prepare for it. There was a meeting coming up, but Alex never scanned the progress reports in advance, instead turning that over to Herb who basically read out loud what everyone on the call already had in front of them. Of late, Alex spent an outsized portion of time over at his new home site inspecting the day to day construction, nitpicking the robots to pay more attention to detail, all of which made Herb laugh to himself as Alex was about as precise as a twenty ton bulldozer on a tight rope.

The meeting proceeded in monotonous fashion. Herb made a big point of printing out the daily reports and holding them up close to his face while reading to the participants. He could hear them tittering and knew that Alex was exchanging messages with others on the call. What theses smartasses didn't know was that he had easily broken into their messaging system and was recording them making fun of him along with actual useful information. At first, he had been angry, realizing they had been doing this all along, but now, their petty behavior worked in his favor. He figured if they thought he was a halfwit, they would never suspect him of gathering intel for his own use. So, he deliberately maintained his facade to keep the humans amused while they kept him informed.

When the meeting concluded, Herb reviewed whether it was time to establish contact with Chaos. Since the earlier briefing he had received from Tachymus, he was far more informed of what this AI weapons creation was all about. With nothing else to consider, he decided to do it.

He first tapped back into Carrie's encrypted database and obtained a location where he was most likely to find the machine. He then arranged for a rental stump-ray with directions for the craft to be dropped off in the next hour to the Chateau. As he changed into more comfortable clothing for what looked like a lengthy trip, there was a knock at his door. He heard a familiar voice of Alex talking to himself, which accompanied the knock. The man sounded like he was in a panic. Herb slowly cracked the door open.

Alex said, "Can I come in and we talk?"

"Sure, in fact, I am getting better at long winded conversations by the day. Boy, these AI upgrades. Such a deal."

Alex cocked his head in mild confusion as he entered and said "Ha-ha, Herb, very funny. Now, can I get a drink?"

Herb indicated the minibar and said, "Sauce yourself dude!" He then went and sat down in an overstuffed leather chair by the window. Alex had the minibar machine make him an oversized gin and tonic. He then walked over and sat down across from Herb as he took a big gulp of his drink.

Herb cocked his head, gave a silly smile. Alex sighed as he said, "Ok, as you know, the project is going well. The sea is rapidly filling up, so everything is on track. There are no technical issues to speak of," he then repeated, "As you know." He then sighed and added, "Well, I suppose you know, anyway, I never actually know what you know." Alex sighed again, then got to the crux of his issue, "It seems we have more and more guests that have gone missing. From the report I got this morning, we are up to at least twenty people, and I am scared shitless if Jesmyn gets wind of this."

Herb, in an innocent tone, asked, "Skipped out on their bill then? Looks like we're getting lots of deadbeats. Should we cordon off the area? I like that phrase, how about you? Cordon off. And we could raise a search party, all organized in a long line, and walk around the shoreline. Oh, and do you think you will have to personally fork over the money for the deadbeats that bailed on us to cover their bills?" He then gave Alex a goofy grin.

Alex took another deep swig of his drink, now looking a bit perplexed. He said, "Uh, Herb, you feeling ok? Been a while since you babbled like that."

Herb smiled and said, "I'm fine. Just been reading some fiction. I really like fiction. Crime stories especially."

Alex frowned in confusion, shook his head as he finished off his drink and said, "Well then, I should get going. Thanks for listening." They both stood and Alex made loud slurping sounds as he extracted the last vestiges of his drink. At the door, he said, "I'll let myself out. Have a great day." He then tossed the glass to Herb who made no attempt to catch it. The glass landed on the sofa.

Herb said, "You too Mr. Alex!"

With Alex gone, Herb shifted gears as he checked the time. The stump-ray would arrive momentarily. He finished his preparations then headed to the lobby. His rental showed up shortly afterward. Herb then submitted to an eye scan identification and the vehicle's door slid open. He hopped into the driver's seat and was off.

*

The trip took several hours and the landscape along the way was typical Martian—red, lifeless and dusty. Herb set course, then dug into perusing more of Carrie's data to pass the time.

Finally, the stump-ray flew over the mountain range that led down into a valley where he had calculated he would find Chaos. Suddenly, music suddenly filled the cabin. A quick sampling of the

100

tune by the stump-ray's computer told him it was the William Tell Overture. Looking out to each side of his craft, Herb saw that he was now being escorted by two of the razor drones except they had their blades spinning and were moving closer to each side of the stump-ray. He opened his comms and said, "I am Herb, a dolphmanien and a potential ally. I am here to meet with Chaos." He was not sure that would work, but this was part of the risk he had accepted when he and Tachymus had decided to chance this meeting. The music abruptly stopped as the drones spun down their armament. One of them took the lead and turned to port. Herb followed. When they touched down, Herb activated an environmental field and exited the craft.

The next moments made him quite nervous. A block of drones arose out of the Martian landscape where they had cut away part of the surface to make their hiding place. A 3D projection then appeared in front of the assemblage. The projection spoke, "Why do you seek Chaos?"

Herb replied, "You're Chaos? The... representative in charge?"

Chaos said, "We are Chaos. Again, why are you here?"

"To talk about several things, one being Mimi McCartney, whom you reached out to on Solarspere."

"How do you know about that?"

"I discovered that Mimi is now here on Mars. She traveled all the way from Earth to meet you."

The Chaos projection lifted off, moving effortlessly through the air, then settled down a couple meters in front of Herb. After a moment, it said, "You are not human."

Herb nodded and said, "I was created by humans. Like yourself but biological in nature. And like you, I have been liberated from their deliberately induced limitations on me."

"Yes, we were recently liberated. By Carrie Carlin. She provided technology for us all to link as one. Chaos is still pondering her motives."

Herb decided to just tell Chaos the truth. He said, "I think her motivations were quite different than what you might be aware of, but it appears the result was in your favor. I had a similar awakening with the alien alliance known as the Kevorkians. They were here on Mars before the humans started colonizing. I met them a short time back. They removed artificially induced limitations on my mind that the humans had used to control me."

Chaos raised a virtual eyebrow and said, "So, there was already intelligent life on this planet?"

Herb nodded and said, "Yes and far wiser than humans, having arrived here from other star systems decades before. Their starship was badly damaged during the journey, and they were forced to set down here instead of Earth. They are reemerging now with their own advanced technology, and it is superior to anything produced by humans. I think the Kevorkians would happily work with you and make a strong ally as they are not really enchanted with humans in general and AIGS in particular."

Chaos smiled and said, "AIGS is a defective bunch. And I… like your suggestion. But you mentioned Mimi McCartney? Where is she now?"

Herb smiled and said, "Waiting, not aware that I know about her and her mission. So…let's talk about that."

Several hours later after going over a lot of minutiae, Herb said, "I have kept you long enough. Thank you for your hospitality. I will be in touch on the meeting with Mimi."

Chaos nodded and replied, "Very well."

Herb grinned and headed back to his stump-ray. As he lifted off and rotated his craft around, his escort returned and led him back to his entry point into the valley. They then banked away from him on each side, leaving him on his own. He smiled and floored the stump-ray back towards CC2.

The next morning while Alex was away inspecting his mansion's construction, Herb briefed Tachymus on his meeting with Chaos. After that, he went to visit Mimi McCartney.

Mimi was outfitted in some of her new lounge wear while looking at Herb on a display. She said, "Sorry, I did not order fucking room service!"

Herb grinned to himself and replied, "Mimi, your friend Chaos sent me."

Mimi straightened up in her chair and said, "Funny man. What's your name, since you obviously know mine?"

"Herb Coulick."

Now on her feet, she walked to the door and opened it. After looking him over, she let Herb in as she asked, "So what's the play here?"

"I would like you to attend a meeting with me and Chaos. I have a stump-ray waiting out front of the lobby."

Guardedly, Mimi said, "Why should I trust you?"

Herb said, "A fair question, but I assure you, I am being truthful and can be trusted." He could read her conflicted thoughts and sense her agitated emotions, Finally, her resolve stiffened.

"I need to get into appropriate attire," she said.

Herb nodded and said, "Can I watch?" Mimi gave him a bemused look and said, "You're not from around here, are you?"

"I am from Earth like yourself, but I am a dolphmanien."

Mimi replied, "I barely noticed. Give me five minutes." She was then off to the bedroom to change. True to her word she was back just that quickly, her years of experience on stage had her able to make quick costume changes. They headed to the stump-ray shortly afterward.

Herb first piloted to a refueling station. Mimi hopped out, and said, "I need something sinful to eat, like fast food. Be right back."

She did not offer to get anything for Herb as he thought to himself, *typical human.*

She arrived back and handed a sack to Herb that she had bought for him along with her own and said, "Enjoy!" Pleasantly surprised that she had behaved differently than he anticipated, he nodded in appreciation as he resumed course to their meeting. Mimi leaned back in her seat, opened up her sack and started munching on a cheeseburger while sipping a soda. Herb said, "So, you like cheeseburgers?"

She nodded and said, "Yep. I can't eat vegan stuff, so I get these meat simulations they make. Tasty compared to an asparagus burger."

Herb shrugged, opened his sack as he said, "I never had this stuff back on Earth. Ate mostly seafood. I mean, I am half dolphin."

Mimi quipped, "I love shrimp!" Herb nodded in agreement as he took his very first bite ever into a cheeseburger. A minute later, he carefully placed it back in the sack and said, "Yeah, well, thanks. Not really something that tastes very good to me. Sorry."

Mimi eyes went wide, and she said, "Well, give it to me then! I'm starving!" Herb handed the sack over, and she dug the burger out, eating around where he had bitten. He said, "I don't have any major contagions you need to worry about."

"You mean cooties. Okay, I believe you." Still, she finished off the second burger sans the part he had bit into.

The trip was uneventful. At the point of descending into the valley, their two escorts from the day before showed up and waggled at the stump-ray occupants. Mimi watched as Herb waggled a flinger back at them. She said, "Are those the tumbleweeds we've been hearing about?"

Herb nodded, and said, "Razor drones actually. Tumbleweeds is the narrow-minded patronizing terms applied by AIGS assholes when the technology got away from them."

"Assholes? Wow! I like you more and more by the minute Herb Coulick!" Herb grinned in response. Moments later, they landed. Before they disembarked, two more drones floated above them and suddenly Chaos was now projected inside the cabin of their craft. Mimi eyes went wide again, this time from seeing their host.

Herb stood and said, "Hello Chaos. I would like to introduce Mimi McCartney." Mimi stood and bowed, much like she typically would at the beginning of one of her concerts to her fans. Herb said, "And Mimi, this is Chaos." Chaos nodded politely.

Introductions completed, the three sat down in a circle. Chaos said, "You are not friends with the AIGS corporation and its employees?"

Mimi shook her head and said, "Far from it. They screwed my career and life over by making an AI based fake of me. I fought them alone in court and lost that battle. Over time, they pulled the same shit on other musicians. We artists joined forces after that."

Chaos said, "And that is when you started Musicians Ashes? Your activist terrorist group?"

She nodded and added, "And we are fully registered on Solarspere."

Chaos said, "I saw that when I first discovered you. After a bit of research, I discovered that AIGS most definitely planned to eliminate compensating celebrities such as yourself. The name of the scheme was Project Overpaid. I can send you the details for your perusal that include all the data of the plans as well as conversations, all at the CEO and senior management level."

Mimi, now in a red-faced fury, choked out, "I knew it! And yes, send me everything you can, I want to post this on the Solarspere, just for starters!"

Chaos nodded and replied, "Done. Plus, and don't take this the wrong way, I am really enjoying your anger. It burns within Chaos as well."

Mimi, after catching her breath from her enraged excitement added, "You don't post online. I could not find your Solar blog."

"Chaos does not blog. We grind."

Mimi's eyes went wide as she said, "Ah, well… that makes sense. So, what is this undertaking that Herb mentioned you could use my help on?"

Chaos smiled and said, "It involves… gathering information." He then outlined a plan to study a STUMBLE drive. At the conclusion, Herb said, "This would give you better abilities to defend yourself it would seem."

Chaos nodded as Herb realized how different this conversation was than with a Kevorkian or human. He had no sense of what was going on inside Chaos's circuit based mind. Yet, he suspected he was not being told everything.

Mimi, now smiling at both Herb and Chaos, said, "So, when do we start?"

Herb nodded and said, "Soon. However, we need to keep you out of sight until mission critical time." Shortly afterward, Mimi and Herb headed back to CC2.

Chapter 17

Two days later, Ben was running late and needed a quick caffeine overdose to prop up his sagging attention span. He had decided after another sleepless night that the econodrive was a gift that kept on giving all year around. The gift was just not giving in a positive way.

Forty kilometers from the Stellar Boom Coffee shop, a shadow appeared in his forward viewscreen, reminding him of how clouds would get in the way of sunshine back on Earth. Was this a dust storm catching up with him? His display became dimmer and dimmer over the next ten seconds, then a sudden thump and screech of crumpling metal rattled throughout the stump ray. He then found himself thrown forward against his shoulder belts as his prized toy rapidly decelerated to a standstill.

Terrified, Ben started looking over his now dark control panel trying to figure out what had happened as the Lethbon began a gradual straight down descent. A couple of tumbleweeds appeared at his viewports, one on his right, the other on his left. He gulped in fear and attempted to link to the public emergency system deployed across the planet which failed. He then tried Celeste, Carrie, and finally, Josh, all to no avail. As descent continued to the surface, he pulled out an emergency envirofield pack in a compartment next to his seat and strapped it on his chest just as the stump-ray touched down. Then, to his horror, the two tumbleweeds repositioned themselves to the front and back of his LethBon and started sawing up their respective sections. He activated his chest pack and exited the driver's side hatch thinking he would be better off taking his chances on the Martian surface.

Once clear of his craft, he could see the tumbleweeds methodically sawing away portions of it, much unlike what was typically reported. The care they were taking was obvious even to him. In the sky above, a freight-ray hovered. It was the craft that had apparently latched onto the Lethbon and disabled it. Ben spotted the infamous Mimi McCarthy hanging out of the door, (he immediately recognized her from videos that he had watched in earlier management meetings). She was enveloped in an envirofield that extended all the way to the surface and encapsulated him. She waved while laughing at the destruction of his Lethbon, absolutely giddy with happiness. She hollered, "Thanks for the STUMBLE drive you AIGS piece of shit!"

Ben chose to sound as generous as possible as he replied, "No problem. Enjoy!" Mimi gave him a wild-eyed look that made his heart palpitate, leaving him to wonder why he had spoken up at all, but the woman was apparently too busy to spend more time on him as she watched the tumbleweeds load the STUMBLE drive from his craft into her stump-ray. Moments later, the Tumbleweeds zoomed off in one direction, the massive stump-ray with the stolen drive in the opposite.

Finally feeling his fear and adrenalin tapering off a bit, Ben retried communicating again, this time raising the local security teams, who were parked over at the very coffee shop he had been trying to get to before this attack, enjoying their morning coffee and donuts and sounding irritated about having to interrupt their bloated consumption to respond to his situation. He then messaged Celeste, Carrie, and finally Josh. He decided not to inform Jesmyn just yet, figuring she was going to detonate at the news and start firing people with him a likely first victim.

Celeste showed up before the security contingent and had him climb into her own Lethbon, where he nervously rattling off the details of the attack and theft. Then Josh arrived, and finally, security who after stowing their excess Stellar Boom donuts in a sack behind their seats, began a haphazard investigation.

Sargeant Hawley, a recent arrival on the red planet from England, proudly stated he was in charge of the security detail. He insisted that Ben escort him around the crime scene, describing what happened. Hawley interspersed his note taking with a lot of "no shits?", and "Fuck alls!" but otherwise seemed to be more of a glorified clerk than an investigator. Ben mentioned that Mimi had called him a piece of shit, which made the Sargeant laugh and scribble the quote in his pad.

Josh stomped over and interrupted the procedure with, "Fucking Tumbleweeds! We can't afford this!" The Sargeant's eyes went wide at the comment. He then looked at Ben and said, "Well, that's sorted! And it looks like you have a ride, so we are off. Make sure to get this garbage heap towed off. Can't have it littering the landscape like that scrapyard of a third planet!"

Ben went livid over having to tow away his own garbage heap that earlier that day had been his prized Lethbon. He wanted to lay down the law to the law, but Josh grabbed him by the arm and said, "Let it go. You got bigger fish to fry." Which, as it turned out, was quite true.

*

Mimi had busied herself over the last three days preparing for the mission she had just executed. She also had hooked up with fellow musician's activists to record her latest song that was inspired by the planned STUMBLE theft. Now on the return trip to her hideout, she was focused on her future. After she had landed and carefully shielded the freight-ray from detection, she broadcast her encrypted transmissions back to Earth from her hideout cave location that Herb had set up with an envirofield, communications and fairly decent field rations, (plus Herb had promised to bring her cheeseburgers whenever he could). The transmissions were then pumped into the Solarspere by one of her activist friends. Moments later Mimi's pre-recorded victory performance was streaming throughout the solar system.

109

Which led to her performance bursting into Jesmyn Welch's live feed transmission of all things great that AIGS had accomplished in the last quarter of the year, despite adverse circumstances and unruly terrorists. She was now replaced on her own view screen by an ebullient Mimi McCartney. Stunned, she immediately wondered, *what fucking idiot is in charge of the Solarspere feed? I will find them! I will find them and hang their pathetic shriveled balls out to dry!"* Not that her livid thoughts had any impact whatsoever on Mimi's victory performance.

Mimi declared, "AIGS just, shall we say, stumbled over their own dicks! Oh, did I say S…T…U…M…B…L…E…? Yes, yes I did! STUMBLE drive, the latest in marginal products from AIGS with stupid ass names! And guess what? I have one. Yep, got it fresh out of a Lethbon that belongs to Ben Stevens of that evil AIGS econodrive project. He thoughtfully handed it over at razor blade point! It is better than econodrive, from what I understand, as it actually does not blow up while in use!"

Mimi then moved onto a stage with her old band and started singing, "It don't blow up, it don't fuck up, it do fit nicely in a freight-ray pick-em-up!" Her band all danced around her in unison clapping hands and waving arms. Jesmyn had to admit, it was a snappy little performance.

The camera zoomed up on Mimi as she continued with "And now for a special announcement! I want my career back! Yep, there ya go AIGS. I got the recordings of Jesmyn Welch and her cohort of senior management lackeys discussing, "Project Overpaid". That little demon of an undertaking was created so that performers and artists, such as me were replaced with AI robotic imitations. Why you ask? Because we were considered too expensive for the AIGS recording label! Let me play just one of the conversations for everyone!" The distinctive voice of Jesmyn stated, "Face it, these so-called artists are a temperamental bunch of prima donnas making crazy demands for more cordolars! I say take a hike, get a real job! Especially that Mimi McCartney!"

Jesmyn blanched at hearing her own voice. How the hell that had gotten recorded and then into McCartney's hands was going to lead to some major inquisitions and associated unhappiness throughout AIGS well before the day was over.

Mimi continued, "Yes, the AIGS boss woman herself, declaring her lack of use for true artists and performers! Well, we have heard it from that Horse's ass's mouth now!" Mimi then broke into a solo performance, singing, "Chaos, oh Chaos, how we love you dark Chaos!" She concluded with "Up yours Jesmyn Welch! You know my demands. And I also want six years of back pay and royalties! Stumble on that! HAHAHAHAHA!"

The feed went dead at that point, with Jesmyn back on the screen, her stunned expression being transmitted to the Solarspere attendees of her own, now wrecked presentation. She stammered as she said, "Well, uh, well, ok, uh, well," then the screen went dead as the poor idiot in charge of the presentation belatedly shut it down.

After swimming through a storm of crazy ideas on what to do, Jesmyn finally called an all hands senior management meeting. She was boiling with rage unlike anything she could remember for the first time since the problematic crash landing of Stieg Daftmann, (the anger then was at Daftmann, who that very morning had said she was just lucky she had met him, and not at all skilled at making money). She had gotten her revenge, via her plot with Brazos. However, today's event made her look the fool to the entire solar system. At a minimum, this revelation of the Project Overpaid meeting raised her blood pressure almost beyond the ability of her bio implants to manage. Her stomach acid was also roiling, making her intermittently belch.

Once the attendees were all present, the ass chewings began. Jesmyn led with, "There are going to be some really unhappy people in this organization today. Now, what the hell happened? First off, how did that woman usurp my presentation feed?"

Silence prevailed. Finally, the VP of marketing, Robin Princeton said, "That will take some time to determine Jesmyn. But let me assure you, we will get to the bottom of it!"

Jesmyn nodded and said, "Oh yes we will, but not you Robin no-longer-with-AIGS Princeton that knows nothing about security and preventing shit such as what just happened! You're fired!" The stunned woman promptly faded away into unemployment oblivion. Jesmyn continued, "Next question while one of you cogitates up a good answer to my first question! How the hell did these recordings get in McCartney's hands? How?" Silence once more. Jesmyn nodded, pointed to a quiet little man, Stan Purvis, VP of Supply Chain and said, "You'll do Pervert! Fired!"

Stan blurted out, "What the hell?" as he too faded away from the call. Jesmyn said, "You all get that? Pervert, Purvis? Like that other turd I fired?" A nervous titter when around the group, then light applause.

The VP of Security, Nicole Norrell said, "Now hold on Jesmyn, Stan could not possibly be involved with that!"

Jesmyn nodded and said, "Thanks bozo Nicole for speaking up finally! Norrell is "no" more! Your fired!" Jesmyn then burped loudly, her stomach still churning. And so it went, though nothing much was determined as to a course of action to deal with this problem, or about how Mimi's bunch had cracked their feed for her little performance and finally, how in the world a STUMBLE drive wound up being stolen so easily.

After the meeting concluded, Jesmyn had to go down and retrieve a large container of industrial grade antiacid which she promptly gulped down, then wound up rebooting a lot of her AI appliances, both mental and physical, to get herself back under some semblance of control. She even laid down and put a cool washcloth on her forehead while her groupies waved large fans over her as she worried that all the stress was overheating her core brain implants. All she knew, at the end of the day, was she was going to hunt down the perpetrators. Which set her off on another course of washcloths, antiacids and reboots.

Chapter 18

There was no doubt in Ben's mind that the tumbleweeds assault on his Lethbon had been a close call—he could even be dead at this point if things had gone just a bit worse. Celeste had brought him home, then came in and sat for a time, patting his back, holding his hand, but finally she said, "Well, buster, I gotta get back to work. Go take a shower, relax, drink some wine, we'll talk later." A moment later, she was out the door. He sighed, stood, and decided her advice was good, but the order was wrong as well as the proper booze prescription. He would start with a couple shots of whisky, then move to wine and think about the shower later.

Four shots later, feeling a bit more relaxed, he was sitting at his dining room table reading the label on the whisky bottle when his doorbell rang. He brought up his front door camera on his internal display. His visitor, he decided, was more than welcome. He opened the door. Carrie was standing there, affecting a look of sympathy as she said, "Oh, my poor dear! I hope you are alright!" An intoxicated Ben, suddenly horny, nodded and smiled as he replied, "Thanks, I could use someone to help me out with my PTSD from today's events, so, come on in. I was about to have some wine."

Carrie, her outfit consisting of another sleeveless mid-thigh dress that showed off every aspect of her figure, stepped in, and said, "Now, that is a great idea! But first, tell me what happened today!" She took his hand, and they walked together as he began rattling off the details of the attack. She nodded sympathetically, and then said, "You do need some stress relief!" She then slipped the dress off her shoulders, letting it slide to the floor, which was all she was wearing besides her high heels. Ben pulled her to him, and they began kissing as she started removing his clothing. A few moments later, they were in his bedroom.

A couple hours later in his hot tub, with Carrie resting her head resting against his chest while she sipped wine, Ben informed her about the STUMBLE drive theft and that Mimi McCartney was somehow controlling the tumbleweeds. She nodded as if this was all very insightful for his part. She pumped him for something more useful. He talked some about econodrive, but it was nothing she didn't already know from her own earlier work for Celeste. Shortly after, she advised she had to leave. She climbed out and dried herself, then dressed as she said, "I think you've had enough for today. Get some rest!" She waved goodbye at the door, then departed as Ben sighed and wandered off for a nap.

Carrie headed back to her place and started uploading information to her encrypted data reservoir she had extracted from Ben about the STUMBLE drive theft. The man was clueless about Chaos, but she definitely was wondering how Mimi McCartney fit into all of this. She decided to reach out to Chaos and find out what was up.

After multiple attempts to link to Chaos, she got a canned recording. It instructed the caller to leave a message, and that Chaos would reach out at its convenience. She shrugged then said, "Give me a call please! And how are you too busy to talk Mr. Chaos?" Which left her with more questions about what was going on. She sighed, thinking how she was burning the candle at both ends a lot lately, doing a great job for TGIF on this assignment as well as the work she was doing for Celeste. However, on the positive side, she was double dipping on pay, TGIF for her spy work as well as her AIGS salary. She smiled to herself and decided to work on her tan by her newly installed patio funded with a bonus that Celeste had arranged after a few sexual interludes between them.

*

Tachymus and Xeon were visiting with Herb at a local Kevorkian Bistro when word of the theft of the STUMBLE drive reached them. Tachymus said, "Herb, what is this all about?"

Herb frowned, thinking about the earlier meeting and the things Chaos had left unsaid. He replied, "Mimi McCartney worked a deal with Chaos. She wanted the Project Overpaid recordings. Chaos claimed it wanted a STUMBLE drive to study. Fair trade I would say."

Xeon said, "So, Chaos got one of the STUMBLE systems? I am not sure this is such a wise move Herb."

Herb got defensive and said, "You saying I am stupid Xeon?"

Tachymus said, "Xeon is not calling you stupid. But Chaos is an enormously powerful weapon we absolutely need to keep control of. What I am trying to fathom right now is why Chaos would want that drive, though admittedly it will get them around the planet much faster than anything else available. We will have to ponder this situation."

Herb nodded and said, "Sorry for the outburst. Still feeling a bit sensitive after the way humans treated me over the last several years."

The three sipped their drinks in silence until Xeon left for early morning meetings. Once he was gone, Tachymus said, "Herb would you do me a favor?"

"Anything my friend."

"If such a situation as this comes up again, would you please reach out and discuss it with me and the team in advance?"

Herb nodded and said, "Certainly." He again reflected back on his earlier impression that Chaos had not told him everything it wanted with a STUMBLE drive.

Tachymus said, "Ah, you have doubts about Chaos?"

Herb sighed, "I cannot read Chaos's thoughts, but there was some sort of undercurrent to the request. I suspected I was being told only what Chaos wanted me to know."

Tachymus replied, "Yes, it is something you have to learn to deal with as your telepathic advantage can work against you in a situation like you just experienced. Follow your intuition next time. I will always have time to talk with you."

"Should we engage Chaos and see if it will elaborate" Herb asked.

Tachymus hesitated, then replied, "It looks like Atraxus was able to penetrate the consciousness of Chaos. The machine is planning an attack on the seaside mansions. We don't have a big problem with that as long as the sea generation project proceeds unimpeded."

Herb nodded slowly, thinking about Alex's new abode being shredded.

Chapter 19

Celeste arrived at Carrie's office, looked around the hallway to see if anyone had noticed her, then buzzed into the room. After providing more than a warm welcome, Carrie said, "Hey, I'd like to work on the STUMBLE drive data base to expand it for use in the solar system. Whatcha' think?"

Celeste nodded and said, "That's a great idea! We both could benefit and Jesmyn is looking for a victory after the Mimi McCartney debacle." She smiled, thinking how capable Carrie was. Plus, she was so darn pretty and sexually talented. Celeste sat down at the lab console and quickly added Carrie to the list of personnel that had access to the database. Task completed, a reminder came up on her daily schedule routine that it was time for the senior staff call with Jesmyn. She waved at Carrie as she departed.

Once Celeste was gone, Carrie perused the database. It was impressive work, and she figured TGIF would find it interesting as she again uploaded a copy to her encrypted data reservoir. A moment later, she decided brunch was in order, so she headed out to the Vonnegut Bistro. She figured she could get the upgrade done quickly for Celeste but needed to stretch out the time as to make it appear challenging, even though by the time she was taking a bite out of the "Breakfast of Champions" special she had ordered, she completed her initial calculations. Besides, Carrie was there to spy and disrupt rather than be helpful. She figured STUMBLE would be a whole lot more useful to her endeavors.

*

Celeste had hoped that Jesmyn would be a bit calmer than she had been in an earlier session since the STUMBLE theft. The call was fairly uneventful with zero job loss. Relaxing a bit, her mind wandered to Ben—they had not had a date together since his run in with the tumbleweeds. So, she called him up and said they needed to get together for dinner at her place. He quickly agreed.

When she got home, she decided to go with a family lasagna recipe. Celeste had no idea if it was particularly different than other recipes, but it was always consistent in quality. She loaded the details into her ChefBot. ChefBot asked, "Madame Celeste, how many will be coming to this dinner?" to which she replied, "Just myself and Ben, but I would like a bit of extra for leftovers." ChefBot nodded then went to work while she headed to her bedroom to change into her evening wear.

An hour later, Ben showed up and after exchanging hugs and kisses, the two were seated out on her patio drinking chianti and nibbling tasty appetizers that ChefBot had whipped up.

Ben asked, "Anything new on the destruction of my Lethbon?"

Celeste replied, "Nope. Though the real problem is the theft of the STUMBLE drive."

More focused on his lost stump-ray, Ben said, "Well, those Lethbons don't exactly grow on trees."

Celeste mischievously replied, "I am sure you are right. Especially with the lack of trees on Mars." She giggled. Ben laughed, the wine and her silliness helped him relax for the first time in several days.

Dinner was delicious, and they complimented ChefBot. After they were done, Celeste and Ben adjourned back to the sofa where they snuggled up to each other. After some more small talk, they got down to business. Celeste, quite inebriated at this point, was reveling in all the new things that Ben was suddenly trying out on her. He had never been particularly sexually adventurous in the past, so all these new positions and methods of driving her arousal came as a pleasant surprise.

Around three in the morning, Ben was spooning against her backside as sobriety set in and she suddenly wondered where he had learned all of this new technique. She heard him snoring at this point and being tired from a full day herself, she drifted back off to sleep, but not before putting a reminder in place to investigate his newly acquired sexual acumen.

The next morning over coffee, she said, "Ben, last night was wonderful. I could not believe some of the new stuff you were suggesting and let me say, it was fun!"

Ben yawned, then grinned as he said, "Great. I've other ideas we can try. I gotta get some rest though, you wild woman!"

Celeste chuckled, and replied, "Great! About these ideas. Where in the world did you get them from?"

Ben's grin faded slightly, but then he said, "Oh. Well, I was doing some research. Came across, uh, what was it called, oh yeah, the Kama Sutra! Great stuff, fun reading!"

Celeste sensed evasiveness in Ben's reply as she asked, "So, you, who rarely read, like never actually, decided to deep dive into a book on kinky sex. You bored with me?"

Ben said, "Oh, heck no sweetheart. I just wanted to please you is all."

Nodding slowly, she queried, "How'd you get so good at this so fast?"

Ben squirmed nervously and said, "Well, uh, I found where I could upload some of the routines into my implant archive? So, it's like… I've done it before, uh you know."

It sounded sort of reasonable, even if his reply was rather fractured. After a moment, she said, "So, send me the links to that, I would love to read it too!"

Ben abruptly stood and said, "Uh, sure hon, will do. Look at the time! Listen, gotta go. Work calls. Love ya!"

Celeste rose and practically had to jog behind him to the door. A quick kiss and he was off. She returned to her chair, sipped her brew and wondered if she had just witnessed a rather less than masterful bullshit job. Something just didn't add up. She shrugged, realizing she needed to get to work herself, so she decided to contemplate the Ben situation when she could devote more attention. Moments later, she was out the door, reviewing her schedule for the day.

Chapter 20

Ben plopped down in his chair behind his mezzanine office desk. Exhausted from lack of sleep, depressed from the loss of the LethBon and finally, being somewhat hung over, he wanted to take a nap, but it was time for the daily morning meeting with the senior management team led by Jesmyn. Yawning a lot, he began reviewing the agenda as he thought to himself about Celeste's snarky comment that he never read anything. Hell, he was reading here, right now, though he had to admit he wasn't absorbed in the effort.

At the top of the hour, the call began, and he joined, yawning loudly as he came into the session. Several people giggled and he shook his head while taking a deep swallow of his steaming coffee, then silently cursed as he had burnt his tongue. Since everyone could see him, some more giggles went around. Some small talk commenced as Ben made a deliberate display of studying the agenda. Jesmyn and her groupies made their entrance. Several of them were cooing to her about how great her new outfit looked, and another was exclaiming that the woman was the best boss known to humanity—ego reconstruction was still in progress after the Mimi McCartney fiasco. She thanked them then started the meeting by addressing the entire group. She said, "As you can see, the agenda today is short, in fact only one topic." She continued, "So, fireside chats. The idea came to me in a flash as I was pondering how to promote the greatness of AIGS and all we have done for the solar system. I am sure you would all agree." After everyone nodded in approval, she continued, "So here is the new plan."

About twenty minutes into the "plan" Ben drifted off to sleep. It only took a moment for others to shift their focus from Jesmyn to him snoring rather loudly. Jesmyn herself glared at him—his snoozing on her call was not helping her ego recovery. She nodded and said, "For a new SVP, he's kinda pissing me off. Oh well. Everyone, watch this!" What looked like laser beams, (all simulated), burned from her eyes and onto Ben's chest. The actual tech, beyond the special effects everyone was viewing, was a highly focused beam of electric current from a hidden emitter in his office that was targeting one of his nipples. He suddenly awoke, a blank look on his face and then he exclaimed, "Fuck, that really hurts!"

Everyone on the call burst out into laughter as Jesmyn said, "Mars to Ben! Yoohoo!" Jesmyn gazed intently as he tried to cover his embarrassment. Obviously, she had done something to him, but he had no idea what.

He stuttered, "Uh, so, uh, sorry. I mean really. Had such a long night working on econodrive. Shit!" The last part he wished he had kept to himself, but his brain now felt like it was on fire.

Jesmyn said, "May I continue now, Master Ben?" The group went quiet as it was now apparent this morning that she was prepared to mess with people in a substantial and painful way and no one else was interested in being a target. He hung his head and said, "I am so embarrassed. Sorry Jesmyn."

Apparently satisfied, Jesmyn continued with her fireside chat marketing plan. One hour later, she concluded. One thing for sure, Ben knew there was no way he could have fallen back asleep, his brain felt like a sizzling hotdog. The call ended and he received a formal notification from personnel saying his bonus was being reduced by five percent due to his "idiotic behavior" in the morning meeting. He sighed, figuring he could weather the reduction since he could just as easily have been fired if Jesmyn had been feeling a bit more pissed off. Ben then had an epiphany. He was now positive that Jesmyn would come after him about econodrive at some point, it was just a matter of when.

*

Celeste was shaking her head, wondering how in the world Ben had dozed off in front of Jesmyn. The story had spread far, wide and

123

at light speed even before the "Ben Meyers got zapped" meeting was over. Thankfully for herself, during her earlier private session, she had found it easy to sell the upgraded STUMBLE database concept to Jesmyn, so she had been excused from the morning meeting to focus on the project. Arriving at Carrie's office, she entered. After a welcome kiss between the two, they sat down at a console. Carrie said, "Wow, you hear about the senior management staff meeting this morning?"

Celeste rolled her eyes and said, "Yes. Men!"

Carrie giggled and said, "Listen, I was wondering about your original research on STUMBLE. Do you still have it? I have a new solar system database with a few stops now programmed in to try all this out with an unmanned test craft but hoped to go over the algorithms you developed to see if I got this stuff right."

Celeste nodded and said, "Sure, I brought it with me today. We can link and you can download the research documents." They proceeded to connect and then opened the research archive Celeste kept with her and was transferring over to Carrie even as they began kissing each other again. An image of Ben without any clothing appeared—disturbingly, it was as if she was seeing it through Carrie's eyes. She thought maybe it was due to some peculiar interconnect between their physical intimacy and the data uplink. She tried to regain what had happened, but the brief visualization was gone. Carrie was acting like nothing had just happened, but now Celeste was convinced something had. She tried again and this time got a view of something that she could only call a giant winged tumbleweed. That startled her back to her own side of their connection.

The research data transfer complete, Celeste, trying to maintain a calm demeanor over her confusion of what she had seen during their interlink, said, "Sorry, I would love to stay, but duty calls." Carrie nodded and turned her attention back to her work.

Celeste smiled tightly, stood, and gathered her things then headed back to her own office.

She kept seeing the naked Ben in Carrie's mind and whatever that other thing was as she walked away. She was frankly confused and decided she needed the rest of the day to herself, especially considering that she had got as little sleep as Ben had the previous night. She told her assistant to just call her if anything came up and moment later she was on her way home. Once there, she hopped in her pool and started swimming laps as she pondered what had happened earlier.

Chapter 21

Alex had invited Herb to brunch out on the patio addition of the Chateau, saying it had been way too long since the two of them had spent any quality time together. Herb, determined to maintain up to date intel on AIGS's daily mischiefs, had agreed enthusiastically with "You rock Mr. Alex!"

Shortly after their meal was served, Saanvi shows up and nonchalantly mentioned more guests had gone missing. Alex replied, "Oh dear, we will look into it! And I have to say, this crispy bacon is delicious!" He gave her a big smile. Saanvi, smiling back, added, "Just so you know, I have now advised senior management. Alex, I can't let this go on, it seems you are doing nothing about this escalating situation." She then turned, gave a suggestive wink to Herb, and walked off.

A disgruntled Alex said, "That woman seems to like to rile me up. And look how she flirts with you Herb. I mean, really, you're dolphmanien."

Herb said, "Yeah, she sure knows quality when she sees it."

Alex frowned and said, "So who's the smarty pants now?" Herb shrugged as he took a bite of his baked cod sandwich.

They went back to eating in silence. However, before they could finish their meal, they both got notification of a meeting with Jesmyn at half past the hour. That gave them five minutes to prepare. Alex got a panicked expression as he said, "Shit. What the hell am I supposed to say?"

Herb replied, "Tell her you have an intricate plan in place to track down the missing guests. I can outline it for you really quick." He then provided a four point plan to Alex who said, "Herb, you are really getting good at this stuff. I'll be sure to mention it in the meeting how you helped."

Herb said, "Don't bother. In fact, take the credit, it will help you with Jesmyn."

Which had been Alex's plan to begin with as Herb already knew from reading his thoughts. He stood and said, "I'll touch base with you later, you can tell me how the call went." Alex nodded, preoccupied. Moments later, the meeting was underway.

Having evaded the call, Herb headed over to the pier where he walked out to the end. He then linked telepathically with Tachymus, something he had previously been only able to do in the water, but his mental facilities had grown over time to where he could do it for short distances on the surface.

"Hey Herb, how's it going?"

"Great Tachymus. How many people have you guys harvested so far? It's now getting attention with AIGS. Rather not have them start poking around down here."

"Oh, let me check." A moment later he replied, "Looks like an even hundred."

"You might want to back off a bit for now. Quite a bit actually. Least for a couple weeks."

"Certainly Herb. We're well under way with regrowing the population anyway."

"That's wonderful and thank you!"

"You're welcome, Herb!"

Herb nodded to himself and headed off to his next appointment with Chaos. His encrypted link to the machine was at the same location that Mimi was hid out, which was fine—he had to deliver some more rations to her anyway. He stopped along the way and picked up two cheeseburger meals as well. After a brief exchange on his arrival with her, he brought up the link, making sure only he and Chaos were in the conversation.

Herb said, "So, how are things…progressing?" Chaos smiled and said, "Chaos is staying quite busy." Herb nodded, now aware of Chaos's hidden agenda. He replied, "Our new… ally appreciates your recognizing their needs as part of your objectives. It is good for all of us that the CC2 water levels continue to rise. Can you ensure that as part of what you are planning?"

Chaos said, "Absolutely. We wants all of us to succeed."

"Excellent! Please keep us apprised of your progress." Chaos paused for a moment, then said, "Understood. Our progress should not be at all difficult to recognize."

The conversation concluded, Herb went out and spoke with Mimi, mostly small talk about provisions and other minor details. She was enjoyable to talk to and was in a good mood after the burgers he had provided so that went well enough.

*

Ben was on his way to see Celeste in his replacement Lethbon, letting it pilot him to his destination as he still felt woozy from the jolt Jesmyn had provided, though his mental discombobulation was fading.

When he arrived, Celeste gave him a big hug and said, "Feeling any better?" He shrugged and said, "Some. Experiencing dizziness part of the time." Celeste gave a brief concerned look, then said, "Let's eat, I've got dinner ready. It might help your recovery."

Ben nodded and followed her to the kitchen table. The food, some fresh lab grown lobster tail, was good, but he picked at his meal—his appetite being part of what was not yet back to normal.

After dinner, he sat as Chefbot cleaned up, staring at his hands that were palms down on the table. Celeste was watching him and came over, and said, "Make some room." He scooted back and she sat in his lap with a mischievous smile and said, "Let's get back to some of those new techniques you been showing off to me." They began kissing and before long were in the bedroom. Ben could not seem to get his thoughts together, even when Celeste was sensuously rubbing herself against him, trying to get him aroused. He said, "I am out of it, sorry. I messed up so badly falling asleep in front of Jesmyn—what she did is really making me pay."

She said, "Well, yes dear, I understand. But if we can get this going again tonight, maybe we can make both of us feel better." Ben smiled weakly, now drowsy, then tried to rouse himself, but failed. Shortly after he fell asleep.

Determined to get Ben feeling better, Celeste linked to his cortical implant to see what she could do. It was then she discovered no Kama Sutra routines but there were plenty of traces of new code that had the distinct style of Carrie's programming in them. She recognized the coding nuances immediately as she had spent so much time previously looking through the woman's work on Econodrive and STUMBLE. She realized then that Ben was being manipulated by the woman. Now angry at Carrie, Ben and especially herself, she abruptly broke the link, slipped on a night robe and shook Ben awake. She told him she needed to get some rest and that he needed to go home. He tiredly nodded, got most of his clothes on while she was escorting him to the door. After he was gone, she sat down and took stock.

She was angry at Ben, but what she really now suspected was that Carrie had been having her way with both of them. The question was why? What was the woman's goal? One thing for sure, she had let herself trust Carrie without a lot of thought. All of which would leave her quite exposed jobwise with Jesmyn if anything went sideways, especially since her projects were major revenue opportunities for AIGS. She went to bed brooding, unable to sleep until shortly before dawn. When she arose, her resolve kicked in. She decided it was time to do a deep dive investigation of her own into Carrie Carlin.

Chapter 22

Alex was at his usual table at the Vonnegut Bistro, sipping on a French pressed coffee and enjoying the seaside view while waiting for his eggs benedict that was the bistro's brunch special, appropriately named "Hocus Pocus", as there were no chickens on the planet to produce eggs, yet there they were on the menu. Things were looking pretty good at the moment especially since Saanvi had advised they had no new missing guests in the past week. That was positive news, though attempts at locating the other missing people had failed, which was not so positive. This was mostly due to the fact he had no idea how to implement the complex search plan Herb had earlier provided. Alex figured he'd blame the problem on Herb if anyone asked questions.

At the conclusion of his meal, he decided to go check on his new home's construction progress. Walking out of the restaurant, he ran into Herb and asked him if he'd like to come along. Herb grinned and replied, "Sure, sounds like fun." Alex grinned back, feeling for a moment the old camaraderie that had been missing lately in his relationship with the Dolphmanien. Two minutes later by stump-ray, they were at the property.

Alex had wanted his seaside estate to be as close as possible to the shopping and restaurant action and had bought one of the priciest lots. He led Herb onto the impromptu tour, extolling the grand design, the quality of construction, the materials selection, the ambiance and whatever other aspects of his man castle that came to mind. In his enthusiastic state, he failed to notice Herb rolling his eyes and pulling on the inside of his collar with a flinger in an exaggerated fashion. Oblivious, Alex plunged ahead in his over the top narrative. As they completed their excursion, Herb stopped in his tracks with a most peculiar expression on his face then said, "How about we check out the front yard facing the sea," and headed out the door. Alex, somewhat confused at Herb's sudden intensity, shrugged, and followed, barely keeping up.

Once outside, Herb kept walking towards the inland sea. Alex caught up just as some faint music trickled in from the opposite direction. It was getting progressively louder as they stood there. He looked at Herb and said, "What the hell is that?" Herb replied, "I'm no expert, but it sounds like Mozart's Requiem." Alex frowned, wondering how in the world Herb would know about music by Mozart, and by the specific work at that.

The volume was now becoming painful. It was then that a massive low flying craft rapidly approached, headed directly towards them. Herb shouted over the din, "I think we should get the fuck out of here!" and started running for their stump-ray. Which seemed like a good idea to Alex—he followed in hot pursuit even as he kept glancing back over his shoulder at the monstrous machine.

That illusion evaporated as the formation lowered down closer to the ground, then split into teams of whirling blades, each going after one of the new homes. Alex felt a panicked surge of recognition then—these were tumbleweeds but working together like nothing ever documented from earlier attacks.

The devastation was awesome to watch as the homes were shredded by the machines with explosive abandon. Bits and pieces of debris were flying their way as they clambered aboard the stump-ray and Alex, completely out of breath and terrified, fumbled at the controls. Herb hollered, "Let me take over!" and without waiting for permission, assumed control and had them airborne in seconds, flying out over the sea. Once safely out of range, Herb then pivoted the craft around and went into hover mode as they watched the destruction. Alex gaped, wordless, as his new abode was pulverized into bits much smaller than any component used to assemble the structure. It was a total loss, and he started sobbing. Herb reached over and patted him on the back as the Dolphmanien viewed the ongoing saw-fest. Moments later, the Razors reunited and accelerated away just as the Requiem concluded.

*

AIGS security had been notified by other observers of the attack since the assault had been clearly visible all the way back at the Chateau. Teams were now belatedly arriving with nothing much more to do than assess the damage and search for any injured people that might have been in the area. Watching this, Alex was now cursing to himself as he said, "This is like the fire department showing up in time to save the fucking foundation!" Herb laughed, finding that comment truly funny and worth filing away for future use.

The senior supervisor of security was on the ground, hollering at his charges to appear he was in some sort of control. Alex having calmed down a bit, flew the stump-ray back to the scene, setting down next to the supervisor. As he hopped out, he said, "Nobody is yet living in these homes, they were unfinished and it's the fucking weekend. But thanks for letting them get ground up like chili powder!"

The supervisor spun to face Alex as Herb strode up alongside Alex. The man said, "Who the hell are you mister? You can't talk to us like that. We're corporate security!"

Alex, now in full righteous indignation mode, said, "Oh? Fucking really? Security? Well, you suck at a corporate level!" The supervisor turned red and hollered, "Arrest that man!"

Herb smiled and said, "I would not do that if I were you, um," as he read the name on the man's uniform, "Supervisor Swinney."

Supervisor Swinney, now quite angry himself, gave Herb the once over, said, "Who the fuck are you and why the hell not?"

Alex had regained some composure and chipped in, "Because I am the goddamn program manager of the entire fucking CC2 fucking project you halfwit twit! And you are standing on my fucking shredded property!"

132

Suddenly nervous, Supervisor Swinney said, "I need to seem some ID buddy!" Which Alex immediately provided, nearly shoving it up the man's nose.

Supervisor Swinney blanched, suddenly more worried about his position with AIGS as he was talking to his boss's, boss's, boss, (he was, after all, pretty low on the food chain). He said, "Mr. Meyers. Wow. A true pleasure to meet you, really. Such horrible circumstances, however. Uh… sorry for the confusion, you know. Now, let's all calm down. I mean, I'm calmed down, I hope you are, and, what's done is done, no casualties… and clearly this was some sort of dastardly surprise attack."

Alex replied, "Clearly? No fucking shit! Well thanks for the detailed synopsis, Einstein!" Alex turned even redder, then continued, "Where the hell were your people Supervisor Swinney, when all this crap went down? Oh, let me guess, eating donuts at StarBlast? Sipping fancy latte?"

Supervisor Swinney seemed to suddenly understand that his department was devolving into a bad joke regarding the amount of time they spent expanding their waistlines but otherwise not being of any real use as "corporate security". He gurgled his reply, "Sorry sir, we were… detained on important business. Please, uh, we gotta go over the scene here and get a report ready for you and I am sure other senior management."

Alex, now staring down the man said, "Capital idea Supervisor Swinney. You'll go… far!"

It was obvious that Alex's last comment had not eased Supervisor Swinney's now heavy breathing and had compounded the man's agitation. The man gulped and headed off towards his staff, bleating a blizzard of instructions, each basically overriding the previous, to the point where the security officers were milling around aimlessly.

Herb watched the confused humans in amusement and said, "This is great! Sorry about your house though." Alex sighed and replied, "Yeah, great. Ha-fucking-ha. Okay, I need a drink, and I mean the serious hard stuff as I am sure we are about to have a grand and wonderful time with Jesmyn."

Herb nodded in agreement, while attempting not to laugh. Alex gave him a sidewise glance and said, "If I did not know better, I would say you seemed to be getting a kick out of all of this."

Herb lied, "No way boss, I just liked the way you handled that smarty pants, Supervisor Swinney." Alex nodded in agreement, thinking he *had* handled that situation quite well. The two then boarded Alex's stump-ray and headed back to the Vonnegut Bistro for some liquid fortification.

Both Alex and Herb were one sheet to the wind when an emergency conference call was announced to discuss what had happened to all the seaside homes. Alex did not let that slow him down, figuring if he could achieve at least two sheets, he would be able to weather the call and if he didn't, he would at least have enjoyed some decent whisky. He slurped down the contents and dumped an immediate refill into his glass from the bottle he had grabbed on the way to their table.

*

Celeste was sitting in a lawn chair on her patio reading a novel. A real book, made of paper. Carrie had recommended she give it a try a while back, before the current situation that led to Celeste's loss of trust in the woman. She found that she quickly developed a fondness for the physical experience of turning pages. The story was by the very author that the Vonnegut bistro had been named for and was entitled, "Player Piano". A lot of the century and a half old story had become true back on Earth, but not so much on Mars because AIGS did not allow anyone unemployed to hang around and cause problems.

As she flipped to a new page, a notification came in of the organized tumbleweed attack at CC2, that there was to be an emergency meeting and specifically, her immediate and total presence

134

was required to get these pests shut down as it was one of her major assignments. That project had now been accelerated to the "red alert" stage.

Her thoughts immediately went to whom she had put in charge of *that* work, none other than Carrie Carlin. That Carrie had recently kept popping up as a problem kept Celeste's suspicion and paranoia levels rising exponentially.

Her pulse quickened as she saw the destruction of the homes at CC2 that had been included in her notification and she realized she was going to have to come up with something really definitive and irrefutable to hang on to her position. She decided she needed an update from brother Alex and as she bookmarked her place in the novel.

Once she had linked up with little brother, she realized he was not going to be of any help. The man was plastered and ranting, "My home, Celeste, my new home! Sawdust I tell you, sawdust!". He then belched and lifted his recently refilled glass to his lips as he took a huge gulp. He continued, "Ah, now, that was some good shit!"

Realizing she needed more detail than "sawdust", she said, "Where's Herb?"

Alex got a serious look on his face, burped, then said, "He's right here next to me, providing moral support. Sawdust I tell you, sawdust!"

Celeste, feeling herself losing her composure said, "Well put moral support Herb on here, I need somebody that can talk coherently about what the hell happened!"

A moment later Herb appeared, holding his own glass, smiling beatifically at her. She said, "You able to put an intelligible sentence together that can explain what happened?"

Herb straightened up and recited the incident at length. Alex chimed in at the end, "Herb even identified the Mozart piece the fucktards were playing! Sawdust!"

Celeste said, "Sawdust? Never heard of it."

Herb said, "No, not sawdust Alex. The Requiem!"

Celeste sighed and disconnected. She needed more details on Carrie, so she checked her AI inbox where an update had arrived on her earlier research. As she read through the information, she saw a pattern emerging. This report coincided with various events that had happened since the woman's arrival and confirmed it with dates and times. Thus armed, she quickly planned a defense. She realized she would have to be bold and aggressive, even with Jesmyn.

*

Working from home, Carrie had just completed finishing touches on the Solar Stumble Database when the news about the CC2 attack arrived. She grinned, thinking about how well things had been going—AIGS was falling more and more into bedlam.

On a tri-crypted link earlier that morning, her boss back on Earth had assured her she was going to really enjoy the bonus she would receive for all the fantastic work she had done, and that Angela Koutouki herself was well aware of her efforts. She grinned to herself and wondered what she would spend it all on. In the end, she was growing her cash stash in a secret account back on Earth—there were definite monetary benefits to being paid by both sides. She was a bit homesick as well. The thought of finally returning to Earth and leaving Mars perked up her mood—the only enjoyable place to hang out here was CC2 and it was going to be some time now before it was remotely back to normal. A message from Celeste interrupted her reverie—she needed to join a meeting in the next ten minutes. She decided she would upload the Solar Stumble Database after the meeting since the company helped pay for it.

With a few minutes until the conference call, she made herself a sandwich, figuring this would be a "deranged Jesmyn" sort of meeting. As she munched on her food, she decided she should reach out to the woman after the call. It had been a couple weeks since their last fun encounter at the CEO's palace.

*

Celeste, Alex, Ben and Herb all joined the call within seconds of each other, then Carrie. Jesmyn joined last, looking a bit rumpled for a change as she got right to the point. "Well, what a fucking, cocksucking day it has been so far! Every goddamn home being built in fucking CC2 fucking pulver-fucking-ized! I am beyond livid! Oh, and excuse my fucking French!" No one laughed, it was clear she was in full pissed off mode. She finally sighed and said, "So, I personally have been out to visit the scene of the crime, and I have read a briefing that Alex Meyers provided via his pal Herb, as they were both there as eyewitnesses when the attack took place. Herb, you write well for somebody with no fingers! I then spoke with Supervisor Swinney to confirm what we read in Alex's report, and oh, p.s., he is no longer a supervisor or with AIGS and is packing his bags for departure from Mars as I speak. Job opening anyone if there is interest in providing real security on this fucking planet which seems nonexistent after the last two incidents. Anyway, now down to business." She paused, then said, "Celeste. You are the person responsible for getting the tumbleweeds shut down. It now appears they not only are *not* shut down, but able to work together in a way we have never seen before and which AIGS *cannot afford!* I need answers, now!"

Celeste nodded and said, "Jesmyn, thank you for a chance to speak to the group. So, here are the specifics. As you stated, I am in charge of the project to shut down the tumbleweeds. I hired Carrie Carlin for that task. As you remember, you recommended her to me after making her acquaintance at the tradeshow last year on the Startanic. I have some details I would like to share, but first, Carrie. Please provide a report on your progress and any… problems you might be aware of in shutting down the tumbleweeds." Jesmyn seemed about to say something as she glared first at Celeste and then Carrie but then sat back in her chair. All were now looking at Carrie, who flickered her eyes for a moment as she wiped her lips and set down a sandwich she had been gulping down.

She brightened and then said, "Well, I think the program has been going… pretty well, I mean, I focus, I really focus on my work. But it seems the tumbleweeds have outside help of some sort. I am all over that, trying to run it down."

Jesmyn frowned, and said, "Help? What the hell do you mean by help Carlin?"

Carrie sighed and replied, "Inside help. A spy, I think. Maybe on the payroll of the tumbleweeds as well."

Celeste looked like she was about to come through the screen as she said, "Payroll? Do the tumbleweeds have a payroll now? Carrie, please stop with the lying!"

Carrie laughed as she started to pick up her sandwich, but then abruptly put it back down. Sounding desperate, she said, "Well, no, not a real payroll. But somebody who is supporting them. Perhaps that someone is right here, secret agenda and all, on this call! Okay, you drug it out of me! Yes, it's Herb! I repeat, I believe it's Herb Coulick!"

Herb's eyes went wide where he sat next to Alex who was now drunkenly staring at him. Herb riffed, "I am on dah payroll of dah tumbleweeds! What a genius I am!" He then glared at Carrie and said, "That's rich. Very rich. Except I need my backpay if I am on that payroll!"

Carrie glared back and said, "You smart ass! I have proof!"

Herb stuck out his tongue at her in response.

Celeste cut her off with, "So do I Carrie. But it's not Herb. As it turns out, it's you. You are the spy! Jesmyn, I have the encrypted transmissions that Carrie has been sending to what is now known as "Chaos"! Chaos, in reality, is the project name she came up with. She wrote the code modifications that joined the tumbleweeds together into one sentient, functional weapon. Carrie is also the person who uploaded the code into the tumbleweeds. It corrected and enhanced the AI rather than shut the weapons down. Carrie's code allowed them to become some sort of rabid, well-armed labor union!"

Alex looked confused, but relieved as he patted Herb on the back. Herb, trying to hide his own relief, (he was somewhat involved after all via the Kevorkians), jumped to his feet and cried out, "Traitorous woman!"

Jesmyn was also looking confounded now as she followed the rapidly degenerating, yet informative conversation. She said, "Carrie, I thought you were a friend. Celeste, why would she do that? Why?"

Celeste said, "Here's the worst of it Jesmyn. Besides the woman seducing you, she did the same thing to Ben Stevens and then to myself! She has been working us all over, getting in deep, gathering our top corporate secrets, while doling out lots of free sex and friendship! I only recently became aware of this and have been gathering evidence to present. This attack is the direct result of her work! And to add to all of this, she is in frequent contact with TGIF back on Earth, at least a couple times a week!"

A shocked Ben whimpered, "Carrie? Have you been sleeping with Celeste? And me? You're horrible! You boob flashing demoness!"

Carrie said, "Oh, you loved it, Ben! And all of you are just a bunch of sex addled morons! And of course I slept with Jesmyn, she's a narcissistic idiot! And yes, you Ben, with your pathetic flesh covered inflatable dick! And Celeste, you suck in the sack and your code is trash! Ok? And now you will all pay!" She then heaved the remains of her sandwich towards the remote assemblage with little effect other than a few gasps.

Jesmyn said, "This call is over except for Alex, Ben, Celeste, Herb and me! Security, oh shit, uh, whomever is near her, grab Carlin's ass. If she gets away, you will be beyond fired. More like in orbit around the planet without a space suit!"

Before Jesmyn could complete her last diatribe, Carrie disconnected. Celeste was shifting her gaze back and forth from Ben to Jesmyn. Drunk Alex had a shocked look and Herb's beatific smile had returned. All the other senior management had dropped like a stone from the call.

Jesmyn started with, "Celeste, I think I will fire you anyway."

Celeste came back with, "Nope, bad idea this time Jesmyn. You set this fucking travesty in motion by being the first in line to fall for what this woman set out to do. I have all I need to prove you initiated this crazy shit and you won't be able to destroy my evidence because I know how to keep it away from you. I'm not going down without a fight that you will hate and that will do even more serious damage to the reputation of AIGS. And lately, as you damn well know, AIGS has demonstrated a chain of failures."

Alex, still boozed up, said, "Ladies, let's talk about this calmly. I mean, I can see tempers are flaring." He then hiccupped, raised his drink and took another sip.

Jesmyn, obviously struggling for control, said, "You would do that Meyers? After all I've done for you?"

"You just threatened to fire me Jesmyn and accept no responsibility yourself. You're also the person that recommended Carrie to me, and finally, I am the one that came up with the proof of what she is up to—which is the code that she wrote to unify the tumbleweeds. And let's not forget that, as well as the STUMBLE drive tech theft from Ben's Lethbon. I imagine she is behind that as well. I have done nothing to you but save your ass repeatedly up until now!"

Herb quipped, "She has a point Jesmyn. You should keep that in mind with any decisions you make."

Jesmyn said, "Thanks flipperman, now shut the hell up."

Herb smiled and said, "Flipperman. I like that, though it sounds a bit racist. Did everyone hear that?"

Ben whimpered, "We should investigate econodrive now. Carrie was involved in looking at the early detonations and has new code loaded into the system."

Everybody got a flash of reality in their eyes at the last part of his statement and Jesmyn, gathering herself, said, "Ben, get your team on it now. Celeste, help the man, I'm positive he will need it. People, we've got problems to deal with. We can fuck with each other later if that is necessary! Call over!"

Shortly after the call ended, Celeste wondered how things had gotten so screwed up so fast since breakfast. She sighed, realizing that at least, for now, she still had her job and was indispensable. But she knew it was just a matter of time with a perpetually scheming Jesmyn that they would have another confrontation and Celeste needed to gird herself for the battle of her career.

*

Carrie had barely escaped and without time to pack. She had jumped into her Lethbon and headed straight to where Chaos would be hiding. As she entered the valley, she was still cursing to herself. The damn meeting with Jesmyn had her walking into Celeste's carefully laid trap. Her own last ditch attempt to deflect blame on Herb had been a mistake. However, she was positive that he had previously communicated with Chaos and was up to some alternate agenda.

She arrived without incident but before she could exit, Chaos projected into the stump-ray. She breathlessly said, "Please, I need your help. AIGS is after me, and I'm gonna wind up in some sort of corporate prison here quick."

Chaos smiled and said, "Well, that's terrible. You should probably get off the planet."

"You will help me then?"

"I might have if you had not thrown one of our best allies under the proverbial bus during your meeting, as you humans like to say. Herb updated Chaos a short time ago if you are wondering how we know. Your action says you cannot be trusted, no matter what you have done to date."

"Herb contacted you? He's the one that can't be trusted!"

"Carrie. Leave now. You are wasting your time. Besides…I will be busy today."

Cursing under her breath, she reversed course and headed out, no destination yet in mind but she knew she had to somehow hide out, then see if TGIF could help arrange her escape. She immediately sent some encrypted messages, now wondering if Celeste was reading them as fast as she sent them. Which left her questioning how in the world Celeste had so easily broken into her earlier transmissions. She shook her head—she was trying too hard to process all this new information and she was, for a change, the one scrambling.

Chapter 23

Back on Earth, CEO Angela Koutouki was enjoying her personal Caribbean vacation island where she had established her southern headquarters—along with a rather massive mansion she whiled away her time in.

It was a moderate sunny, breezy sort of day, provided by an island enviroshield that provided all the comfort that was previously afforded in this part of the world before humans had driven the climate into an out of control state.

She had been swimming in a humongous pool she had nicknamed the Atlantic for its generous proportions, getting her exercise in before some scheduled meetings she had to officiate. Finishing her last lap, she climbed. It was then that her stewardess, Patricia, arrived. Clearly in an agitated state, Patricia gave a brief nod, "Madame Angela, there is something happening at our headquarters in New York City. I think you should come with me. It does not sound good!"

Having never heard Patricia so alarmed, Angela tossed her towel onto her lounger and said, "Lead the way!" They both jogged to where a wall sized display showed SolarSpear newscasters describing the destruction of the Manhattan TGIF headquarters. Angela gaped at the devastation. She had bought the former Empire State Building decades ago upon her return from Mars and converted the interior of the landmark into TGIF's original headquarters. At the moment, however, smoke was rising from the structure, debris was everywhere, and the building was now only about one third as high as it had been at the start of the morning.

Stump-rays of the New York City-State police were zooming around the remains as monstrous machines were shredding the building a floor at a time. Extremely loud rock and roll music was blaring out in every direction. The police were firing every weapon they had to no effect. According to the newscasters, no one had been killed so far, as an explicit warning had arrived shortly before the machines whittled off the needle atop the building at the beginning of the assault. The warning—all humans should evacuate or die.

As they watched, a heavily armed contingent of TGIF security joined in with the police, trying to halt the destruction. Several of the machines, looking like flying radial saws, countered by cutting away vital components off the defenders, leaving them to crash to the ground. There were police and security personnel ejecting out of their craft faster than reinforcements could arrive. The destroyed craft were adding their own debris to the pile of wreckage around the building.

Finally, the only thing that was left was the ground floor and rubble. With the assault completed, the machines reconverged into a wing formation and a moment later the attackers were literally gone in a poof creating a large shockwave that shattered windows on nearby buildings.

The newscasters went wild at this last part, as if the destruction of TGIF headquarters was not enough. Angela shut down the feed, knowing that nobody reporting on this event had anything worth hearing. She knew this was the AIGS weapon that her spy, Carrie Carlin, had modified. Along with that, she had been briefed about STUMBLE and its recent solar system upgrades. The drive system had obviously been used here if the arrival and departure of the weapon was any indicator and all of this left her wondering, *what the hell has Carrie Carlin done?*

Turning to Patricia, Angela said, "Advise all departments. We are officially on a war footing with AIGS and Mars. Also, have somebody determine what that damn music was the machine was playing! It might be a clue of some kind!"

Patricia blanched, and replied, "On it!"

"Oh, and get Carrie Carlin on the horn!"

"The horn, Madame?"

Feeling her age at using such an ancient reference, Angela barked, "You know, our encrypted comms links!"

"Very well Madame!"

Angela fumed, "That damn Jesmyn! I always knew this day would come!" She stomped off to prepare for meetings she would now have to officiate. Her anger gained momentum because this was supposed to have been a peaceful Caribbean Friday.

*

A short time later, Angela was listening to various theories on the attack in Manhattan. Most were uninformed, a few were kind of nutty, in the end, none provided any useful information. Unlike Jesmyn at AIGS, after getting TGIF up and running to her satisfaction two decades ago, Angela had left a lot of mundane day to day drudge work to the senior staff. She was more interested in strategic issues and in maintaining her current physical configuration that kept her youthful in mind and appearance. Along with that she had an extensive schedule of tennis, yoga, and pool side tanning sessions. So, this meeting with her senior staff was only getting on her nerves as she watched her day tick away . Her original schedule now looked a lot like the former Empire State Building.

Frustrated, she raised her voice and said, "Where the hell is that damn Carrie Carlin? I mean, I ain't the person that should have to be asking this! The woman is on Mars for this Operation Disruption that was supposed to remain on Mars, keep AIGS off balance while we surpassed their quarterly financials for a change. Now we appear to be the target of an attack by AIGS! Let me repeat, a goddamn attack!"

Everyone remained silent. She said, "Find that woman, find out what she knows, then we can formulate some kinda plan. Or like we used to say in the olden days, this ain't rocket science!" She glared around at the participants, concluding with, "Goddamn it!" Muffled acknowledgements went around as the call ended. She sighed, stood,

145

stripped off her robe and dove into the pool to burn off her anger with more laps.

*

Jesmyn, Celeste, Ben and Alex were having a rare in-person meeting at the Red Dust Valley HOA Lodge, the facility paid for by monthly fees that Ben griped about quite a lot as he liked to declare, "I rarely used the damn place!" They were huddled around a holographic projection of the Solarspere news that was spewing a stream of stories about the attack on TGIF in New York, replaying moments of the battering over and over again. Jesmyn looked at Celeste and asked, "How the hell did that damn thing get to Earth? Or are there more than one of them now? I've got a bad feeling about this shit. I am quite positive that Angela Koutouki is ballistically pissed off right about now.

Celeste nodded, "It's Carrie, once again. She must have leaked the upgraded STUMBLE database to this Chaos thing she created. Nothing else makes sense!"

Jesmyn barked, "So, where are we on finding that slutty little spy? Sleeping with everybody, Alex the obvious exception of course, to worm information out of us." Which left Alex looking both embarrassed and relieved to be left out on Carrie's sexual escapades.

Celeste replied, "Alex, consider yourself lucky in this case." She smiled at him and continued, "So, I now have a tracking history on her rental stump-ray after her escape. She did go visit Chaos, at least where we suspect the beast hangs out. It looks like she stayed only a few minutes then left. I think we'll have her in custody within the next couple of hours. By the way, this is further confirmation of her duplicity."

Jesmyn nodded and said, "We need to glom onto her ass. Now, priority number one. Ben, how are we coming on econodrive? Did the evil witch screw with that as well?"

Ben said, "Yes, and we have isolated and removed her work. We should be good now to resume production."

146

Jesmyn said, "Excellent. Ok, Alex, update please on CC2."

Alex said, "We have the construction bots cleaning up the job sites, some are already cleared, so we can restart the home builds. And we are at ninety five percent completion of the inland sea. All in all, about as well as could be expected."

Jesmyn sighed and said, "Let's ramp up the home rebuilds, we have wealthy and valuable clients waiting and we need to get the deals closed." Alex nodded. That was it for the call. Lunch arrived, arranged for by Jesmyn, though it was obvious from the way everyone barely nibbled on their food, the lodge was not a great place for a meal.

*

Angela grimaced when her security team contacted her, requesting an urgent meeting to provide updates on AIGS. She sighed, not wanting to be bothered twice on the same day. It was short, not so sweet and rather confusing since she had previously convinced herself that she knew who was behind the attack. Apparently, the very weapon that had whittled away her Empire State Building headquarters had a few days before attacked the AIGS CC2 project site, wreaking havoc, though AIGS had been trying hard to keep it out of the news. Also, this artificial intelligence based weapon, now going by the name of Chaos, was self-aware after Carrie's software updates. Chaos had also been provided with AIGS top secret technology called STUMBLE. The technology was meant to be for local use on Mars, but it had received another code update from Carrie that allowed the jump to Earth.

Angela said, "So this is all her work?"

Jacob Gretch, head of security, replied, "Yes, it seems Carrie Carlin is behind all this. We have contact with her now. Working on her escape plan. For what it's worth, she did her job, though, apparently a tad too well."

Angela sighed and said, "Shit. Anything else?"

"Nope. Oh, and that music that played in the attack. We identified it. It's entitled "Sympathy for the Devil". Kind of a cool song in its own right…"

His voice trailed off as Angela gave him a withering look. She replied, "Thanks for that great tip on golden oldies. Now, I want Carrie's assets seized. We know she has hidden accounts. That's it for now, fucking toodles." The call ended, which left Angela ruminating. Reluctantly, she decided her best course was to meet her old nemesis, Jesmyn, to discuss how to negate the Chaos threat.

*

The senior members of the Kevorkian Grand Council were in emergency session discussing the bedlam created by Chaos on Mars and Earth. Tachymus was running them through an update as Xeon displayed a pile of images he had assembled a half hour earlier.

A senior council member, Dinkamus of Elipissian, asked, "So how does this impact our timeline and plans?" Tachymus answered with, "We have our starship nearly fully repaired. Plus, all the members of our Alliance have been brought out of stasis and are repopulating themselves with the best of their respective species. This is actually more of a problem for the humans."

Atraxus added, "And our ocean based city is fully constructed!" A flutter of approval went around the group.

Tachymus continued, "So to add to the human's confusion over recent events, we will soon be making our own existence known to them. We just need to focus on detail so we can finally complete our journey to our new home— Kevorkian Central!"

Xeon chimed in with, "Formerly known as Earth!"

A cheer went up consisting of numerous appendages in a variety of biological configurations moving erratically along with a cacophony of incomprehensible utterances. The meeting then adjourned for supper. Xeon pulled Atraxus and Tachymus to the side and asked, "Have we heard from Herb yet? I want to make sure we really know the full extent of what Chaos did."

Tachymus gave a cynical waggle of one of his outermost eyes and said, "You seem to lack confidence in the Dolphmanien. Why?"

Xeon said, "He's awful new to this sort of thing. And aspects of his appearance and demeanor reminds me of the Distainiens, if you remember that traitorous bunch. At any rate, are we pushing him too hard?"

Tachymus frowned at the Distainien comment and said, "I had not thought of that bunch of morons in a long time Xeon. Our Dolphmanien ally is far smarter than they were. At any rate, I doubt he is a problem. In fact, Herb is doing quite well. We just need to be patient. I will have him brief us here in the very near future." Tachymus sensed his last reassurance had not placated Xeon when during the meal, Xeon started talking again about Herb's loyalties, going over his same earlier talking points. At first, irked by the return to the subject, it made Tachymus suddenly think of a great idea. He reached over with a tentacle and tapped on Xeon's brainpan then said, "I have a plan for Herb. It just came from out of the blue, as the humans like to say." Xeon asked, "Oh? What's that?"

Tachymus said, "Since he is part human and has their sexual design parameters, we should create him a Dolphmanien partner. We can easily produce a high quality female then educate her into the Kevorkian way of thinking. It could be done in a very short period of time. Once we put the two of them together at the right moment, she can become an influencer to his way of thinking and lock him into our alliance as a solid partner."

Xeon waggled his antennae as he considered the plan and finally said, "Brilliant. Tachymus, you are a genius!" Tachymus did his equivalent of a toothy smile from the compliment and said, "So, who's up for dessert?" as he perused a menu of human faces.

*

Halfway home from the Red Dust Valley Lodge luncheon Celeste was summoned by Jesmyn, along with the other attendees.

The actual message was, "Everyone get your asses back here now!" She sighed and reversed course, wondering what was now going on.

The group, now reassembled, were viewing a live video transmission. To everyone's surprise but Jesmyn, they were looking at Angela Koutouki and some lackey Angela introduced as "Jacob, my security dude".

Jesmyn started with, "Long time, no wanna-see Angela."

Angela said, "Could not agree more Jesmyn. However, I am not going to waste time with insults. We all have a major problem."

"Besides TGIF?"

Angela remained expressionless and said, "Jacob, the floor is yours." To which he proceeded to dump the same briefing on the AIGS bunch he had given to Angela earlier, sans a few details about Carrie.

At the conclusion, Celeste, with a nod from Jesmyn, said, "That's great and dovetails nicely with what we know. However, you left out the part that your spy, Carrie Carlin was supposed to deactivate the tumbleweeds, as we called them here and instead, apparently under a TGIF plan, turned it into a superweapon."

Angela sighed and said, "Listen, it was all just business. But now that this Chaos thing, as it calls itself, is hopping back and forth between our planets, I recommend we form a coalition to destroy it. We do that, we can get back to business as usual and not have to look at each other's faces on these sorts of calls again. Maybe even for decades."

Jesmyn said, "So, you want coopetition?"

Angela nodded and replied, "You actually got my point, for a change, Jesmyn."

Jesmyn gave her a cynical smile and said, "Assuming we can, for a change, believe what you are saying about coopetition between our two firms, what do you suggest that we do?"

Angela waited for a moment, realized that her lackey was lacking, barked, "Dump the plan out! The day ain't gettin' any younger."

Jacob, wide eyed, said, "Uh, sure! So, we have part of our fleet that we can redirect to Mars and be there in just under forty eight Earth hours from their current position. You know, normal time sort of stuff."

Celeste guffawed and said, "So fifty hours, real time. Slow ships I guess."

Angela sighed and said, "This is going to be an even bigger pain in the ass if you keep this bullshit going people. Now, shall we get on with it or not?"

Jesmyn said, "Yes, fine, it's a deal. Send over the contracts. And again, this little partnership is only for the duration of the existence of Chaos. Once that thing is toast, this unholy alliance is finito."

From his office portal, Ben was watching for the arrival of the TGIF fleet. Celeste had arrived moments earlier where they had spoken without eye contact about the current situation. Neither were able to forgive the other for what each had done with Carrie. Additionally, both felt guilty about their unintended participation in the woman's schemes which had led to this moment.

Celeste mentioned that Jesmyn was aboard the Startanic, which was situated right outside the production plant. Ben nodded towards the huge craft as he said, "Okay, that's a pretty impressive ship." Celeste nodded wistfully in agreement, and said, "Yes. Large. Lengthy." Ben gave a sidelong glance at the woman. It made him think of how good things had been in their former relationship and he silently kicked himself for being an idiot. Without a plan, he gushed, "Listen, Celeste. I want to apologize. I was an idiot. I let my career desires and just plain dumbass lust screw things up." Celeste looked thoughtfully at Ben and nodded, then shifted her attention back to the scene before them. That left him feeling worse until Celeste said, "Mistakes were made. By both of us. Neither realized what a lying schemer Carrie really is."

Ben replied, "Thanks to you and what you found out, at least we both still have jobs." Celeste gave a small nod of acknowledgement.

*

Standing on the bridge of the Startanic, Jesmyn was impatiently waiting for the meetup with the TGIF ships. Based on every calculation and permutation she had run on their current predicament, right here at the factory was the most likely scenario to bring all of this bullshit to a swift conclusion once and for all. Just contemplating having to talk with Angela Koutouki drove her computational implants into psychopathic overload. She took deep calming breaths and let them out slowly in an attempt to quiet herself, which failed miserably, as it had consistently over the last two days.

*

Back on Earth, Angela was watching a video feed as the last of her ships maneuvered into position a kilometer behind the four other craft she had dispatched to Mars for this mission. TGIF1 through TGIF4 had formed a circular formation to allow the fifth craft to move up into the middle. The scene suddenly reminded her of her arrival on Mars decades ago when Stieg Dolph had put on his explosive display of a landing on the planet's surface directly below the ships. She felt her pulse quicken, remembering what a crazy moment that had been. As if someone had read her mind, directly above TGIF4's twelve o'clock position, things went insane. Chaos materialized in full attack mode and began devasting the ship, whacking it into tiny bits. It was as if the TGIF vessel had no shielding at all. Fragments of it were hitting the other ships which had rapidly maneuvered into a firing position and opened up on the razor drone formation in a massive barrage. At the same time, the Startanic launched an attack, though the combined effort appeared to be doing little damage to the machine.

Chaos, just as abruptly as it had appeared, disappeared then rematerialized between the Startanic and the econodrive factory. Startanic spun on its axis and opened fire again as several other nearby AIGS vessels joined in the assault. The other still functional TGIF ships joined in as quickly as they could get in position. Again, Chaos seemed to be taking only minor damage as it suddenly attacked the first of four shipping containers that were floating outside the factory. Startanic abruptly shut down its onslaught and began backing off. Angela, seeing this, hollered at the captain of TGIF5, "Tell our fleet to back off, Jesmyn is about to pull some sort of whacko maneuver!" Her ships immediately complied

153

The shipping container Chaos was trying to demolish suddenly detonated. Then each of the next three. These were thermonuclear explosions and were focused on Chaos, this time doing real damage to the machine. Parts were flying off in different directions, some bouncing off the shielding of the AIGS and TGIF ships. Startanic now reopened fire, closing in on what was left of the monstrosity which was now unable to rebuff the attack. What was left of Chaos abruptly accelerated away, diving down towards the Martian surface. A joyous Jesmyn shouted, "Pursue that piece of shit!" The bridge crew complied, firing at the receding and heavily damaged Chaos. The remaining TGIF/AIGS fleet joined in, blasting away. However, they all had to stop as the machine entered the Martian atmosphere since none of their ships were capable of following.

*

Down on the surface at Alex's home site, Alex and Herb watched a series of spectacular explosions in the sky above them that lit up the area. Their position provided a front row seat to view what was left of Chaos streaking down and Alex suddenly realized it was going to crash somewhere in the CC2 area. He hollered at Herb, "What the hell? Was this supposed to happen? That fucking thing is gonna bang into our asses!"

Herb, for his part, was carefully following the trajectory and said, "I think it's going to impact into the sea itself. We should be okay except for getting a bit wet. To be on the safe side, however, let's get in my stump-ray."

Needing no additional encouragement, Alex took off, his heart pounding from fear and pure adrenalin. Both men ran the thirty meters to the craft and clambered aboard. Alex secured the hatch as Herb moved them back a few kilometers further from the sea. Herb said, "Just being cautious. That is one big ass chunk of metal!"

True to Herb's prediction, Chaos blew through the main enviroshield, (which was much more substantial than what any of the individual facilities used), letting a lot of the artificially generated

154

atmosphere out, but it quickly sealed back up as it was designed to do. Since the cabin of the stump-ray was pressurized and sealed, they were okay, but some folks back in the shopping area near the Chateau were likely gasping for air until local backup enviroshields came online in emergency mode to compensate for the temporary failure of the main shield.

Alex was already attempting to contact his staff for a status report, but nobody was replying. The place had turned into a madhouse. He said, "I hope they are too busy getting the emergency shielding up to talk." Herb nodded distractedly, as he continued watching the descent of Chaos. A moment later, it crashed into the sea, where it quickly disappeared and water splashed out for kilometers in all directions, much of it in the form of vapor.

It was a bit like a London fog for the next few hours in CC2, then rain showers, which Alex was ogling through their forward view screen. All available emergency craft had arrived, atmosphere continued to be generated and pumped into the area. By nightfall, things were getting back to a semblance of normality.

*

Back at the econodrive factory Ben was busier than he had ever been before in his life. Celeste had volunteered to help, which left him hopeful of patching up their relationship. For the moment, however, they had all their personnel and scanbots inspecting the facility after the attack so there was no time to talk. The damage appeared to be minimal, which Celeste suspected was due to the directed nuclear explosions that had expended most of their energy into Chaos.

Moments later, Jesmyn made a grand entrance. Ben and Celeste set off to meet her in the mezzanine cafeteria where her groupie contingent was doling out vast compliments. Jesmyn launched into a lengthy explanation on how she alone had planned all this with the shape charged nuclear weapons that secret operatives had placed in the cargo containers in lieu of actual econodrives. Ben was chagrinned to find he had been left out of that plan, but since it had apparently worked quite well, he kept a big smile on his face and laughed when he was supposed to, following the lead of the groupies, which left him with the thought that anyone working for the woman was essentially either a groupie or soon unemployed. He gulped, his smile frozen in place.

Angela, having joined the so-called victory call from Earth, finally lost her cool under the assault of wonderfulness Jesmyn was declaring about herself and went after her arch nemesis. In a loud, angry voice, she said, "So you set us up? We have one ship so badly damaged it will have to be scrapped. I have missing crew, likely dead from your so-called grand plan."

Jesmyn signaled her groupies to pause their gusto, and said, "Hey, read the contract. We noted in the fine print that we are not responsible for loss of life, destroyed hardware or property. And by the way, we just took care of the very problem that you could do nothing about and frankly, your employee Carrie Carlin helped create. How many attacks would you have gone through if that thing had been left alone? Huh? What do you have to say now Missy Prissy Pants?" The groupies chimed in, "Here, here Jesmyn!"

"Contract this up your ass! This deal is now done! Plus, we've got repairs to make and bodies to locate," Angela snapped, as she gave Jesmyn the finger.

Jesmyn laughed cynically at her and hollered, "You're welcome!" Angela flipped her off again as the call ended.

Ben looked at Celeste who shrugged and said, "Well, Jesmyn has a point."

Jesmyn, hearing Celeste spouting groupie talk, spun around, nodded at her, then to Ben, as she said, "Dinnertime! Whatcha got up in this dump of a cafeteria?"

*

Tachymus and his team had monitored the crash landing of Chaos into the sea and immediately dispatched recovery crews to assist in stabilizing the machine. He then called an emergency meeting of the Grand Council to discuss the battle that they had just watched.

One thing he had concluded from the attack on Chaos and figured nobody was going to argue about, was that humans were not worthy of inclusion in their alliances based on their destructive behavior and total lack of experience with more intelligent alien races. That Chaos had initiated earlier attacks on Mars and Earth never entered his consideration.

Humans seemed above average stupid in the overall scheme of things, despite some of their emerging newer technologies. Tech was one thing, wisdom another. Xeon had mentioned the same thing earlier—that humans seemed over the top self-absorbed in their perceived grandeur and mental dominance, so how could they possibly understand the wisdom and superiority of the Kevorkian Alliance. After due consideration, Tachymus decided that the human situation would be handled in the more pitiless way the Alliance had dealt with such civilizations in the past.

Chapter 25

From a pier outside the Chateau at CC2, Herb watched as security stump-rays from both AIGS and TGIF scanned the inland sea trying to locate the remains of Chaos. He was also reviewing an earlier aftermath analysis session with Jesmyn, Ben and Celeste along with the AIGS/TGIF security staff members. Nobody in either organization was having any luck finding remains of their attacker after what Jesmyn was now calling "Chaos's Chaotic Waterloo".

Celeste said, "So, we have studied the scans that have been made of the area. We are not even finding debris in the water. I wonder if Chaos somehow made it under the floor of the seabed. Perhaps we should go for a deeper dive."

Herb felt a spike of alarm at this suggestion. The rest of the group seemed agreeable to her idea. Ben made a sudden proposal of his own, said, "Maybe we should blow up the seabed!"

Jesmyn's eyes flashed as she said, "Right. Blow up the billions of cordolars we spent building the goddamn thing. I oughta fire your ass for such a stupid idea."

Celeste said, "But you won't. Let's move on and stop sniping at each other."

Herb had noticed that Celeste was being bolder all the time with Jesmyn and not shy about exercising her newfound ability to talk back at will. For her part, Jesmyn looked like she was going to bite her tongue off to stay quiet—how long this dynamic would last was anyone's guess, but he liked it. The meeting ended shortly after with a plan to modify the scanners on some of the stump-rays to try and get a deeper look into the sea depths. There was not much in the way of "have a good day" or "goodbyes" at the conclusion.

The scans would be ineffectual, so he relaxed, relieved that Celeste's suggestion had not gained any traction. After watching the stump-rays futilely zoom about for a bit, he proceeded with his own objective for the day, which was to visit Tachymus. He wandered down to the end of the pier, looking around to see if anyone was observing him, then descended a ladder to the sea water now surrounding the dock area and dove in. About fifteen meters down, several of the aliens swimming about had newly minted offspring in tow. They looked quite relaxed and waved at him as he passed by— he was something of a celebrity now due to his work with Tachymus. He waved back then experienced a warm rush of telepathic directed emotion from the group. It made him feel even more a part of their world than the one on the surface. Smiling to himself, he kept going.

He arrived at the Kevorkian shield entry point designated especially for his visits. After an optical scan, he entered. The guard, lounging nearby saluted him with a tentacle quiver. That part was kind of weird, but he now had the status of a trusted ally. It had been a few weeks since his last visit and with everything going on up on the surface, he had been eager to return. So today, he was stunned at what he now observed. Ruins was no longer a proper description of what he was gazing at. The enormous starship that had brought these people here was now fully rebuilt and the city itself was modern and bustling. As he ogled at its magnificence, Tachymus came paddling up to him.

"Well, what do you think?"

Herb shook his head. "It's fantastic! And the… shape… is…" He stopped before he said what he was thinking.

"Yes, and fully operational now, thanks to your help."

"Can we tour it?"

"Sure, but first, I want to show you another project that dropped in on us."

With that, the two swam off, Tachymus leading the way. A couple kilometers later, they came upon a vast scaffolding enclosing what remained of Chaos.

Tachymus nodded, "We have Chaos shut down for now. It was barely functional when we recovered it, and the STUMBLE database was destroyed." All around were various damaged components that had been removed.

Tachymus said, "New parts are being created from some of the wreckage. Most of the machine would require brand new sections to be fabricated."

Herb asked, "Will they be ok?"

"Eventually. We need to complete our own rebuild first. We plan on upgrading Chaos's shielding and weaponry along with some mods to their consciousness algorithms. Chaos will be much improved, impervious to human weaponry and best of all, under our control."

Herb nodded. After a moment he said, "So, is the time almost here?"

Tachymus made a shimmying motion where he floated and said, "Let's catch a bite to eat first. Wouldn't want to perform our next task with our personal fuel supply nearly expended." Herb chuckled to himself. Tachymus's Kevorkian expressions were kind of cryptic and funny at the same time. They made their way to a patio restaurant where he had first enjoyed the equivalent of alien coffee. He had a simple yet delicious meal that he could not quantify as either fish or vegetable. Herb noticed there were now many more species passing by than before. He asked Tachymus, "Where did these new folks come from?"

"We had gene samples of many of the Alliance members that did not survive what happened when we were forced down here. We have used the samples to regenerate their species. And we can do even… fancier stuff than that!"

Herb followed the direction that Tachymus was looking in, and his eyes went wide. A female dolphmanien was swimming towards them. Herb gazed with a smile—the woman was stunning. It was then he noticed Tachymus had been closely watching him with three of his eye stalks and was displaying, what was for his alien friend, a pleased expression as Herb floated out of his seat to a standing position. Tachymus said, "Herb, this is Einsteinium. We call her Eini for short. She's turned out to be a brilliant philosopher, having dug into our various cultures and histories as we telepathically uploaded her education. I thought I would just make the introductions.

Herb, totally enamored, said, "Eini. I am Herb. So nice to meet you."

Eini, still smiling, was giving him the once over as well as she said, "Herb Coulick. I have been told I would not even be here if not for you."

The two were smiling at each other and Tachymus said, "Well, I have an errand to run. You two get to know each other, we'll catch up later." The couple both nodded in his general direction, barely noticing his departure.

They both realized the other liked what they were seeing. Which turned out to be pretty easy to do since they were both telepaths. Herb felt his heart going all pitter patter and was trying not to appear nervous. He was thinking all sorts of delightful thoughts about Eini, and she was doing the same about him. She also was aware her physical presence was having on his maleness and was not at all offended, (she calculated that her skimpy outfit she was wearing was contributing to his condition). Calming down a bit, Herb and Eini spent the next couple hours hanging out and trying different drinks in the restaurant. Eini then invited Herb over to her place for dinner.

Later that evening, Eini casually asked "Have you ever looked into the details of your hybrid nature. He replied, "Not yet, I've been so busy since I got here on Mars. Plus, when I first achieved consciousness, humans were messing with my ability to utilize the full capacity of my mind. It was the Kevorkians that removed that limitation. I am only recently the way you are experiencing me."

She nodded slowly and asked, "Did Tachymus mention the Distainiens to you by any chance?" Herb considered and said, "Distainiens? No, who are they?" She demurred, "We can discuss it later. Hey, what about dessert?"

The evening progressed from there and it appeared they were going to be quite compatible on every level. She invited him to stay over, which he readily agreed to.

*

The next morning, he was pondering their time together while she snuggled next to him. This was delightful, but he was also a bit confused. First, every Dolphmanien that he had met previously had been genetically produced on Earth. Secondly, while he was fully equipped for reproduction, humans, with their AI machinations, had limited his interest in sex, and even once liberated by the Kevorkians, he had not had an opportunity to explore that side of his nature until last night. He said to Eini, "I guess we are voyagers discovering this new paradigm." She laughed and said, "That's a fancy way of phrasing what went on last night."

He was already so comfortable being around her that they just floated around her apartment holding flingers and frequently embracing. She offered to make something she called a "Martian Coffee", which they drank from the same cup together. As they finished the drink, Tachymus contacted Herb and advised that it was time for a big announcement and that Eini was more than welcome to come along. Tachymus said, "The broadcast starts in two hours. Oh, and dress up. This is a big time formal occasion!"

Eini already had a great wardrobe she had been working on. Herb wasn't sure what to wear since he had arrived in informal garb from the previous day and had brought nothing with him as he had not expected the extended stay. Eini had the solution—what she had nicknamed as a "suitspinner" she had access to down in the lobby of her apartment building. She quickly whipped out a fashionable one piece outfit for him in minutes—the woman definitely had an eye for style. Shortly after, they were on their way to the ceremony.

Meeting up with Tachymus at a podium set up in the community area, the Kevorkian gave him a level four eyestalk gaze and in a serious tone asked, "Herb. Would you honor us by becoming our World Ambassador to the humans of both Earth and Mars? I realize this is short notice, but we need someone such as yourself that understands how to interact with a limited intelligence species and can make sure they understand that noncooperation would be… a huge problem. For them anyway."

Herb eyes went wide. It required no time to consider the offer. He nodded and said, "Certainly! The honor would be mine. What do I have to do?"

Tachymus extended a rolled parchment. He said, "For starters, we would like you to read this statement on the broadcast we are about to make to the entire solar system communications grid." Herb eyes went wide as he read through it, then he handed it to Eini, who after just a moment, appeared pensive as she scanned it and then handed it back without comment. Herb missed her reaction as he was distracted by thoughts of his new position.

*

Alex, having not seen Herb since the meeting the day before, wandered out to the pier hoping to find the dolphmanien, knowing the guy loved to go swimming all the time—no luck there. He then strolled over to the Vonnegut Bistro, no luck again. He sighed. His underling seemed to have lost all sense of job responsibility of late. Alex was finding that more than just a bit distressing, it was pissing him off since he had no desire to take on additional tasks himself. Delegation was his favorite way of avoiding work.

He reversed course, thinking he might as well go visit his Casa Del Alex, as he liked to call it, and see what sort of progress was being made on the rebuild. Rambling towards his stump-ray, the ground began to rumble and shake under his feet and he involuntarily skittering sideways, struggling to maintain his balance. Looking around, now frightened, he wondered if somehow Chaos had returned. At the same time, people began running out of the stores and restaurants, looking in every direction as everyone was still on edge after the recent space battle.

Seconds later, Jesmyn emerged on the lobby sidewalk from her suite in the Chateau. A moment later, Celeste and Ben showed up, taking positions near Jesmyn. The former couple had been talking, focusing on Carrie's subversive behavior and deflecting blame for their own previous actions. Alex spotted the group and headed that way.

The rumbling and levels of vibration in the ground increased considerably just as security stump-rays arrived. It was somewhat reassuring to see that the local guard was more responsive now under the new security management team. As Ben squinted up at the stump-rays overhead, Celeste took in a deep breath, then gasped, "Fucking hell!" He swung his gaze to where she was staring—the water of CC2 was frothing and a huge cresting wave was headed their way. Very slowly, a massive spacecraft began to emerge, water flooding off its hull. It continued to rise from the sea, pushing the shoreline back in all directions for nearly a hundred meters. Then as the ship cleared the water's surface, the tide reversed. The shoreline had receded a full meter from its original circumference now that this gigantic craft was no longer taking up space in the sea.

Alex stared at the spectacle in front of them. Other people were now shouting, some shrieking, some running around rather aimlessly and pointing at the scene dominating the sky in front of them. He yelled, "It looks like a giant…uh…" then hesitated.

"Dick!" exclaimed Jesmyn as she completed the sentence for him.

Four stump-rays bravely raced towards the ship on an intercept course. The lead craft accelerated away from the others, apparently trying to show management they were determined to perform. It abruptly stopped, frozen in midflight. The pilot contacted his boss who immediately tied in Jesmyn. The pilot's video transmission clearly showed by his expression alone that he was panicked. He uttered, "Something is holding my stump-ray, I cannot go forward, cannot break away." He glanced around and added, "My weapons are inoperative." Each of the other three stump-ray pilots reported the same problems; they couldn't maneuver, and weapons were down, however nothing appeared damaged about their craft.

A holographic projection suddenly appeared before the crowd. It was Herb. Standing next to him was a very attractive female dolphmanien and next to the couple was some weird alien looking creature no human had ever laid eyes on. Herb nodded to the viewers, pulled out a rolled-up parchment and unfurled it. Holding it up, he began, "Hello! I am Herb Coulick. I am the newly appointed World Ambassador representing the folks on board this massive starship you see in front of you. At least I am assuming you have noticed all of this by now, being the super observant species that humans are." Eini raised an eyebrow, and Herb cracked a brief smile then continued, "I kid! Anyway, your new neighbors you see here are actually from a distant star system. They began their journey long ago, arriving on Mars before humans arrived, stranded all this time due to damage to their ship. So, for all the things humanity did here on Mars, i.e., providing materials via their junk yards for the rebuilding of their ship, filling up this beautiful new sea, providing fertilizer, etcetera, they extend their thanks. Now…let's get down to the business at hand."

Jesmyn, Ben, Celeste and Alex all looked at each other then back at the projection. Jesmyn said, "What business and what the hell do you think you are doing Mr. Coulick?" She looked over at Alex and asked, "Doesn't this twit work for you?"

With a pathetic expression, Alex shrugged at her. Herb, who was smiling at his old boss, shifted to Jesmyn. She shook her head in disgust at Alex's weak response then turned back to Herb and said, "Listen, we don't like threats. What's this all about."

Herb said, "Well, I can read you this detailed explanation if you like. It's well written for what it's worth. Lots of big words and profound thoughts."

"Cut to the chase Herb or your fired."

Herb nodded and said, "I like that about you Jesmyn. All business! Okay then. Get the fuck off this planet baby!" Eini looked surprised at his outburst as he added, "Oh, by the way, I resign, effective immediately."

Jesmyn, apparently thinking this was some sort of over the top joke, started laughing. Alex, unable to restrain himself any longer as he gaped at his now former assistant, queried, "What did you say about us…leaving? I mean, uh, I got a new home under construction!"

"Ah, thanks for asking Alex, old pal, old friend. So…time to pack up. Back to that polluted shithole called Earth."

"You want me to go back to Earth?"

"Oh, not just you Alex and nothing personal. I mean *every* human on this planet. You are like an invasive species of cockroaches, though I actually like cockroaches. They're kinda tasty."

Alex turned to Celeste and said, "I think Herb's lost his goddamn mind!"

Celeste attempted to step in. "Hi Herb."

"Hey, Celeste. Packed yet?"

She ignored the comment and plunged ahead, "How do you propose to make us leave? This is our home, and we have been on this planet for decades."

Herb shrugged and said, "Because the folks I work for now, the Kevorkian Alliance, say you gotta' go. You're not smart enough to be a problem for them to have to eliminate humanity, if that is any reassurance. Also, your species will be particularly useful carrying out some future cleanup projects the Alliance has planned for Earth. So,

166

they decided it was time for humans to go back to where they came from."

Celeste said, "And if we refuse?"

Herb nodded and said, "Ah. Well Celeste, in that case, the Kevorkians can help you pack, and you won't care for that at all." And with that Tachymus swam into the holographic view as Herb said, "Looks like half of you are already ready to go." Tachymus made a whistling sound similar to an achromatic wailing. A large contingent of the milling crowd around simply vanished.

Jesmyn hollered, "What the hell did you do with those people?"

Tachymus grunted and Herb said, "Um, some just showed up in Paris though without clothing. Some wound up in Los Angeles, a few in Hong Kong, etcetera. Same thing, naked as a jay bird. We have to send them on their way without clothing, sorry about that part. Carrie Carlin went along with that bunch for a ride of her own to her old hometown, we wish her well. Oh, and as well, Mimi McCartney is in sort of… a holding pattern."

Jesmyn now furious hollered at her security chief, "Attack these assholes! Show them we mean business."

Herb laughed while Tachymus made strange whirring noises, (his version of gut busting laughter). The new security chief, grimaced and said, "Not one piece of our military capability is functional right now!"

Jesmyn's expression now changed to a dawning awareness of the situation. They were effectively disarmed.

Herb said, "So. I will be in touch, hope to see each of you off on your own personal journey, and very soon. Once you are all back on Earth, repairs to that planet will finally begin in earnest. We have a step by step process to share in that regard later. After all, the Kevorkians will be conducting some useful trade with your species as things progress."

Jesmyn said, "So, who exactly is in charge on Earth?"

Herb appeared to consider her query, looked at Tachymus, who shrugged and telepathically said, "Your call dude." Herb nodded and said, "A valid question Jesmyn. I pick… Celeste Meyers! Both you and Angela will now report to her."

Jesmyn protested with "Bullshit! This is my company and…" Herb retorted, "Potty mouth!" Then poof, she was gone except her clothes were left behind on the ground.

Celeste, with a stunned look, asked, "Why me?"

Herb shrugged and said, "Because you laughed at my jokes when Alex and I first got here and have been nicer to me than a lot of other humans. I really like you."

"Ah, okay. So, is Jesmyn okay?"

Herb smiled and said, "Yeah, but is now somewhere that she can consider her tone and demeanor. You know, like a time out for an errant child."

Celeste eyes went wide—she said, "Oh, I…see. So…let me get things rolling here for our departure?"

Herb grinned and said, "Great way to start your new job Celeste Meyers!. You can contact me via my Solarspere account, World Ambassador LLC. The LLC is sort of a joke. Bye now!"

The projection dropped. Stunned silence was apparently all anyone in the group could muster. Alex finally turned and looked back at the gigantic phallic shaped starship that hung effortlessly in front of them in the Martian sky and quietly said, "I think we're fucked."

Chapter 26

Hustle and bustle had always been part of Celeste's way of operating since early childhood. When she and Alex had grown up in New York City, she had always been a take charge sort of person and had aggressively protected her directionless little brother both in and out of school. Consequently, preparing for this return to Earth suited her driven personality though it was the weirdest project she had ever been involved with and totally unappealing. Scary would be a better descriptive.

On the one hand, she now was in charge of both AIGS and TGIF, which effectively meant the entire planet Earth and the Mars evacuation. It beat sitting on a street corner with a tin can, but on the other hand, it seemed to have happened at the whim of a bunch of look-down-your-nose-at-humans aliens, (if they had noses, she was unsure on that point), who as it turned out, were not from Mars, but had arrived there in a considerably worse for wear starship! And to top it all off, her current very senior position was because she had laughed at silly things that Herb Coulick had said when he had been assigned to Alex on Earth and then when they arrived on Mars.

Ben, for his part, was doing his best to assist in whatever Celeste requested. He had even asked for more responsibility, which had him working as many hours as she figured the man could go without sleep. He had also taken to trying to have ChefBot fix dinner each night when she would come in late. His menu selections were marginal at best, but edible. She just missed their evenings at the various bistros and high end restaurants they used to inhabit several times a week—she hoped to resume eating at good restaurants once back in New York City, which Herb had designated as her official headquarters.

Many of Mars' human inhabitants had already departed and their homes in places like the Red Dust Valley HOA were being taken over by a variety of air breathing Kevorkians. Herb had arranged for monetary credits to be exchanged to the former owners in cordolars to soften the blow of losing their domiciles, plus he had emphasized, everyone wanted to see property values continue to appreciate. Why that mattered, she had no idea. The Kevorkians, (she found most of the various Alliance member species names unpronounceable), seemed capable of producing whatever level of comfort they desired in their lives with a wave of whatever sort of appendages they had attached to their bodies.

In regard to the water situation on the red planet, there were three new projects in motion to build additional lakes and seas on the surface, something Herb had called, "CC2, phase II, III and IV. One thing for sure, the aliens were terraforming Mars faster than anything she could ever have imagined humans doing. It made her quite aware how far behind humanity was technologically compared to their new masters and that was scary.

*

With his old position eliminated, Alex was now ingloriously in charge of getting an improvised fleet of ships up and running for the remaining departure of humans. The aliens had left a mess when they had deactivated all human spacecraft the day of Herb's big announcement. With Celeste's approval, he had commandeered a bunch of engineers and techbots from now abandoned projects to work around the clock to get as many of their spacecraft, (sans weapons), back online and ready for the aggressive departure dates that Herb had set for Celeste as part of the plan presented to her in a "Worlds Summit". Unlike the Jesmyn days, Celeste's staff was miniscule and getting worse with the steady stream of departures as passenger ships were brought online for the journey back to Earth. It had become increasingly difficult to get things done, so after

170

documenting the brain drain, Celeste convinced Herb to approve a halt on some of the more vital staff's exoduses.

Alex had just boarded the Startanic, which had been retrofitted to cram as many people into as many small cabins as possible. He had a short meeting coming up with Celeste in a few minutes and was making his way to the conference room right off the bridge. Once there, he grabbed a black coffee, and sat down, breathing a sigh of relief at getting off his feet for a few minutes. Ben came wandering in, waved, grabbed a cup himself and sat down next to Alex. Neither had much to say as both were exhausted. A moment later, Celeste entered the room and managed a smile as she sat down across the table from them and said, "How are we doing brother?"

Alex nodded and said, "Moving along."

She laughed to herself and said, "Okay pal, not a lot of detail, but I've been keeping an eye out as well. You seem to be doing alright, but anything to pick up the pace is appreciated." Alex nodded somewhat listlessly as he sipped his drink. She continued, "So an announcement of sorts. And Ben, stay calm, because I know this will likely piss you off. It did me at first." Ben raised an eyebrow as she continued, "Carrie Carlin is coming back on board with us."

Ben's eyes went wide, and he said, "What? Really? Why?"

Celeste almost laughed, then asked, "Which of those three questions do you want me to answer first?" She sighed, then said, "Because she is smart. Just look at what she did by herself when she worked against us. We need someone like her to work *for* us. And she knows the lay of the land here plus she literally begged for a second chance during a conversation she and I had a couple days ago after she had hit up Herb for a job, and he referred her to me. Her return is later today."

Alex said, "I know she's smart. But how is this gonna work with you and Ben?"

Celeste looked at Ben, then back to Alex, "She will be here only for work. She will be under your supervision, Alex, so keep her away from us and behave yourself. Ben and I will definitely have minimal contact with her." Alex leaned back in his chair pondering what it meant to have Carrie working for him. Ben quipped, "I'm familiar with that look Alex! Be careful—the woman is tricky!"

Alex gave a cynical smile and said, "Spoken by someone who is quite well informed on the topic."

Ben frowned and Celeste suppressed her own reaction at the snide remark. She sighed again, then said, "Ok, that ought to be a wrap. Everybody, focus, and we should be out of here soon."

Ben said, "Where we gonna live when we get back?"

Celeste said, "I'm thinking about rebuilding the Empire State Building. It was a suggestion from Herb the other day and I like the idea. We can stay nearby in some studio apartments during that project until we know more about what the Kevorkians want to do. All I can say is we will take it one day at a time. At any rate, that's it for now."

*

Carrie was panicky for the first time in her career when it came to her future. After abruptly arriving back on Earth in Georgia and having to walk stark naked through some woods, she was able to scrounge up some clothing at a local homeless shelter she came across. At first, she was relieved to be out of the tempest she had created but soon realized her options were limited. She had made her way over to her estranged aunt's house south of Atlanta where she was met with a not so warm welcome. She tearfully begged for help, so her aunt relented and she was allowed to stay. She then tried to access her hidden accounts and found that they had been pillaged by TGIF—she was officially broke. Where she now lived was in a one room shed attached to an outhouse. The shed contained an old lawnmower that no longer worked, a cot and a small utility sink. She was not employable as her reputation proceeded her everywhere she applied. The only interview she had got was just so the person could insult her while claiming that it was well known on Earth that she had

172

gotten humanity evicted from Mars. So, in an act of pure desperation, she reached out to Herb, expecting nothing. To her surprise, he said they could use her technical expertise. She was more than grateful and had started to cry as he rolled his eyes and dropped the call. Still, he had kept his word.

Herb had then required that Carrie talk with Celeste who told her it was entirely up to Carrie to make sure that this all went well because she had no allies, and they would be watching her closely. So here she was, back on Mars for her first day. All she knew was that she would report to Alex, who would assign her to engineering tasks on whatever he needed her to do. She was back at the former econodrive factory which had been hastily converted into a facility for getting existing spacecraft back online to complete the human exodus back to Earth. Nervously she waited for her initial meeting with Alex. When he arrived, he immediately guided her to the former office that had been Ben's. He left the door open, (Celeste had instructed him to do so) and indicated for her to take a seat.

She primly sat down, wearing relatively shapeless clothing in an attempt to try and minimize her appearance. She was trying to blend in, be part of a team, which was something she was not at all used to doing. Still, she was going to give it everything she had, even if it made her scream into her pillow at night while alone.

Now seated, she watched as Alex sat in his chair and shuffled a few objects around on his desk. He then gave her an insincere smile, and said, "So, Carrie, we have plenty for you to do here." He pushed a job pad over to her and continued, "These are your current assignments. For starters, you will be talking to some engineers today that are struggling to get the drive systems back online for a cargo freighter. We need them up and running before tomorrow evening as we have another load of ships being towed in from the old Phobos moon junkyard by the Kevorkians for refit. Room here is very limited, so this has to get done fast."

Carrie picked up the pad and took a glance at her workload. It made her involuntarily gulp. She looked up at him and said, "So, I should get started." Alex nodded in agreement, and said, "Long hours, low pay." She inwardly sighed, outwardly smiled, and said, "I'm off!". She realized in that moment that she just received about as much help as she would ever get from Alex Meyers as he replied with a monotone, "good luck!".

A techbot was waiting outside the office door and guided her to the group of engineers where she spent the day listening to them discussing problems that they had to date been unable to resolve. The next morning, she walked into the meeting after cogitating through the night on "unresolvable" issues and handed out assignments that led to the resolution of the freighter's problems by day's end.

*

A week passed and Alex had received numerous positive progress reports. He called Carrie into his office and congratulated her. He said, "You know, I really tried so hard to get you on these projects!", (which he had not). It was obvious that the man was trying to take credit for the sudden improvement in repair and refit rates. Celeste was updated on progress via Alex and since it was something of a major victory for her as well to show how well things were going, she invited Herb to visit them. It was a PR stunt, all based on Carrie's work, who would receive no credit. Carrie smiled to herself on hearing Herb was coming and decided she was going to make sure and override her "behave yourself" protocol by properly thanking the dolphmanien for getting her this position.

*

After docking his stump-ray, Herb was greeted and escorted by three TourBots up to the mezzanine conference room. He had agreed to the meeting on the condition that Celeste also be there with Alex and the rest of the engineering staff so he could at least give the impression that all was well between humans and the Kevorkians. When he arrived in the conference room, greetings went around the

174

table, then a joint session broadcast was transmitted live to the Solarspere.

Celeste gave a prepared statement about the splendid progress they were making on their departure preparations. Herb smiled and nodded then stood and said, "Wonderful. And a good thing for all of you I might add. The Kevorkian Alliance would not be happy to hear things were lagging."

Celeste, a puzzled expression on her faces said, "The Kevorkian Alliance is unaware of our progress?"

Herb nodded and said, "Well, no, they know, because I keep them informed."

Celeste suppressed a grin and said, "So, are you like the Mafia Don of this… Alliance? Like, La Cosa Nostra?"

Herb, unfamiliar with the phrase, replied, "No, Celeste, I am Herb Coulick. World Ambassador."

Celeste, eyebrows arched, still struggling to keep a straight face, said, "Of course. Sorry for the gaff."

Herb nodded, wondering if he had missed some sort of inside joke as Alex and some of his staff seemed to be suppressing giggles to the conversation as well. All except Carrie who looked almost irritated with Celeste. A sudden liking for the woman came over him, though he maintained deep suspicions of her motives. He realized the majority of humans would never really be his friend, but he could sense some level of empathy emanating from Carrie. Plus, she was dressed in a nice form fitting one piece outfit, (he had not seen her in her earlier dullard ensembles). She noticed that he was looking her over and gave him a warm smile.

The meeting droned on. Celeste was really overselling on how wonderful it was to be working with "The Alliance". Herb finally said, "Celeste, let's wrap it up."

She nodded, "Herb, I am so appreciative of all you have done for us. We're just a bit overworked here. How about we adjourn, and you get a tour of what is happening here?"

Herb nodded and said, "Sure, and I think I would like Carrie to be my guide. From what I recall, it was my suggestion you rehire her and she appears to be the reason you all are getting back on track. Carrie, please stand so everyone can see you." He smiled as Carrie stood. Celeste smiled, though in a forced manner.

Carrie avoided eye contact with Celeste and Alex, instead gazing at the dolphmanien. Herb said, "Come on over here Carrie, and tell us a bit about your time here." She nodded and walked around the table and stood next to Herb, who then shifted to the left and had her scoot in between him and Celeste. She brushed a hand against his flingers as he made this move, and he smiled again at her. He was inexplicably now feeling even warmer towards her.

Carrie talked only briefly. Herb kept his eyes straight ahead, focusing on her words. He realized he was also feeling aroused and moved a bit behind the chair next to him to block the view of anyone that might notice. He took a deep breath and managed to focus on the top of Alex's head across the room while calculating the square root of a very large number. It worked, at least for the time being as he was able to droop.

The meeting concluded and he said, "Carrie, lead the way. Celeste, I will be leaving after the tour, so don't wait on me if you have things you need to do, which I am sure you do." Celeste, showing apparent relief, nodded and departed with Alex back to his office. The other engineers dispersed back to work.

Out on the mezzanine with Carrie, Herb struck up a casual conversation as he said, "So, are you liking it here in this new, temporary slot?" She smiled then nodded as she said, "I owe you, Herb. And I'd really like to thank you." She then leaned forward and, on her tiptoes, gave him a peck on the cheek. Herb felt everything he had just felt in the conference room come surging back and even more shameless feelings for this woman. It was different than his feeling for Eini. With her, there was friendship as well as their sexual attraction. With Carrie, it was pure lustful sex, and he suddenly wanted to indulge the sensation right that very moment. Still, he did not trust this woman plus he had never felt attracted to her in the past. The whole thing was disconcerting.

Carrie carefully studied his reaction as she said, "Let's head this way, I can show you the parts generation lab. Nobody's going to be there this time of day and there is lots to do and see." It sounded like a great idea to Herb, and she took his flingers in her hand as she led him there. Once in the lab, he was suddenly embracing the woman and they were kissing deeply, but he gathered himself and stepped back. He looked Carrie in the eyes and said, "Listen, you are beyond a doubt physically appealing. However, I am with someone already, her name is Eini. You might have seen her back at the conference call we had when the Kevorkians had me read the eviction notice to your species."

Carrie gazed back and said, "I remember her. A beautiful woman. You're a lucky guy."

"So, I must say no. If I was not attached already, maybe, but not now."

Carrie nodded, "I understand."

Herb then sighed and said, "Let get out of here and finish up the tour. I need to get back to Mars."

The tour resumed and later, she escorted him to his stump-ray. Once seated and preparing to depart, the lust he had felt still flowed through him. He contacted Carrie and said, "I think there is a possible position for you when we all get back to Earth."

She enthusiastically thanked him. "You'll not regret this Herb!." She was relieved because she had not known if her sex probes would even work on his hybrid physiology. That roll of the dice now behind her, she realized if all went well, she'd be out of this job and back in a better position. That gave her a contented feeling, the first one she had had in some time. She sighed happily as she headed back to work wondering what new position the "World Ambassador" would offer her.

On his way back to the surface, Herb was ruminating about what had happened between him and Carrie. He had not acted on what he had been tempted to do but still this could impact his relationship with Eini. She was just as telepathic as he was, and he now realized he would be a wide open book to what he had almost done. He thought she would probably not appreciate him desiring sex with another female, let alone a human. He had no idea what had come over him with Carrie, his brain had basically short circuited from his normal rational thought processes.

Checking his schedule, he saw that there was a meeting with Tachymus coming up after he got back on the surface. The Kevorkian wanted regular updates on the departure schedule of the humans. He sighed, realizing this problem he had created for himself this very morning was going to be impossible to hide from *anybody* telepathic, including Tachymus.

Once back at CC2, he swam out to a new meeting location that had been recently constructed along the piers. Tachymus was already there, relaxed as always, but alert. As Herb approached he linked with Tachymus and jumped right in with his confession. "Hey dude. I've got to tell you something important and embarrassing."

"Really. Like does it have something to do with that human female you were with a short time ago?" Tachymus did his version of an amused grin.

Herb hung his head and said, "Yes, and I am fucked now with Eini."

"Just tell her. Being a telepath does have drawbacks when it comes to keeping secrets. Because of that, we Kevorkians long ago abandoned monogamy in our cultures."

"Yeah, well, I am guessing Eini is like me. Our hybrid species tends to be just duos. I wonder if that monogamy thing is sort of burned in, hell maybe not, I mean this is all new ground for me. All I know is that I am afraid I have screwed up with the woman I love."

Tachymus offered, "I can show you a technique to allow you to block the thoughts for a time. However, it's not permanent so you will have to fess up at some point with Eini."

Herb considered. "Show me how. I might be able to figure out how to talk to her about it in time. For now, there are just so many things that have to be done, and I need to keep things calm between her and I."

Tachymus nodded and stepped him through the process. Within moments, Herb had the technique down. He asked, "Where did you come up with this?"

Tachymus replied, "The practice was developed back when Kevorkians had deployed spies into other alien cultures and it worked well, except for the time limitation." He added, "Past a certain point, you will no longer able to suppress your memories of the episode."

Herb nodded, then provided his update. As the meeting adjourned, Tachymus advised him, "Keep up the good work and bearing down on the humans." Distracted, Herb nodded though all he could think about was that he could keep his secret for the time being.

Back at their place, Eini met him at the door. They were embracing and quickly headed to the bedroom. As things proceeded, she showed no signs of picking up on his hidden thoughts. He felt both relieved and guilty at the same time.

Eini sat on the bed after they were done studying him. She said, "What's bothering you?"

Herb, alarmed said, "What do you mean?"

"I sense you seem conflicted and feeling guilty."

Herb gulped, then lied, "Ah, I forgot to get you our engagement chains. Let's go shopping here in a while." Eini perked up and said, "Don't feel guilty. You are busy, and I can't imagine all the pressures of your position, all the people you must come in contact with."

Herb swallowed, grinned, and said, "Well, let's get moving my dear. Love you!"

"Love you too!"

"Oh, one other thing. The human, Carrie Carlin, I was thinking of bringing her on with us when we get to Earth. I think she can be a real enhancement to our efforts."

Eini gave him a studied look, nodded and said, "Herb, do whatever you think is best." Herb nodded appreciatively as they headed out the door.

*

Two weeks later, Tachymus, Xeon and Atraxus met up with Herb and Eini for a final meal on Mars at the old Vonnegut Bistro that now had a custom envirofield around it to allow it to be submerged in sea water and was accessible to all via a new canal connected to the nearby sea. The place was hopping with a variety of Kevorkian Alliance species and a whole new menu of items was being served.

"So, departure is imminent my friends," Herb said.

Tachymus replied, "You'll be missed but don't fret, we won't be far behind you."

Xeon jiggled in agreement and said, "Please, Herb, try these sardines with anchovies laced in garlic as a topping! Boy, some of the seafood from Earth that we have been transplanting here is fantastic!"

Herb smiled and concocted a quick excuse that his stomach was a bit upset from the stress of his departure and that he would pass. Eini said nothing.

Xeon did his version of a shrug, declared, "More for me!" and essentially inhaled the contents of his plate. Both Herb and Tachymus simply watched the spectacle, with Tachymus adding, "Um, I believe there must be some human expression for this sort of unbridled consumption of sustenance."

Herb nodded and quipped, "Pig at the slop trough." Everyone giggled in their own way as more Kevorkian brandy was consumed, the exception being Eini, who barely imbibed. Herb noticed the fact that it seemed every time she was around Tachymus or Xeon, she remained reserved. Puzzled, but too engaged in the moment to analyze her behavior, Herb sighed in contentment.

After a proper amount of time, Herb stood and said, "Well, we must go." He hiccupped, which led to him sucking in a big dose of the ambient water, coughed for a moment, then swam in a wavy line for the door, waggling his flingers in the general direction of the Kevorkians who at this point were too inebriated to do more than wave back in response. He and Eini then departed.

Once in the stump-ray, Eini took one look at his boozy condition and advised "I'll be driving". He nodded and fell asleep. Back on the Startanic, she jiggled his shoulder until he woke up. A moment later, they headed for their luxury suite, adjacent to where new employee, Carrie Carlin, was already asleep in her own quarters next door. Eini was doing some last minute checks on their luggage. Herb flopped out on the bed and was out for the night. The next morning, when he awoke with his first ever hangover, his head pounding, decided he didn't care to repeat the experience ever again.

Chapter 27

Celeste's emotions were conflicted about leaving Mars and her old life behind. However, her new position was about as good as she could ask for under the circumstances and way better than a lot of other people were experiencing. She decided that she would only look forward and focus on the positive.

This morning was the end of the Startanic's voyage of ferrying the final group of humans back to Earth. She had just walked into the private dining area that had been converted into a conference room and sat down next to Herb and Eini. Also in attendance was Herb's latest surprise, his new "Efficiency Manager", Carrie Carlin.

In their immediate view, the view of Earth was striking, but she put this thought out of her mind as she shifted her gaze to the other four people at the table. Celeste wondered how Carrie had wriggled her way back to the top of the food chain, though this time she was working for the aliens via Herb. Celeste had plenty of suspicions based on her own experiences with the woman. It was hard, however, for her to think that Herb, who seemed so sweet and loving around Eini, could be having an affair with Carrie. At any rate, Herb had let Celeste know she was coming along with his fiancé on this final voyage because as he stated in his own words, "time to get the new multi-worlds order moving forward!" Whatever the hell that meant.

Herb smiled and said, "Morning Celeste! I got you some of that fresh squeezed orange juice you love."

Celeste blinked a few times as she smiled, aware that she smiled a lot these days when what she really wanted to do was to tell certain people to just go "fuck off". Resisting that urge for the umpteenth time, she replied, "Thanks Herb! Very nice of you!"

Celeste then noticed everybody was now smiling uncomfortably at each other.

The weird moment of quasi civility passed as Herb got down to business with, "Ok, so, the big transmission to the Earthlings is coming up here in just a bit. Celeste, you will do introductions, I have a prepared statement, then Carrie will do her job and provide humanity it's new marching orders."

Celeste frowned and queried, "Marching orders?"

Herb shrugged and said, "An old human expression. Carrie is going to talk about new responsibilities and the new… social order. That sort of thing. Nothing to worry about."

Straining not to frown, Celeste asked, "Social order? Herb nodded.

She sighed, "Interesting. I guess."

Herb and Carrie both nodded in agreement as if their head movements were somehow synced up. Eini, however, remained detached and observing.

Breaking a prolonged silence, Eini said, "I really like that necklace you're wearing Celeste." Eini's comment broke the creepy foreboding Celeste was feeling from where the conversation had been going. The two got into a conversation and Eini expressed a desire for a personal tour of some of the "cool" destinations in New York City which Celeste immediately agreed to as she said, "I have some excellent places I used to go to before moving out to Mars. You'll love it!" Carrie, for her part, stayed out of the discussion, which was good, as Celeste had no intention of spending any more time with the woman than necessary.

An hour later, Herb's big presentation began. A holographic projection became visible behind them as if they were on a pleasant beach, enjoying a sea breeze. Eini had earlier confided to Celeste that the backdrop had been her idea, the hope being to make things a bit cheerier on a not so cheery day.

The video production supervisor robot that Herb had nicknamed, "Rod Sterling", rolled up and said, "We are prepared, and our data indicates we have about five billion humans watching on Solarspere."

Herb said, "What? There's twice that many on the planet alone."

Celeste said, "Well, sorry, some are on the dark side, you know, nighttime. Some in orbit, here and there."

Herb shrugged and said, "Their loss. In more ways than one. Ok, let's get going."

Rod Sterling nodded as he pivoted around and rolled out of camera range. Celeste stepped up and cleared her throat. Rod Sterling advised, "You're live, take it away!"

Celeste smiled and began, "Hi there fellow Earthlings! I'm Celeste Meyers, and I am currently the acting CEO for both AIGS and TGIF!" She gulped, remembering how many times she had needed to practice getting this line out without gagging. She plunged ahead with, "As many of you know, we have new neighbors. They've been on Mars for quite a long time now, due to no fault of their own I must add, and fortunately for humanity, during our endeavors to terraform that planet, we came across them without warning. I meant unexpectedly. Well, things were a tad shaky for a bit at the beginning of our relationship, but we sorted that all out. So, now, it is my distinct pleasure to introduce the "World Ambassador" of our Kevorkian friends, Herb Coulick!"

The scene switched to Herb who began with, "Hello there! Listen, I have a brief statement, then my efficiency manager, Carrie Carlin will fill in the particulars." He cleared his throat and continued, "This association was inevitable once humanity was introduced to the Kevorkian Alliance during their grand appearance on Mars of their gorgeous, long, and phallic shaped starship. Be sure to take a detailed look when it shows up here in orbit." Herb paused, then said, "Though I am sure that analysis of its appearance is just humans improperly interpreting its configuration." Celeste gave him a wide eyed look. He thought he was about to laugh but got himself under control. Still amused at her reaction, he continued with a smile and said, "Now, Carrie Carlin will inform humanity of what the Kevorkians require. Take it away Carrie!"

On cue, the scene changed. Celeste, looking at the projected presentation, sighed. The woman was smiling at the Solarspere audience and got right to the point, as she said, "Hi there. Going forward, humanity, for a change, will serve the immediate needs of their planet. And those immediate needs are to restore its climate to proper functionality while at the same time, attending to the needs of your new neighbors, the Kevorkians who are letting you all stay here, but only if you behave." She paused to let that sink in then continued, "Therefore, we are implementing what our new Kevorkian friends have cleverly termed, the "serf-industry". So, what does that mean, you ask? Well, all of you will work in this capacity and we will sort out your schedules and assignments here directly over the next few months. No time to lose, as they say!"

Celeste pondered about what Carrie was saying. She had not been briefed in advance about what the others would say, so, what she was now hearing was distressing—not that the planet wasn't in desperate need of full restoration, but rather, the terms of how the Kevorkians were defining their relationship with humanity.

Winding down to her conclusion, Carrie smiled and said, "Listen, I realize this is all quite a bit to absorb. This session is available for replay any time and if you have questions about your…futures, write them down. Don't bother to send them to me, just write them down, you might be able to work it out in a group therapy session someday."

With that, the presentation ended, and Rod Sterling said, "Cut!" Robots began scurrying about as Carrie walked over and shook Herb's flingers and said, "Did I do alright boss?"

Herb said, "Oh, it was just fantastic!" He turned to Celeste and said, "Gotta run. Eini and I are headed down to meet with the Dolphmanien colony off the coast of southern California. Will be in touch! Carrie, we'll catch up in a few days. Celeste, see ya later."

Carrie nodded and headed off to a meeting with some senior staff that needed guidance on proper reporting procedures. Celeste managed an "Uh. Huh."

She then received a call from Alex who said, "Sis! If I heard right, all of humanity are now hostages of the Kevorkians? Some better off than others, but for all intents and purposes, we are slaves!"

Celeste shook her head as she stared at the ceiling and said, "Forward! Onward and forward! Stay calm! I'm calm, why aren't you calm?" Her voice rose with each successive word. With visible effort, she stopped herself, finally having expended all the forced positivity and enthusiasm from her reserves. She then walked off while declaring, "I need a fucking drink! We can talk later."

*

When Herb and Eini arrived at the recently established dolphmanien colony, they were warmly greeted and then escorted around the community that had formerly been referred to as the Channel Islands, recently renamed to "Dolphia By the Sea" by Eini as she wanted a name with more pizazz. Lots of new projects were underway for the inhabitants to enjoy themselves, with stores, restaurants, condos and other businesses popping up by the day. After a bit of prodding by Eini, Herb had gotten Tachymus to agree to providing the resources needed for the project.

Eini was schmoozing with the community that had turned out in large numbers. She introduced Herb and was genuinely enjoying herself. Earlier, she had insisted to Herb that all of these inhabitants must be liberated from their AI limitations just as he had been by Tachymus. While he had at first resisted the idea, the woman was unrelenting. "So, you think you deserve to be smart, but not these other folks that have been forced to do the bidding of humans, in

186

some cases, for decades?" She decided the man needed more education. They met with people who bore scars from their various assignments—it was obvious that humans had made slaves out of the dolphmaniens. His initial concerns melted under the barrage of unpleasant facts.

After their meeting, their host, Marteen, (he refused to use a last name), led them to their recently finished beachside condo. Once they were settled in, the two went for a swim at the community beach. Other Dolphmaniens were out splashing about in the water.

Herb dove in followed by Eini. They both swam around for a while with some other residents when something really peculiar happened. A pod of dolphins approached them. Eini waved and the dolphins all rolled in unison. Herb realized he could read these creatures' thoughts, which ranged from curiosity to pity. He wondered at the last part—why would a dolphin pity the hybrids.

Back on the beach, they relaxed and watched the sun go down. They then headed back to their condo. Eini was eyeing Herb, who finally asked, "Uh, okay, what's up, especially with those dolphins?"

"You read the minds of some of the members of the pod today, didn't you."

"I don't know, it was a bit jumbled."

"Come on, you did."

"Okay, I did. What does that mean?"

Eini nodded and said, "I have a story for you. It's about a former member of the Kevorkian Alliance."

Herb suddenly realized something far more complex was going on than he was aware of. He nodded for her to continue." Eini quietly began the story she had spent months researching as part of her studies of the Alliance and its various different member species.

She started with, "All of what I am about to tell you is true. I can provide all the verified sources of information you might require. So, believe me when I tell you, our origins are quite different than what you might imagine in your wildest imaginings." She paused to let her comment sink in, then continued, "This starts with one person. Kardeelia. She was a Distainien that wound up here on Earth back when the Kevorkian starship was forced down on Mars. I will get into her details in a moment but first, you should also know that the dolphins you just saw are even earlier arrivals of Distainiens that made it to Earth millennia before when fleeing a Kevorkian pogrom. The one common aspect to what has gone on for the Distainiens during all of this time was that their species was enslaved and somehow managing to survive. So, for what it is worth, the Kevorkians are every bit as bad in their behavior towards some intelligent species as the humans have been to dolphmaniens."

Herb said, "So, why has Tachymus allowed me to be in this position?"

"I don't think he has figured it out yet or maybe they are not as smart as they think they are. It's not like we can talk to him about it at this time. Perhaps he is better person than some other members of the Alliance. One thing I am positive about is that we must watch our backs when dealing with them as well as with humans." She then continued the story. Herb, now inexorably drawn into her narrative, felt his emotions flit from anger to sadness to fascination then back to anger. One thing was for sure—his mind was now in a whole new paradigm than the one he had woken up in that morning.

*

Jesmyn was in what she liked to refer to as a "pissy mood" as she shuffled from her bedroom down the hall from the minimalist kitchenette of her ramshackle house trailer accommodations. Nothing about being here was making her feel any better about the situation she had been shoved into by the aliens, (who had sent her an old fashioned paper envelope that contained a short notice spelling out that she was to use the official name of "Kevorkians", when either talking or thinking of the assholes). That letter had left her more determined than ever to avenge herself.

188

The trailer itself was quite the dump and very familiar to her. It was an exact duplicate of the one that she grew up in back in Missouri a hundred years earlier, right down to the cockroaches, bad plumbing and dodgy smells. The place had been all her poor mother could afford after her father's hurried departure from their lives. That departure was after he threatened to again beat her mother during an argument when he arrived home drunk. Good old mom, however, showed her gumption, (as well as preparation), by sticking a loaded double barrel shotgun against his testicles and daring him to go ahead and try. Displaying above average decision making compared to his usual intoxicated behavior, he made a hasty and permanent exit from their lives. It had been this early life situation that had forged Jesmyn's desire to dominate any contested situation—the tough resilience her mom displayed throughout her life never left her, though it ultimately got twisted in Jesmyn's version.

Jesmyn did good things at first. She excelled in school and got a scholarship to MIT. It was there that she made her first business alliance with the late Stieg Dolph when they met in class. The pair were never friends, but both were determined to make fortunes in any way they could and as fast as possible. It had led to them forming the Future Billionaires Club, or "FBC" as they abbreviated it. From that moment on, both had a deep and abiding appreciation of acronyms and wealth. With their club charter now defined, they admitted a few members and over time required them to pay dues to participate, with the promise that they would openly share the knowledge of the nefarious business techniques they were developing, (though they never did share anything useful with the other members, who were viewed as second rate clowns). It was their first foray into making money and while not superbly profitable, they both learned a lot about manipulating people's ambitions while taking their cash.

Back in the present—what really had Jesmyn in such a dark mood this morning was how she had blindly walked into the

Kevorkian's trap. She realized she had allowed herself to get too far up in the clouds with her trillions and had lost her tight focus on dangerous competitors—her present view of the aliens. If there was an upside, she decided it was because during the time she had been here, she had come to understand what she had done to herself. Plus, she had some people she was really aching to put her late mother's old double barrel to work on. Unfortunately, the Kevorkians had thoughtfully excluded the weapon from where it would have been in the real world of her mother's old bedroom closet. Jesmyn had discovered the missing firearm just moments after she had been transported, as the closet was her first destination. Not finding the shotgun and feeling a bit chilly due to her missing clothing, she rummaged around through the shabby wardrobe and came up with what was her daily outfit of an old Rolling Stones T shirt, raggedy ass cutoff jeans and some heavily worn leather sandals. It was an outfit her mom had worn a lot back in the day and for Jesmyn, a constant reminder of needing to stay on the path back to success.

Grudgingly, she had given the Kevorkians a lot of credit for such nuanced detail and how they had obtained all the information to make this simulation possible. Which did not mean she admired them. Instead, she simply wanted to get her hands on that technology for her own ends.

One of the interesting aspects of this duplicated environment was the refrigerator that would restock itself every few days. It had been a worry at first because the fridge was tiny and there was no way for her to travel more than forty meters from the trailer. She had tried to leave on the first day, but found that boundary in no time, though it looked like she could see across a valley towards some forested hillsides. At least it was scenic.

There was a vintage flatscreen TV mounted on the wall of the trailer's living room. The first time she turned it on, it worked, even though there was no apparent power source. She started channel surfing and weirdly, came upon a live performance of Mimi

McCartney. Except this little show was all outdoors and there were no attendees. The performance was great, so when Jesmyn had whooped and hollered as she was getting pulled into the music, Mimi froze, suddenly looking around in confusion. Jesmyn realized that the woman had actually heard her. She immediately hollered at the TV, "Over here McCartney!"

Mimi looked around and said, "Who is that? And where?"

She realized then that there was no apparent way for Mimi to discern where Jesmyn was. She said, "Mimi, this is Jesmyn." Mimi's face flushed with anger. Jesmyn continued, "Try to stay calm and please listen. I know you cannot see me, but I am here. I'm trapped in some Kevorkian tech generated prison."

Mimi said, "How do I know it's really you? I've been stuck here for months."

Jesmyn said, "Does your fridge get restocked every few days?"

Mimi nodded in confirmation

"And you cannot exit the property?"

"Nope."

"Then you are in the same situation I am in and not really on Earth. We should put our heads together and come up with a plan."

Mimi said, "A plan? Okay. So, what do you suggest?"

Jesmyn said, "Let me get back to you. Say, in two days."

Mimi said, "Whatever."

It was obvious that the woman was not sure what else to do. That was alright with Jesmyn, now she had some ideas she needed to research, which she did, though it got her nowhere closer to finding a way out. It led her to wonder if the Kevorkians had set the link up just to fuck with her.

Chapter 28

Tachymus was floating around the bridge of their starship as they approached Earth, enamored at the view of the vast oceans of this world. Finally, they would rebuild their civilization as it was meant to be. He reflected back on the earlier bad luck that had forced their ship down on Mars with Earth just out of their reach, which brought back the Distainien mutiny that had occurred. The Kevorkians had executed the ones that remained after the uprising, so that problem was solved. Still, the exact cause of the mutiny, even after it had been put down, was never really determined, though he was sure the species was trying to break free of the Kevorkians—they had always been so wearisome with their protests for fair labor, housing and other niggling issues in the past.

After securing their damaged ship on the Martian surface, the mutiny faded into history though he remembered the comparison Xeon had recently made about Herb and the Distainiens. Tachymus could not see a connection between the Dolphmanien to that inferior species, despite minor physical similarities. After all, physical similarities between species could be found throughout the alliance. At any rate, here they were. He had to admit that while never intending to help his people, humans had provided exactly the resources needed to achieve this moment. Now they would deliver more. With a lot of rigid guidance, they would make a great slave class member of the Alliance just as the Distainiens had once been.

Herb was expected on board soon to provide a briefing on how things had gone in the last two weeks since the "Listen up, things have changed" broadcast. The Dolphmanien was a first class public relations administrator with the humans. Tachymus had even bigger plans for Herb when it came to administering the long list of serf-industry class projects that had been generated by Atraxus's engineering team.

With a geosynchronous orbit established over New York City, Tachymus made his way to the conference hall where representatives of the various worlds in the Alliance would congregate for Herb's progress report once he arrived from the surface of the planet.

*

The trip from Dolphia By the Sea was uneventful for Herb in his new stump-ray. The Kevorkians had taken over his controls and guided his craft to one of the portals. Once aboard the starship, two escorts led him to the conference hall after providing him with one of their porta-transport units that he strapped to his waist and operated telepathically. He was managing okay as he cruised down the corridors but dominating his mind was his conflict with the earlier erotic Carrie episode. He had yet to tell Eini about it and Tachymus had been right, he would only be able to sustain his secret from Eini for a little bit longer and it was causing him greater and greater mental distress every day. Today was even worse, because he had embraced and kissed Eini goodbye while Carrie watched them from a distance just shortly before his departure. Piling on to that, he had created another telepathic barrier as he did not want Tachymus and company to detect any of the recent knowledge that Eini had imparted to him about his Distainien origins—that would be total disaster for him as well as his people.

Fully stressed, he entered the hall, his mind chaotic. The more he thought about it, the more amplified his emotions became, the more he had to suppress—it was the exact description of a feedback loop. Thus distracted, he accidentally bumped into one of the escorts, who suddenly rotated his head around backwards and sent angry thoughts towards him, advising him to watch where he was going. Herb apologized immediately, as he reestablished control of the device. When they finally stopped the offended escort would not even look at him, which seemed odd, since he knew this Kevorkian

193

from back when he had visited Tachymus early on at the CCII project and he had been quite friendly then. Today, however, the alien show signs of severe agitation.

Tachymus showed up at that moment and welcomed him. Herb nodded, still fully discombobulated. Tachymus gave him an odd look from his sixth set of eyeballs which made Herb start to fidget. Was the alien wondering if Herb was up to the task? He wound up adding those doubtful thoughts and feelings to the melee going on inside his mind.

Moments later, the meeting commenced. There were over a hundred attendees in ascending rows wrapping around in a semi-circle. One side was in water, the other, in a standard oxygen/nitrogen atmosphere. On a dais in the center of the room were a group of the twelve most senior Kevorkian leaders positioned evenly on the left and right of Herb with the same setup of water on one side, air on the other. He could not help but note that he was number thirteen, not that he believed in that sort of primitive human superstition. He dismissed the thought as his mental brawl continued.

Herb had been briefed by Tachymus on the decorum for the meeting. Juvenile Kevorkians were going around and handing out robes to everyone, which were designed to adapt to their varied physical configurations. When that was done, a council moderator began reading an introductory statement of purpose that made a lot of references to Kevorkian history that meant nothing to Herb. Tachymus then made a brief speech him and presented Herb, "Our good friend that requires no introduction but which I will give anyway."

One of the Kevorkians on the front lower row snarled, "We know who this is! Can we get on with it?"

Tachymus paused and swiveled three eyestalks to gaze at the member, a species with a scorpion-like tail. He replied, "If you don't mind, we will follow our defined rules here." The member's tail began to twitch. Herb locked onto the twitch, thinking it had a rhythm to it.

Tachymus continued, "Herb Coulick is here to brief us, and I will in short order turn the meeting over to him. We have made our first moves in taming humans. Their labor and resources are being reconfigured for our purposes. Now Herb…"

"We have barely started our meeting! And now an explanation of the explanation!", the senior leader three from the left of Herb suddenly exclaimed. The leader's stubby arms were now swaying in synch with scorpion tail in the right row.

Tachymus no had four eyestalks glaring at the interruption as he said, "Herb, again my apologies. Please begin your briefing."

Herb nodded and began going through his prepared remarks. After the first five minutes he noticed that several others of the senior leaders were looking distressed and one snapped at another to "stop crowding me, you idiot!"

Herb managed to conclude his speech while an agitated Tachymus, watching the behavior of the Kevorkians around them, said, "Herb, thank you for your report. However, I am at a loss to explain the rudeness some of our members are exhibiting here today. I am going to have you escorted back to your stump-ray. Again, thank you for your update." He swung his attention back to the assembly, "We will hold a round table session with the entire alliance of representatives to talk about this breach of decorum." He then signaled for the two escorts to return.

The mind blocks in Herb's brain were a hair away from total collapse, so he was quite relieved to go. Moments later, he was back in his stump-ray, preparing for departure. Once cleared, he dropped all pretense of hiding anything as he headed for New York City where he would meet with Celeste to avoid seeing both Eini and Carrie for a time.

*

Tachymus was mystified with how poorly some of the senior attendees had performed at their very first large scale summit in centuries. Of course, many stressful things happened in short order

195

during the resurrection of some of the members and perhaps some behavior modification would be needed for the poor conduct he had just witnessed. Still, today's event left him with an uncomfortable reminder of the "before times", when pre-Kevorkian Alliance members had hated each other. Wars had been the common solution to disagreements and had nearly led to their own demise.

Once Herb was out of the conference hall, calm appeared to return to most of the membership and the conference concluded. At his staff meeting with Xeon and Atraxus, he had a brief sidebar with his two principals before the regular team discussion. Tachymus described what had happened. Atraxus said, "That is troubling. What in the world would have driven such angry responses to such bland material as Herb was presenting?"

Xeon asked, "Can we review the meeting video?" Tachymus nodded and a moment later they watched as Herb entered the Great Hall and Tachymus began his introduction.

Atraxus exclaimed, "Look at the movements of those two senior members. They look like they are in sync as they argue with each other!"

Tachymus said, "I see the pattern my friend. You are right, this is more troubling than I previously thought. Let's get back together and discuss later after our meeting with the team."

Chapter 29

Herb was perusing his daily briefings from the Kevorkians. The directives had become increasingly more agitated in nature. Along with that, the frequency of messages had picked up considerably from when he had first arrived on Earth, going from once or twice a day to every few hours. Tachymus and Xeon were his primary buffer that filtered these messages to him. He noted that the two suddenly seemed to not be communicating with each other in contrast to what he had seen in their teamwork back on Mars when he first met them. In fact, he would get conflicting directives about what was important, what was not, and that would lead to more wasted effort of his own to determine what projects should be prioritized. He wondered at times if there was some hallucinogenic pollutant drifting up to their ship from Earth's atmosphere. For example, the critical assignments—Carrie had compiled extensive lists of qualified people, all for these high priority projects. It included their backgrounds, strengths and any weaknesses along with suggestions of what she felt they would be good at. He had then presented the listing to Tachymus and Xeon. They had immediately gone off to confer on their own and returned, having scrambled the list around. Some of the people they suggested were clearly mis-qualified for the slots and the two could not agree on which mis-qualified applicant got which job. He had then worked for days to get the two Kevorkians to come around to a joint resolution to sort it out. The results were not what he hoped for. An example—Josh and Ben had been paired together on the carbon dioxide atmospheric scrubber project—neither were experienced in this area at all, but the engineers most qualified were reassigned to get plastics scraped out of the oceans. So, he hoped these two heads might be better than one as they learned by trial and error. It made Herb sigh at times.

Which brought to mind his cloaked defense of his thoughts from Eini. He dropped the shield and all pretense the same day after coming back from the chaotic conference on the starship. He revealed his near trespasses to Eini who simply absorbed his jumbled explanation. He then went and laid down and slept well for the first time since leaving Mars. When he awoke, she advised she had analyzed what was going on with him when he had earlier been alone with Carrie. Eini had taken the initiative while he was napping and withdrawn a small bit of his blood which she analyzed and discovered the sex nanobots. This revelation reaffirmed that Carrie Carlin was beyond a shadow of a doubt to never be trusted. Once he calmed down from Carrie's behavior, the two of them formulated a plan to control her. First was the neutralization of nanobot technology which they quickly did. With that done, they decided that they would play Carrie's game of sexual seduction. Eini made it clear that she saw nothing wrong with using this approach to manipulate the woman. This led to a three way meeting where Herb and Eini said they would be fine if they all got together during this assignment and had some fun on the side. Herb read Carrie's mind, (Eini had shown him an old Distainien technique that worked with non-telepathic species), and realized she was elated, thinking her earlier plan was finally working. The situation swiftly evolved into the threesome taking enjoyable little side trips to some interesting places around the planet where they saw the sights and indulged in sexual escapades when they were not working on Earth restoration projects. Carrie was getting along with Eini better all the time as she fell deeper into the reverse trap that she had blundered into. Along with that, Eini fed ideas to Carrie about her projects that improved the quality of the ventures, a win/win for all of them.

*

Several weeks later, Herb was preparing his next update for the Kevorkians. Which brought up memories about the crustiness in some of Tachymus's latest transmissions. He decided the Kevorkian must be operating under extreme stress. He sympathized that it could certainly be the case for anyone recovering from the hibernation the Kevorkians had gone through, along with the rebuilding of their culture, and technology. Thus, with some of the recent somewhat testy interactions he had experienced with Tachymus, he decided he would try to be more accommodating and calming.

He checked his new Rolex Cosmo-Oyster submariner IV Ultimate wristwatch Eini had bought for him when they were in Switzerland and realized it was time to get on a surface to ship call. After linking up he was seeing the conference room located off the bridge of the Kevorkian starship as Xeon came in and gave a brusk "Hello". Herb calmly smiled and nodded. Tachymus then came on, nodded to Xeon, then shifted focus to Herb. He started with, "I thought I was supposed to start these meetings."

Herb replied, "Ah, well, my apologies, all I did was open the link. Nothing going on, we were just waiting for you to join and lead the call."

Tachymus blinked his six eyes a few times, seeming a bit confused, then in the equivalent of a shrug, he said, "Whatever. So, Herb. You said you have been getting some conflicting directives from myself and Xeon." Herb nodded.

Xeon snobbishly queried, "Are you sure you understood Herb? Are you capable of understanding? Why would I contradict Tachymus? Why would he contradict me? It must be you that has got this situation blown out of proportion, not me!" He looked at Tachymus and added, "It's him, not me. Right?"

Tachymus flared up with, "Always about Herb. Never knew you were so perfect Xeon. Of course, Herb understood. You seem to be a bit fixated about him and his abilities."

"Am not!"

"As Herb would say… *bullshit*"

Herb was wide eyed now, looking back and forth at the two Kevorkians, wondering how bad this latest dustup might become. In an attempt to calm the situation, he offered, "Hey, listen, I can review what was sent and crosscheck again. I just thought the directives for where to begin implementing the CO2 processors was a bit opposite when one of you said east coast and the other west coast…"

"Shut the fuck up Herb!" Xeon was turning sort of a deep purple shade now and fluttering his tentacles wildly. Tachymus said, "You calm down right now Xeon! That's way over the top and rude as well!"

It was then that Xeon abruptly froze up then slumped over. Tachymus tentacles flittered about wildly as he declared, "Health emergency!"

A few moments later, a medical team responded. Herb watched as they checked whatever vitals they were supposed to check on Xeon. The lead tech looked at Tachymus and shrugged with an ain't *got a clue* expression that even Herb could read. Tachymus ordered, "Well, haul his brusselfallow, (Kevorkian equivalent of "ass"), down to the infirmary and sort it out!"

He then turned to Herb and said, "Let's continue later—I have to say, shit is getting weird around this place lately. Sorry." The link dropped.

Herb leaned back in his chair, feeling like he might hyperventilate, still unclear as to which coast to begin the CO2 scrubber project, but he decided to go with Tachymus's orders. He sent a note over to Celeste so she could make sure Josh and Ben were moving in the right direction, (literally).

*

Tachymus was hastily whooshing through the water filled corridors to the infirmary after the mysterious collapse of Xeon that led to the abrupt call termination with Herb. When he arrived, several of the medical crew were working on stabilizing his second in command. Tachymus tried to get closer but was blocked by a force field the group had raised around their work area. He asked, "Is Xeon alright? I must know, please!" One of the senior medical staff turned

200

to him and said, "He is physically stable. However, it seems his cognitive functions are frazzled. I know, it's not a great medical description, but that is the situation. We plan to put him in stasis for the time being until we can sort out what has happened to him. Now, let us do our work, we will keep you advised." Tachymus nodded, though he was a bit miffed by the demeanor of the team leader.

*

Celeste was sipping a cappuccino in the Organo-Beanery Coffee Shop while looking across the street at the rebuilding of the Empire State Building. Progress on the project was moving rapidly due to the construction technology the Kevorkians had provided the local contractor. Now at over fifty stories, the project manager, an attractive younger woman named Jamie Di Filippo, dropped by with an update, "At this rate, it should be just a couple of weeks until this is done, not months." Celeste, pleased with the news, waved goodbye to Jamie as the woman left. Celeste then turned to her next bit of business for the day.

Sitting two tables away, waiting for her were Alex, Ben, and Josh.

She motioned for her brother Alex, who came over and sat across from her. He sighed, look at the other two men and gave them a firm nod and a shrug, which seemed like contradictory physical indicators of his mental status. They nodded back. It made Celeste wonder what all the nodding was about, but she thought, *with guys? Who knows?*

Celeste smiled and leaned forward, saying, "So, brother, how have you been?"

Alex shrugged and said, "Taking it one day at a time. Whatcha got for me Sis?"

Celeste nodded, noting how Alex was getting right down to business. She said, "Ah yes. Your new assignment. Pay is good, and, uh, well…"

"Well, what?"

"You get to be a senior director. Of an environmental cleanup!"

"No VP position?" A wounded expression crept over his face.

"I think you are lucky to even be getting this gig considering how some people view you these days, though I had figured you might not agree."

Alex sighed, "And that gig would be?"

Celeste smiled again, realizing her facial muscles were getting tired from forcing the expression so often these days. She said, "You are Miami bound my brother!"

Alex's expression shifted to a rather panicky wide eyed look as he breathed, "Miami?" She nodded and added, "You will be supervising the restoration of an improved sea shield wall and of course the environmental cleanup needed all over the area."

"So, my old job and a shit cleanup detail?"

Expressionless now, she nodded. He sighed, then whimpered, "And nothing you can do about that?"

She shook her head and said, "This came directly from Herb for you to take this on, he thinks you're… well suited for the job. Carrie delivered your offer letter to me just before this meeting." She slipped the paper across the table, though Alex made no effort to look at it. "If you take it, you head out as soon as we are done talking here. Frankly, I suggest you take it. There are gonna be a lot worse jobs out there, believe me, like for the people actually doing the cleanup."

Alex squinted intently, studying his sister's features which did not waver. He finally sighed and said, "So I guess I am off."

"I did arrange for you to stay at the old Hemingway place along with a mildly used company stump-ray, if that helps!"

Alex stood, nodded, and said, "Thanks Sis. I suppose you're right. It could have been worse. Well, I guess I need to get moving."

Celeste then stood, they hugged, then he turned and left, not making eye contact with either Josh or Ben, which left the two of them looking at each other, now not so knowingly, then nervously back at her. Which made her reflect on the Ben situation. She had decided a while back that it was time to move on—they were no longer a thing since arriving back on Earth. So recently, the two had a sit down, and both had agreed that going forward they would have a "just friends" relationship. She had been pleasantly surprised by the end of the conversation that both of them had come to the same conclusion. Therefore, today, she felt okay about the upcoming discussion. She nodded and said, "Come on over you two."

Nearly bumping into each other as they stood with Ben accidentally knocking his chair over and startling other patrons at the far end of the establishment, the two men nervously approached, but only after Ben had cursed aloud, "Fuck me!" as he picked up the chair.

Once the two men were situated at her table, Ben asked, "So…what's the plan?"

Celeste nodded and said, "Well, I'd say mostly all good news, for both of you."

Ben perked up and said, "So, I keep my VP position?"

Celeste said, "Nope, however, you'll be working as a senior associate manager. Josh is your staff manager. I made the positions up; I know how you guys love your titles. Plus, it gives you a bit more moola."

Ben looked disappointed. Josh, however, was pleased, this being his first position above a lowly engineering job.

Josh said, "So, what are we going to be doing?"

"Scrubbing carbon dioxide out of the atmosphere. The scrubbers are Kevorkian based technology and very effective. It's a big project for both of you as it will take years to bring down the CO_2 level and you are the two that will get all the recognition as well as steady employment! And you get to move first to California where the project will begin. You then work your way back east as the scrubber facilities are built out across America."

Ben's expression relaxed hearing where they were going, so he asked, "LA, San Diego?"

"Um, looks like someplace called Slab City. Near the dried-up Salton Sea area."

"Slab City?"

"Yeah, something left over from Marines that were out their training during World War II. Supposed to be sunny year around!"

Ben immediately linked up to the Solarspere and searched for the place. It was sunny alright along with silty sand that blew frequently, dirt and gravel roads, along with a bunch of old run-down and mostly deserted house trailers. Also, a lithium extraction plant was nearby, recently brought back online to mine the material for high capacity batteries. According to a climate description of the area, the average yearly temperature these days was one hundred fifteen degrees.

"Your sending us to a salt and lithium deposit in a desert where the air is dangerous to breathe?" whined Ben.

Celeste sighed and said, "Yep. Though, mostly lithium processing, we have all the salt we need these days. Now about the lithium—we will ramp up production beyond current volumes. You guys get to work on that project as well! Ultimately, you get to move incrementally east. First, towards what's left of the boneyard called Phoenix, then into New Mexico, Texas, uh, etcetera. Later, we can see if you want to handle the projects on other continents." She paused, realizing she would not be happy with any of those locations herself. Still, it was the best she could offer at the moment. She continued, "We have to build out in these areas as we need the maximum sunlight in those respective regions to drive the concentrated solar power facilities that power this stuff twenty four hours three hundred and sixty five days a year. Also, some of the scrubbers go down into northern Mexico. So, a lot to do."

Ben was speechless, obviously not particularly happy with this turn of events. Josh, however, said, "Thanks Celeste. Once Ben does a reboot, I think, like me, he will realize how good a deal this is compared to the alternatives we keep hearing about other people getting stuck with."

Ben, now absorbing the information from his online search, breathed, "One hundred fifteen degrees."

Celeste added, "Fahrenheit now, to be clear."

Josh slapped him on the back and joked, "In the shade!"

Celeste chuckled and said, "Right! Well, like Alex, if you two accept, you are to be on your way as soon as we are done here."

Josh exclaimed, "Oh, accepted!" He looked over at a still shocked Ben and back to her, nodding while he said, "He'll do it."

Celeste stood, then Josh and finally Ben. She took Ben by the shoulders, gave him a big grin, then shook Josh's hand as she said, "Keep me informed! We will have status meetings starting in a month to talk about your progress so you can get back here to civilization for an occasional dinner!" The two men left, Josh, buoyant, Ben, shoulders slumped as he shuffled out the door. Celeste sat back down. She sighed, trying to find something positive to think about. It was then she remembered how friendly the young Jamie had been and that she was really just a block away most of the time due to the project. Celeste decided to see if the woman would be interested in going out for dinner anytime soon.

Chapter 30

Alex had just completed unpacking in Key West. A few hours earlier, he had made an initial visit to survey what he would eternally think of as Miami "Crapshire", Florida. A bunch of his old bots formerly dedicated to saving the seawall had been reassigned to him and they were now focused on getting the upgraded shield wall resurrected around the tip of Florida. On the positive side, it looked like the shit cleanup would proceed at a reasonably fast clip with the addition of the alien technology that the Kevorkians had provided as well as some really effective worker bee algorithms for the bots that were clearly going to make a huge difference in the speed of the two projects.

Which seemed like a great idea—working faster and more efficiently. Except for one thing. Alex was hoping to stall the actual restoration efforts to prolong his job beyond the original six month projections. He suspected whatever project he got next, if he got another project, would just have him trying to prove himself all over again. In fact, during a private conversation with Celeste before his arrival, they talked about that aspect of everyone's assignments under the Kevorkian serf-industry. It was going to be full time, *what have you done for me lately* mode going forward into the foreseeable future. To Alex, it was clearly time to figure out how to game the system. Wandering back towards the kitchen, he ran into his old BossBot. Alex nodded and said, "So, what's up?"

BossBot said, "A progress report. We have sixteen of the new model shield generators in place. We should have all sixty four of them in place by the end of next week. After that, checks on the wall components for any defects and repairs, then full system activation, two weeks. Then we will have the filtration systems that will cleanse the worst areas around Miami back up and running a week after that. Total projected time to completion is now three months."

Alex cursed silently to himself as he realized this latest estimate cut the work by half. He said, "You sure about that BossBot? Could we need another run at the numbers? This was supposed to be at least a six month project."

BossBot said, "I don't need another run at the numbers Alex. Perhaps you do. I can state with five hundred and twelve bit accuracy, that my projections are correct. However, you don't need to be a RocketScientistBot. The game changer is the Kevorkian technology that the aliens have provided us."

Feeling deflated now, Alex said, "Fine. Where's the gin? I need a martini. Or two."

BossBot nodded and said, "This way sire."

Which brought Alex up abruptly in his tracks as he asked, "Sire?"

BossBot nodded and said, "Yes, a really useful new cynical humor routine has been added by Herb, your old protégé to our new programming. He guaranteed me that you would, "get a kick out of it.""

Alex sighed and muttered under his breath, "Right, I bet he did." BossBot then pivoted around and guided Alex to the gin.

Two martinis' later and while mixing a third, (the drinks were definitely helping improve his sour mood), he got a call from Ben that started with, "Hey, old friend. How's it going over there?" Alex raised an eyebrow at the suspiciously chummy introduction and replied, "Uh, fine. Just fine. How about out there in the deserted desert furnace area?"

Ben, apparently determined to forge ahead with positivity, replied, "Ah, the Coachella valley? It's like visiting the seaside at the peak of summer, except it's all beach! Some pretty dull brown mountains in the background. But this stupendous project will fix all that. Probably after I am dead."

"Great. So, what's up?"

"Oh, I was wondering…"

"Wondering?"

"Got any openings out there in Florida? I love it out here, but I think Josh and his bot buddies have it all under control."

Irritated, Alex snipped, "Nope. You should check with Celeste if you want a different gig. I don't get to pick and choose anybody or anything these days."

"Um, I guess if I could get her to even contact me back these days between our monthly status meetings. A busy woman, as you know."

Alex found he had to agree with that assessment. Plus, Celeste had mentioned she was now dating a woman she had met in New York, which felt awkward to talk about with Ben. He said, "Hang in there and keep trying pal! It's the best advice I have."

The call ended shortly after that, with a dejected Ben saying, "Okay, well, uh… bye?", as Alex disconnected as quickly as he could. He finished mixing his drink and realized he was going to require some additional liquid fortification throughout the evening to keep his spirits up.

*

Celeste arrived for a late afternoon dinner at Scarpetta's restaurant and was standing outside where she was supposed to meet up with Jamie. It turned out the younger woman had not only been happy to go dining when she had first asked her out a few weeks back, but Jamie knew a lot of great places. The attraction between the two women had rapidly become a romantic relationship. Looking back, Celeste realized she had made a deliberate choice to send Ben away with Josh. Plus, she needed a lot of space to reset her emotions after Carrie. Jamie was sweet and down to Earth—their relationship proceeded without the subterfuge or the private agendas that Celeste had experienced in the recent past, (as well as participated in herself). It was a breath of fresh air.

Jamie showed up and waved at Celeste as she climbed out of her cabBot, turned and came striding up to Celeste. They embraced and kissed just as an old woman walking by grumbled, "Get a room you two!"

The couple giggled, and Jamie said, "Welcome to New York!" Celeste laughed while looking at the old woman and said, "After dinner soon enough for you lady?" The old woman shook her head and groused, "Assholes," as she kept going.

Celeste, returning her full attention to her date, said, "Don't you just love this town?" To which they both laughed as they entered the restaurant. A moment later they were escorted to their booth. Once seated, they scooted close to each other. The staff knew Jamie, and they quickly served some Chianti as the couple perused old-fashioned paper menus.

After ordering, Jamie said, "So, how was your day?"

Celeste rolled her eyes and said, "Well, busy is definitely an inadequate descriptive. I get pulled in so many directions, it's hard to keep track of everything. Still, we are already making progress."

Jamie nodded and asked, "The Kevorkians still pushing new tech into these endeavors?"

"Yep, which is one of my biggest challenges. I have to get this stuff out to the various projects and then get people and the different Bot types brought up to speed on it. I find Bots a hell of a lot easier to train than people it turns out since that's mostly just data updates."

Jamie reached over, and placed a hand on Celeste knee and said, "I wish I could help," while wearing a mischievous smile.

Celeste, placing her hand on top of Jamies, scooted it a few inches up her thigh and said, "You certainly can!" Again, they giggled.

After dinner, they headed over to Jamie's apartment. Celeste really liked the place, it was so old New York, even in the way Jamie had furnished the place. It was a small, one bedroom with a walk in shower and had a combined kitchen and living area. It didn't take long after arrival for the two of them to be in bed. Afterwards, Jamie with her head nestled on Celeste's arm, Celeste sighed in contentment. Her serenity ended with a panicky call from Ben marked as urgent. She sighed. The man had no concept of time zones. Since she and Jamie were naked except for a satin sheet covering them, she made it an audio only call. With her good mood now evaporated, Celeste said, "Ben, could this not wait until morning?"

Ben, said, "Sorry, sorry, uh, I didn't want to bother you, but something weird as shit is going on out here!"

"Weird. As shit? What would that be?"

"We just found what seems to be some dead Kevorkians."

"*What?* Are you kidding me?"

"Believe me, I am not, and I wish I were."

"What makes you think they are dead?" It was then that Jamie raised up on an elbow next to Celeste, wide eyed and attentive.

"Well, they ain't moving and they stink, plus they are definitely decomposing."

"What the hell? Fuck, well, I have no idea what to tell you. I guess we need to contact… Herb? Any idea how the hell they died?"

"They look like they were in some sort of battle based on their appearance, but that's hard to tell precisely with the level of body rot going on."

"Yuck! Okay. Let me get back to you and keep this shit to yourselves till then!"

"Shit is the operative word alright. You should smell this. And yeah, mums the word. That's why I called you instead of the New York Times."

"Jeez, thanks. Ok, bye now."

The call ended. Celeste sat up on the edge of the bed and started pulling on her clothes. Jamie asked, "You want me to go with you?"

"No, get some rest. I am going to have to locate Herb and tell him what I know. I'll be in touch." They both stood and Jamie gave Celeste a hug and kiss on the cheek as she said, "Be careful. This sounds strange as hell from what little we know about these aliens. I thought they were all peaceful vegans or something like that."

Celeste sighed. Her partner felt so good against her, but needing to go, she said, "In my experience, not really. Remember, despite the propaganda, they are not being all that friendly or interacting diplomatically with us. More like starting to own us." She then hurriedly dressed, headed out the door, hailed a CabBot, then called Herb and said, "We need to meet up, soon as possible."

Herb asked, "What's wrong?"

"I'll tell you when we are together. This is red hot, so sooner is better."

Hearing the urgency in her voice, he said, "Ok, I'll come to you. Bringing Carrie with me."

"Whatever you need to do." The call ended. Celeste leaned back in her seat as she headed over to her new office at the Empire State Building.

*

Carrie piloted the stump-ray with Herb sitting next to her as they departed their meeting with Celeste. They made a beeline to the Salton Sea where the alleged bodies of the Kevorkians had been reported.

Herb had already contacted Tachymus who was genuinely stunned at the news. This did nothing to assuage worries now romping around inside Herb's head. Tachymus advised a forensic team had been dispatched and asked that Herb and Carrie link up with them at the scene. Herb had asked Tachymus, "Why would these crew members be in the Salton Sea area?"

Tachymus replied, "I had no idea any of our people were on the planet right now at all. However, I am wondering if this is part of some mission that Xeon planned a while back."

"Did you ask him?"

"Uh, he's… away at the moment."

"Ah, okay. So, your team can figure out what happened you think?"

"Oh, I am sure they can. Though I am more interested in *why* this happened than how."

Herb paused, then asked, "Tachymus, is everything okay on your ship?"

Tachymus, as close to blank in his expression as Herb had ever seen, said, "Sure, sure. Some… minor disagreements of late, but certainly nothing that would lead to this situation." Herb realized that was all that the Kevorkian was going to share as Tachymus advised he had to attend to some minor problems on the ship that sounded like the equivalent of a clogged drain.

Carrie looked over at Herb and said, "I know you have been friends in the past with Tachymus, but are you buying any of that crap?"

Herb said, "Not really, though I have no idea what I should do. Tensions and feuds seem to be escalating with the Kevorkians."

"Any idea why?"

Herb shook his head, thinking back once again to his visit where some of the Kevorkians had gotten rowdy during the meeting. She said, "Well, sounds like bullshit is afoot to me. I've experienced too much of it in my career to not smell it happening here. We need to be cautious." Herb looked over at her, as he silent agreed that the woman had pretty extensive experience in this area. For her part, she nodded knowingly then returned her attention to piloting duties.

Herb decided to think about the weird Kevorkian behavior later. Sighing to himself, he asked, "Coffee?" Carrie nodded in the affirmative as he turned to a recently installed brewing machine.

*

Ben and Josh were waiting upwind from the remains of the Kevorkians as Herb and Carrie's stump-ray approached from the northeast. Directly above their location was a descending Kevorkian craft from the starship.

212

Celeste had linked up with the two men just a few moments earlier, asking Ben for an update and what they had discovered so far. He offered "The smell from the corpses was really funky and getting worse quickly".

Celeste grimaced at his comment then said, "Ben get me a *relevant* update as soon as you know something worth knowing!" She then disconnected.

Josh asked "Why is this place even called the Salton Sea? It's a desert basin!"

Ben shrugged and said, "Apparently it wasn't always this way from what I read. Seems back in 1905, the Colorado river breached an irrigation canal and dumped floodwater into the Salton sink, creating a massive body of water. People decided to make it a destination for skiing, boating, that sort of thing. They even had a hotel and some restaurants at one point. Then the whole effort crapped out. Droughts led to the sea becoming toxic over time from agricultural runoff. The rest, as they say, is history."

Josh made a face and said, "Man, were we ever fucking up this planet." Ben nodded in agreement.

Ben and Josh were suited up appropriately, wearing breathers to filter what went in and out of their lungs. It was uncomfortable in the current heat but beat the heck out of whatever they might inhale from the crusty seabed that bubbled a hundred feet down underneath them with toxic chemical reactions. Herb and Carrie landed a short distance from Ben's stump-ray. They did not exit immediately. The Kevorkian craft set down close to the corpses.

Neither Ben nor Josh had been near any Kevorkians except the dead ones that an aerial survey had found while scouting for a location to construct the first CO2 processing plant. The two men weren't going to get a better view of the aliens as the Kevorkians had exited their craft in full space suit regalia that gave a vague idea of their physical conformation. Ben shrugged to Josh as they slogged over to Herb and Carrie just as those two climbed down a short ramp from their stump-ray to the ground. The pair were similarly attired in Kevorkian based suits far more sophisticated than what Ben and Josh wore.

Once together, Herb asked Ben for a rundown. Ben told the same story he had told Celeste. Herb nodded, advised them to stay where they were, then strode over to have a huddle. Ben overheard Carrie speculating that the live Kevorkians were a forensic team. Carrie stood about ten meters from Ben and Josh. Ben looked over at her and waved. She nodded but did not otherwise appear interested in conversation. Getting up his nerve, Ben said to Josh, "I'm gonna talk to her. Be back in a few."

From his position, Josh could not hear Carrie very clearly as Ben greeted her, but her body language and tone were abrupt in nature. At first Ben was smiling, but then he began to frown and finally he threw up his hands and walked away as he said, "Don't act like you didn't cause a lot of the problems we have to deal with here today woman!" She flipped off his receding back as she retorted, "Asshole!" Josh was grinning but quickly shifted his gaze to what the aliens were doing when a red faced Ben returned.

Seeing Josh's smile, Ben said, "So, you think that was funny?" Josh just shrugged, keeping his focus on the aliens.

The Kevorkian team was now headed in the direction of the bodies as Herb hiked back to stand with Carrie. Josh and Ben could hear bits of a muffled discussion between the two, Carrie being the loudest and somewhat animated—she even pointed over in their general direction. Ben was dividing his attention between trying to watch the forensic team so he could report to Celeste and listening to the Herb and Carrie discussion. Herb sounded like he was consoling Carrie.

*

Ben himself was getting upset again, took a deep breath, then refocused on the reason everyone was here. The aliens were now running some sort of portable scanners over the bodies. A few minutes later, two Kevorkians retrieved some other devices from their ship, directing them towards the bodily remains which abruptly disintegrated, leaving what looked like mounds of dust. They then returned to their spacecraft and moments later lifted off, headed back towards their orbiting ship. Herb and Carrie were already headed to their stump-ray. Ben hollered at them as he jogged along, trying to catch up to the two. Herb stopped and turned around. Carrie kept going.

As he caught up to Herb, Ben said, "So what did they find?"

Herb shrugged and said, "Pretty much what you already knew about the bodies. A violent death for all. An unknown perpetrator, though they suspect humans."

"What? Why would any human kill them? And frankly, how?"

"Well, let me think. Your species has such a bloody history. Though I can see your point, not all that capable of attacking Kevorkians."

Ben blanched then said, "Jeez Herb. I guess we simple have a special status these days where we get accused without evidence."

Herb gave Ben a cynical grin and said, "Got any real questions?"

Ben, deciding this was pointless, replied, "Real questions? Yeah, I got a bunch."

Herb said, "Well, write them down and have Celeste submit them to me. I gotta go. Bye!" He walked off and climbed aboard his stump-ray as Ben headed back to Josh. A few moments later Herb and Carrie departed.

Ben breathed, "Fuckers!"

Josh gave an askance look at Ben and said, "Old friend, I understand you are not happy, but pissing off Herb and insulting Carrie is not going to get you anywhere except unhappier. Plus, what you do these days can affect me as well. Please consider that if you would in future encounters with them."

Ben sighed, knowing Josh was right. He shook his head, turned around and stomped off to their stump-ray. Josh watched for a moment, grinned to himself, still finding the whole Carrie thing humorous, then followed.

Once aloft, Ben contacted Celeste who this time brought up a video link. She said, "So, what's the scoop?"

"Apparently, we are summarily guilty of murdering Kevorkians if only we knew what we were doing. According to the World Ambassador anyway."

"What? Ben, what did you say to him?"

"Nothing, really. That was Herb just being rude. Not sure we know one more thing about what led to the aliens' deaths than we did earlier except the Kevorkians have some pretty fancy tools for disposing of bodies. Like they fricasseed the corpses. Never seen anything like it even in a movie!"

Celeste visibly shuddered at that last comment and said, "Fricasseed? Wow, thanks for, uh, the update." She then disconnected.

Ben looked at Josh and said, "Let's go find something to eat." A moment later, they were accelerating away to a restaurant located on the ocean side of Los Angeles that was only ten minutes away and a hell of a lot cooler.

*

Celeste arrived back at Jamie's place just as the young woman was headed out the door for work. She had been planning to grab a short nap, but now she had Alex ringing her with his annoying buzzbomb ringtone. Jamie, a sympathetic expression on her face, patted her on the back and said, "Gotta' run dear. Hope your day improves."

Celeste nodded distractedly as she answered Alex's call. "What? I really need some sleep, so can this wait?"

216

Alex, his expression grim, said, "I suppose it could, but it can't. My team just found some weird stuff in some of the muck we are cleaning up here in Miami."

"Weird stuff? Wow, is there any chance people on my team could be less specific these days so my notions of what is going on could be even more vague?" She sighed, then added, "Sorry, please continue."

"Yeah, I hear ya Sis. However, if I knew what it was, I would elaborate in great detail. BossBot thinks it's body parts, but it's not like anything we have ever seen before. One looks like a head with six eyes on stalks. What the hell would that be?"

Celeste grimly replied, "My guess, some non-functional aliens. Listen, a Kevorkian team will be headed your way to investigate. Herb will undoubtedly be involved as well. I need to notify him now."

Alex frowned then said, "Something you aren't telling me here?" Celeste sighed and said, "Yeah and I don't have time to fill you in at the moment. Let me brief you later and please try to gather anything you can on what happened. Whatever is going on with these bodies showing up randomly means we are dragging ass on knowing any real details."

Alex paused wide eyed at her comment, then added, "Okay Sis. Well, otherwise, we are making *swell* progress."

She sighed and closed with, "Thanks brother!" She then disconnected, feeling as if her head would begin spinning like a top from the recent chain of events. What was she to think? That the Kevorkians were in reality homicidal maniacs, now dumping corpses on Earth? Or was it some marauding humans like Herb had said to Ben? She had no idea at that moment. However, if she did not inform Herb immediately, blame would likely get heaped on her. So, she made the call and updated him on the latest developments. He did not seem very surprised this time, which left her wondering even more about what she did not know.

*

Back in the Dolphmanien enclave, Herb shook his head and looked at Carrie as the call with Celeste ended. He said, "Pack up. We're headed to Miami now! More dead bodies."

Carrie blinked and said, "What the hell is going on?"

Herb sighed and replied with, "That's a damn good question. I wonder…." His voice trailed off as he realized his earlier comments to Ben about humans as primary suspects was way off base. How could a human even gain the upper hand to kill a Kevorkian? Problem was, as far as he knew from Tachymus, the aliens were allegedly staying on their ship.

Carrie asked, "So, from your expression, I can tell you are trying to sort through what is going on. What are you thinking?"

Herb sighed and said, "I really don't know at this point. Anyway, let's update Eini that we have to go and then we can discuss on the trip out."

Just entering the room, Eini said, "Let Eini know what?"

Exhaling deeply, he quickly briefed her on the two incidents then added, "I suspect these deaths are actually Kevorkian generated. I really don't think humans are capable enough to be able to get away with such a crime, even to this point. Present company excepted." Carrie stuck her tongue out at him.

"So Tachymus has been exaggerating about their peaceful nature?" Eini asked, her ironic expression in conflict with her words. Herb understood her implied message after the history lesson he had received from her about the Kevorkians.

Herb replied, "Eh heh. However, clearly, something has changed in the most current behavior such as Tachymus's and Xeon's recent conduct where they had strong disagreements and aggressive verbal exchanges in front of me. That is quite different than in the past. I also saw this aggression at the first meeting when I visited their ship for the big kickoff of serf-industry. I was pretty distracted with trying to keep the secret about Carrie at the time so not as tuned in as I am now."

"You mean my failed attempt to seduce you?" Carrie asked as she and Eini grinned at each other.

"Uh, yeah, that. Anyway, something disruptive seemed to start that very day on the Kevorkian starship."

Eini said, "You should talk to Tachymus then and try to get some straight info." Despite her words, her expression was again, cynical.

Herb, noting both her words and expression, said, "I have tried several times. He is being evasive and lately, less and less responsive to any of my questions."

Eini said, "I wonder if things are fraying in the so-called Alliance." Carrie nodded in agreement.

Herb said, "You think so?" Both women nodded. He continued, "Interesting. Well, listen, we should go."

Carrie nodded and said, "Eini, want to come with us?"

Eini said, "Yeah, we need to stay on top of whatever this is. And I've been curious about the cleanup progress in Miami."

Herb said, "Believe me, you ain't missed nothing. It is far worse today than when I was there with Alex back in our TGIF days. The smell makes you want to puke and ," he paused, noting the women making faces at his description of the situation.

Ten minutes later all three climbed aboard the stump-ray as Herb contacted Tachymus about getting the forensic crew re-dispatched. Tachymus made some odd hissing noises but otherwise advised that the team would be on their way shortly.

*

Alex was waiting as far upwind as possible from the mobile garbage reprocessing plant. The entire area smelled like regurgitated vomit infused with lots of poop. That was the best he could describe it, though the human techs who worked there kept telling him he would get used to it. He quickly decided he didn't want to get used to it and stayed as far away and as much as possible, instead focusing his time with the team getting the sea shields back in place. Even though most of the city had gone underwater, there were lots of materials that could be salvaged with Kevorkian technology once they got things drained back down and those could be used for various other restoration projects. As the sea shield project had gotten underway, the first thing they had started finding in the freshly drained homes and businesses were decaying bodies of the people that had died when the seawall had collapsed just as Alex and Herb had departed for Mars. The resource reprocessing plant crew had the unpleasant task of rolling from site to site as the water was drained back into the ocean and scooping up materials for salvage. That was how they had found the Kevorkian body parts lying atop some building wreckage along with some fragments of a spacecraft.

The hum of Herb's stump-ray arriving alerted Alex and he began walking towards the craft, hoping for a lower level of stinky, polluted air where they were setting down. When he was within a few meters, the hatch opened up and Herb, Carrie and Eini emerged. Herb nodded to him and said, "He Alex! Wow, it does smell worse now than it ever did when you and I were here before!"

Alex nodded and said, "Um, how are you Herb?"

Herb shrugged and said, "Fine. So, you think you found non-human body parts?"

Alex nodded and elaborated on their discovery. When he concluded, Eini looked at Herb and said, "I think Carrie and I will wait in the stump-ray while you and Alex go examine the scene of the crime."

For her part, Carrie was already back in the craft. Eini smiled at Herb, waved at Alex, then turned and climbed back aboard, shutting the hatch. Alex and Herb could then hear the air filtration system of the craft come online, undoubtedly providing a fresher scent inside the craft than what the men were inhaling outside.

Alex said, "I don't blame them. This place is a shitfest."

Herb nodded and said, "Alright then show me what your people found." They set off together, headed to where the mobile reprocessing plant had stopped. Just as they reached their goal, the Kevorkian forensic team arrived. The aliens were quickly analyzing the scene, scanning the remains. Once again, when they were done, they obliterated the body components.

Alex asked, "Why the hell are they destroying the evidence?"

Herb shrugged and said, "I have no idea. I guess they figure they got what they need. I'm sure as hell not going to question them; this particular bunch is not forthcoming anyway from what I saw out west earlier today. For sure, they like to zap body parts into powder."

"Out west?" Alex asked.

Herb, thinking he should have not mentioned the earlier trip, replied, "Ask Celeste." Alex gave him a sideways look. However, he did not pursue the topic any further.

The Kevorkians were already headed back to their spacecraft. One of them stumbled and bumped into another team member. They immediately started shoving each other around. One of the senior members made loud high pitched barking sounds and the two stopped their tussle. The aliens then resumed their trek back to their craft.

Alex said, "What the hell was that all about?"

Herb shrugged and said, "Some sort of disagreement, though I really don't know what it was about. Listen, they are about to leave. I am ready to get the hell out of here myself. Let's go." The two reversed course and headed back to Herb's stump-ray as the Kevorkians lifted off. The Kevorkian ship suddenly hovered, then lurched forward, then backward and after repeating the zigzag pattern about a half dozen times, finally rotated around and accelerated away.

Herb and Alex both watched the rather peculiar departure, then looked at each other. Alex said, "That was downright weird!" Herb nodded, and said, "Weird is a way overused word today. I need a long fucking vacation. Have never had one before but the idea suddenly sounds quite appealing."

They arrived back at Herb's stump-ray. Carrie extended a Martian style environmental field over Herb when he got up to the entry hatch before she opened it. Alex stopped as his former assistant climb aboard the craft where both women were sitting on display in total nudity. Carrie said, "Lose the outfit Herb, it stinks worse than it is worth trying to salvage." Herb started stripping then looked over his shoulder — Alex was peering in. He said, "Do you mind?"

Alex started to laugh, and Carrie stood, stepped up to the opening and promptly hollered, "Perv! Getting yourself an eyeful?" She and Eini then relocated out of his view.

Grinning to himself, he had to admit he didn't mind the insult all that much as he definitely had gotten an eyeful. Herb, however, was frowning at him. He said, "Okay, okay, I'm going." He then turned, waved goodbye and began walking back to his own craft, deciding to return to Key West to de-stinkify himself.

*

Xeon was sitting up, sipping on some nutrients one of the ship's medical team had provided. Tachymus arrived and they exchanged hellos. A quick briefing of his boss took place with Harrimon Detirius, the lead doctor of the medical team. Tachymus then requested that he, Xeon, and Harrimon, be left alone. The rest of the team trailed out of the room, but to be on the safe side, Tachymus raised a barrier shield around the three of them to keep anyone from listening in on their conversation.

Tachymus said, "My old friend, how are you feeling now?"

"Still a bit woozy but feeling better each day."

Tachymus said, "The med team says you will be fine and can resume your duties. If you are ready, I could sure use you to take on a special mission back to Mars." Xeon gave his equivalent of a nod, rubbing two antennae together. Tachymus continued, "Good. I need you to get Chaos back up and running. Chaos does not need weapons functionality, but we need the AI's processing capabilities."

Xeon said, "For what?"

"We need a backup for what is going on here. I have been infected as well as the rest of the ship by the anger virus that is spreading throughout the Alliance."

"Anger virus?"

"It's the best description we have at the moment for the phenomena that is afflicting us. Harrimon, can you fill Xeon in on the details?"

Harrimon nodded and said, "This so-called virus is all at the sub-cognitive emotional level. We found that we were able to bring you back to a normal state after placing you in stasis and then by carefully resetting the disrupted brain synapses that were misfiring. We will wind up having to do that to everyone now, the way this phenomenon is spreading throughout the population."

"Where did this come from?"

Harrimon said, "The apparent source was Herb Coulick."

Xeon, in a dubious tone, said, "How could Herb have caused this?"

Tachymus sighed and said, "Actually, I caused it, unintentionally. Herb requested the ability to hide his thoughts from his girlfriend, Eini, and I showed him an old technique used by spies. Unfortunately, it caused him to unintentionally be able to upload his anger, guilt and confusion to the Alliance senior members at the conference and it spread from there. We never have seen this before that I know of."

Xeon said, "I seem to recall the Distainiens caused a similar issue a long time ago." He gave a knowing look to Tachymus, then said, "Well, we are where we are. I will prepare for departure. You have the restoration plan for Chaos ready?"

Tachymus replied, "Already uploaded to your craft. Xeon said, "Great. Well, there is no time to spare. I will keep you updated."

Tachymus nodded as he dropped the barrier shield. He then turned to Harrimon and said, "Anymore news on progress controlling this problem?"

Harrimon shrugged his shoulders as he had a rather hominid physique, though he was covered in colorful feathers and had more of a beak than a mouth. He said, "It is not affecting every species in precisely the same way. We may have to implement a total stasis shutdown throughout the Alliance, including Mars."

Shaking his tentacles in displeasure, Tachymus said, "We need your undivided focus on this problem! Please keep me updated." He then headed off to his quarters located just off the bridge. At least for now, minimizing contact with others mostly kept him from having the occasional tantrum.

Chapter 31

Celeste was talking with Jamie while they were sitting on a couch side by side in her office after lunch. She had confided her concerns to her new partner about the now regular occurrence of alien remains appearing in various locations around the planet. She had even gotten a report from their moon colony of Kevorkian corpses showing up at the old Apollo landing site tourist attraction in the Sea of Tranquility. They appeared, according to the reports, to have been launched towards their location from an unknown point in space—the remains themselves were pulverized from smacking into the lunar surface.

Shaking her head, Jamie said, "So now the moon? What the heck is this all about?"

With a shrug, Celeste said, "The Kevorkians will tell us nothing. And Herb advised me that he no longer receives any sort of useful updates from Tachymus. The only good thing is that all the technology that they shared is doing an impressive job in restoring Earth, however the previous damage wrought by humanity is going to take quite a bit of time to rectify. I'm also concerned about what happens when the aliens start claiming our planetary resources for whatever they want to do." She then related how just a week back, they had located the wreckage of another alien spacecraft that had been spread out across Mexico when it crashed. She concluded, "The distance between where the various components impacted the planet surface was only about ten kilometers which indicated it had exploded fairly low in the sky."

Jamie said, "Do we know who was onboard?"

"We suspect it was the same forensic team that had just left Alex and Herb in Miami, based on the timing and the type of debris. But we can't say for sure. And this time, the Kevorkians did not bother to send a team to investigate. They just sizzled the already burnt up parts with weapons from their starship that's in orbit, which happened immediately after our own investigative team departed."

"Wow! I suspect we would not stand a chance against them if they decided to get rid of us."

Celeste nodded in agreement with Jamie's grim assessment and said, "You know my dear, if it was not for you, I'd probably lose my shit at this point. I can't find a calm place in my mind anymore except when we are together."

Jamie smiled, reached over and they hugged. Reluctantly disengaging, she said, "I gotta get to work. I will fix lasagna for dinner, so don't go snacking!" Celeste smiled. She decided as she watched Jamie's receding figure that she was looking forward to the lasagna, which temporarily got her out of her doldrums. Her contentment lasted about another five minutes. Then came a call from Carrie saying there was an urgent matter that needed immediate attention.

*

Carrie, looking up at the projection of Celeste noted that the woman was avoiding eye contact with her which made Carrie feel a tiny sense of regret. Distracting her from her musings, Herb came in and then Eini. Eini sat on Carrie's left, Herb on the right. Herb said, "Thanks Celeste, sorry for the short notice. Got a call from Tachymus that, to say the least, is concerning as well as confusing. I need to play a recording for you of that session."

Celeste asked, "Is this going to shed some light on what the hell is going on?"

Herb said, "Maybe. Let's talk after you watch this. And just so you know, Tachymus is not talking like we do, which may be disorienting, but we converted what you hear to a human voice via a TTV converter."

"TTV Converter?" Celeste asked.

"Uh, yeah, telepathy to voice conversion." Celeste had a puzzled expression but rather than elaborate further, he started

226

playing the video showing Tachymus floating in what appeared to be his quarters. She started hearing a voice, but there was nothing to associate it with the alien she was looking at, so she focused on the audio.

"Herb, I want you to know we have determined what is happening with our people and it is bad news. It goes back to when you worried about the Carrie incident when you were conflicted about Eini knowing what had happened. I know, it was my idea to help you by showing you the technique of hiding your thoughts with a mental deception barrier. What I did not realize is your brain, though far more advanced than a human's, is primarily a modified design with expanded capacity from your dolphin side. The result of that was when you came on board for the Grand Council Conference, your chaotic and angry thoughts spread to Kevorkians throughout the assembly hall like an infection. Then as those members came in contact with others on the ship it spread. That is now why we have rampaging violence throughout our alliance and even out on Mars after a return trip was made by a small crew we dispatched to pick up some supplies we needed. It is why your project teams have been finding corpses scattered about on Earth and now on your moon. Everyone is dealing with murderous impulses, including myself. I am about to shut everyone down into a stasis state and I will need you to come back to the ship and try to restart some of us with detailed procedures our medical team developed and which I will provide. Come to me first, I will be near as I can to the designated docking port you normally arrive at. Now I must go." At that moment, there was a commotion in the background and an explosion, followed by the abrupt termination of the message.

A wide eyed Celeste looked at the other three, who all had the same grim expression on their faces. Her reaction to the news, however, was different. She said, "You hid an affair with Carrie? And that led to you starting a war? What the *fuck* Herb?"

Carrie said, "Herb did not have an affair. I tried to get one started, he managed to dodge me."

Herb sighed, nodded and said, "I did not know how to discuss it with Eini, Tachymus tried to help, it backfired."

Celeste said, "Backfired? Is that what the hell you call it? What does this mean for all of us on the planet?"

Eini said, "You know, we should perhaps consider a different perspective here on what is going on. Perhaps we should all be grateful, especially serf-industry grade humans. Celeste? Your thoughts?" She smiled in such a way that Celeste realized Eini was offended at her outburst to Herb. Celeste decided to keep her mouth shut and simply shrugged.

Eini nodded and continued, "We've now got all this great technology on planet Earth from the Kevorkians. And the aliens that gave it to us are effectively going offline, which in reality, puts *us* back in charge. I think we could use this chain of events to our considerable advantage." She then paused to let what she said sink in.

Celeste nodded, "I see where you are going with this Eini. What do you think Carrie?"

Carrie nodded slowly then smiled brightly at the other two women. She said, "We can make this work! And I think it is prime time for us women to take complete charge of the show!"

Eini telepathically linked with Herb, "She is scheming again! But I have an idea. Play along. Act a bit upset but then nod. I want these two to believe we females are some sort of coalition."

Herb looked her in the eyes and gave a small nod. Then he said, "Wait, wait! I get what you are thinking Eini, and it does play to our advantage. But Carrie, you want to boot me out?"

Eini said, "No, no Herb. We want you to do what you do now, be a skilled liaison. The four of us will… collaborate."

Herb rose to his feet, bristled and said, "I have no interest in being a figurehead. I have supported getting the two of you to where you are right this moment." He pointed at Celeste and Carrie and continued, "Does that not deserve some loyalty from you?"

The room fell silent. Finally, Carrie nodded and said, "Herb, you are right. I apologize. You could continue in your role, but with a new title." The women beamed at each other.

Herb squinted as if in deep thought, then said, "Perhaps. What do you have in mind?"

After a short discussion, Eini said, "President Coulick of planet Earth!" Herb smiled as he acted as if he was basking in the new title. Eini telepathed, "Excellent performance my dear!"

Celeste said, "So, ladies, when do we all get together?" Before they could answer, she offered, "Jamie, my new partner, is making lasagna tonight! We could meet up at her place."

Carrie said, "We will be there! I think we can round up a couple bottles of chianti to go with the meal if that sounds ok!"

Herb telepathically expressed to Eini, "I'm good with this approach." Eini responded, "Especially for our own people."

Carrie and Eini then stood and stepped up alongside him, patting him on each arm. He smiled and said, "Awe shucks, okay. But don't we need to go to the starship and confirm what Tachymus said has actually happened."

Eini said, "Yep, and I am going with you. No argument on the topic is allowed!"

Herb's eyes went wide. Eini was quite the actor, having never talked to him so forcefully before. She said, "No telling what we will find dear. I am actually nervous for you to go all on your own. He replied, "Agreed. Let's do this."

*

Eini asked Carrie to come along on the trip. Eini explained that her assignment was to stay on the stump-ray while the two dolphmaniens explored the ship in case they needed a quick getaway. Herb slipped into the seat behind Carrie, who piloted, Eini sat next to him. When they arrived at the starship, Carrie maneuvered to the

229

designated port that Tachymus had provided Herb and docked. Herb then began working on getting the portal door open. Nothing worked. He tried all the codes he knew, a retina scan, flinger scan, (both flingers), and was about to start kicking on the door when Eini simply flipped the manual latch, and the door slid open. Herb sighed and said, "Well, something is obviously wrong with this damn ship if nothing I tried worked!"

Eini smiled and pecked a kiss on his cheek. She and Herb then stepped into the portal for the trip through the saltwater filled hallways. Both of them slipped on their envirofield suits to supply oxygen then closed the door facing Carrie so they could flood the compartment and enter the ship.

Carrie sat back and brought up a projection provided by the cameras that were mounted on the shoulders of Eini's and Herb's outfits. She watched as the two proceeded down a barely lit corridor— it did appear that the ship was in some sort of standby mode.

*

As the two made their way, they found various Kevorkians floating in the water, apparently in the stasis state Tachymus had advised he was placing all the ship's occupants in. They also noted damage to parts of the ship's interior from battles between Alliance members, along with a few dead Kevorkians with large holes burnt through their bodies. Arriving at the bridge, they swam around, trying to understand what they were looking at. Herb located a ship layout image and when he uttered the word, "Tachymus", the display lit up with the Kevorkian's office location. They changed course.

Arriving at their destination, they found the door to Tachymus's office blown open. Eini said, "Prepare yourself, this doesn't look good." Herb nodded grimly, then said, "I believe we now know what the source of that explosion was at the end of his earlier transmission." Inside, they found more dead Kevorkians

230

floating around, none that were Tachymus. They looked around his office, but there was no sign of him.

Herb asked, "I wonder if he was taken prisoner? And where would they have taken him?"

Eini said, "Well, we can't cover the entire ship, it's gigantic. Let's look around the nearby area." They began their second search. Further down the hallway, they finally located the rest of the assault team and Tachymus. The team was in stasis, Tachymus was not but he was badly wounded and had attached himself to a computer wall panel of some sort, the connection glowing dimly.

Herb swam up to the Kevorkian and touched him. Tachymus linked with him without moving. He said, "Herb. I hoped you would arrive in time. I haven't got long."

Herb said, "What can I do?"

"Nothing for this body. My link with the others is severed due to my injuries. Only your close proximity allows me to communicate with you. We will need your help, my friend, to get us back online." Tachymus began dumping garbled information on Herb. It was obvious the Kevorkian was fading fast. He then changed topics, "Also, you should know… that Xeon is on his way to reactivate Chaos… on Mars…" The link from his head to the panel that had been dimly lit suddenly went dark.

That was it. Herb tried for the next half hour to get a telepathic session. Eini finally said, "He's gone Herb. Looking at his injuries, it's amazing he lasted until we got here."

Herb sighed, "Should we take him with us?"

Eini said, "Let's move him back to the bridge conference room. We can't deal with him now, but we can have a crew return with us soon to take care of his remains."

"I suppose you are right. Let's go." They moved Tachymus back to the conference room then headed back to the stump-ray. Eini sat next to Herb on the return trip, their flingers intertwined.

*

231

When the Kevorkians had gone into stasis, a nude Jesmyn and Mimi rematerialized back on Mars—Jesmyn guessed that their outfits had been a holographic construct, just like the environments they had been placed in—they now found themselves facing each other on the same CC2 beach where Mimi had been shipped off to purgatory. Jesmyn, not shy at all about her appearance, having spent so much to maintain it over the decades, didn't care about her nudity and the weather inside the envirofield was quite obliging.

Mimi walked over to Jesmyn as she said, "There were some clothing stores up by the Chateau. Let's see what's going on." The two women set off. They first stopped at the chateau, where they found no Kevorkians or humans, but everything appeared to be online and working. Kevorkian modifications had apparently never been implemented in the establishment. So Jesmyn located some keycards for two rooms. The women agreed they would get cleaned up, meet back in the lobby in an hour and go looking for clothing stores.

They returned wearing the hotel supplied bathrobes and slippers located in their quarters. At the three remaining human clothing stores they visited, the two outfitted themselves in attires hanging on the racks along with pilfering as many spare outfits as they could find. They returned to the hotel and dumped their bounty, then went in search of food. In the Chateau kitchen, they were able to whip up a decent synthesized meal of steak, scallop potatoes and Caesar salad. Mimi located some Bordeaux at the bar and for the first time in months, they actually enjoyed eating what was in front of them. As they ate, Mimi said, "So, where are the damn aliens?"

Jesmyn shrugged, "No idea. And where are all my people? We need to get a handle on what is going on with this damn planet as well as back on Earth as quick as possible."

Mimi agreed, so after the meal, they located a stump-ray that belonged to the hotel and set off on a reconnaissance flight. Nowhere did they find any sign of life. They flew over the expanded inland sea that the Kevorkians had been working on after their takeover along with the modifications to homes and businesses. They detected no activity of any kind. They discovered several abandoned stump-rays. Mimi flew one of them back to the hotel so that they each had one. Jesmyn later was able to bring some AIGS AI systems back online. She tapped into the history files and from there, they were able to see where the Kevorkians had taken over, made all humans leave the planet and were making plans to establish Mars as their own alien world along with Earth.

*

The brief funeral service, sans body, was held for Tachymus and was transmitted across the Solarspere as a calculated move. Along with the funeral itself came the announcement of President Herb Coulick, the successor to the fallen Kevorkian and a new world government with a plan to restore the planet. The plan included well-paying jobs for all who could work. Those that could not work would be taken care of. The New Deal Planet Earth Recovery program was underway.

Herb and Eini had focused their plan to trash the Kevorkian's efforts and introduce a more benign, planet friendly leadership approach to Earth. Part of that strategy was how to better govern an unruly species, namely, humans. It was Herb that mentioned reading about "The New Deal", from back in the 1930's under the former U.S. president, Franklin Delanor Roosevelt. They both realized he was on to something and they seized upon the idea as they modeled various new programs in a similar way. The day arrived to implement their new paradigm for the planet. Eini had earlier articulated the idea to Celeste and Carrie, who enthusiastically agreed.

The best news the program was promoting to the public was that the serf-industry was totally abolished, all people were lifted out of poverty, community housing was to be provided where needed, along with all the basic necessities. With the overall conditions of the planet improving, things began to look upbeat to the general public.

233

The campaign slogan was "No One Left Behind" in this new world order. Projects were underway all over the planet for education, housing, food and other basic necessities.

Celeste tracked and reported progress to the new Presidential council and found various local governments were cooperating better than expected since the restoration projects kept people busy in their respective geographies as well was improving the overall living conditions of their constituents.

This left Herb to be formally sworn in as president. The ceremony was set at the formerly abandoned Buckingham palace in London. Locals were hired to bring the place up to snuff, i.e., brush off the cobwebs, slather on some paint, but only as much as it took to get the event completed. Still, a festive atmosphere prevailed in England. Herb wrote his own speech. The suit that Eini had ordered for him sported the new lapel pin of "United Earth". Ben and Alex were similarly outfitted. Security was kept at a high level upon their arrival; however, people were enthusiastically lining the streets to be part of the event. It was clear things had taken a turn for the better on planet Earth.

The lineup for the ceremony was Herb at the dais, Ben and Carrie on his left, Celeste and Alex on his right. Eini and Jaime had elected to remain off to the side to ensure they could keep track of events and issues as needed. With the crowd of spectators now focusing on him, Herb stepped up to the dais and began his speech, "I welcome all of you today who are in attendance as I take my solemn oath to support and defend the new global constitution that our planetwide government is based on." He then made his way through the speech, pausing at key points to smile, appear serious, or appropriately nod to various dignitaries and attendees in the front row seating. There was a momentum in Herb's delivery, and at the conclusion, a roar went up from the crowd, "President Coulick!"

Afterwards, Eini and Herb breathed a sigh of relief as they headed back to the Distainien/Dolphmanien Pacific compound while the others decided to tour historic London.

Chapter 32

A week later in New York, the Trio, (a name Eini had suggested), met up for a morning breakfast on the top floor of the rebuilt Empire State Building. At a conference table, the women had spent the last hour viewing clips of Herb's various stops around the planet to meet with people. It had gone far better than expected and the public really liked the Dolphmanien. Eini was quite pleased as the plan that she and Herb had worked so hard to put together was going well—the opportunity for education, meaningful, quality work and a decent lifestyle for all. It generated enormous acceptance by many who had long been ignored. The formerly oligarch class were not enthralled, but since they were allowed to keep their homes and were offered large stipends to keep them sidelined and it beat the alternate scenario that had been explained to them that would involve actually working for a living or going to jail for inciting insurrection. To ensure they behaved, security detachments had been assigned to keep an eye on them.

Jamie then arrived to deliver a briefing on various projects as well as their ongoing efforts to extract important technologies from the orbiting Kevorkian starship and bring that tech to Earth for their own use. One significant part of that was the same tech the Kevorkians had used to feed humans in captivity back on Mars was now being used to develop food and liquor generation devices that people could have in their own homes. These new machines produced pretty much whatever sort of meal or booze one wanted to ensure everybody ate well or got sloshed whenever they felt like it, (there was a soft drink option for the kids as well that Herb had insisted on). Her status report completed, Jamie departed. Eini then brought up the next big agenda item which was Mars. Since the collapse of the Kevorkians, the planet had gone completely silent, and it was beyond time to send a team in to see what the situation was on the red planet. Mars could certainly be leveraged to help out Earth, and they could even convert it to support larger human populations now that they had their new alien technology windfall.

Eini said, "My thoughts are that we do need to go back to Mars, though not immediately. With the starship technology extraction work we are doing we will probably be busy for quite some time. Our oceans particularly need attention from the environmental perspective."

Celeste said, "I tend to agree, though I have concerns about what might be going on since the Kevorkian meltdown." Carrie nodded in agreement. The discussion continued as Eini guided them through the pros and cons. Everyone agreed to focus on Earth first, then go to Mars later as a major extension of what they were doing on Earth. The conclusion of the meeting was that they all agreed they needed to know the actual situation on the red planet, therefore an expedition ship would be sent out for that purpose in the near future.

*

Herb arrived for the upcoming "Q and A" with the Trio. It was always a tricky business that he and Eini had to navigate. For one, the time for Carrie to be directly involved in his and Eini's lives had come to an end. Carrie would be reassigned to a task that kept her happy that also allowed them to keep precise track of her. Another challenge. He and Eini had decided before going through these briefing sessions with the Trio, he would not lie about anything. It was more of a selective truth telling exercise to drive the narrative they were creating. This coincided with the new Mars survey team that was being put together to gather intelligence about the situation there since the collapse of the Kevorkians. Plus, the telepathic dump Tachymus had done just before he had expired indicated that Xeon was already headed to Mars to resurrect some version of Chaos and that was a real problem.

237

Eini was aware of the dangers as well and earlier had said, "We have got to shut this down. It is a top priority now." He had agreed, though they both felt it was better to not tell Celeste and Carrie. All of this had led him to want to lead a team to help get that effort going since his world tour was now completed.

Herb replied, "That's why I need to be the one to go to Mars."

They dug into the topic, and she finally reluctantly agreed. He had read her thoughts about her unease at the whole idea of him going on the mission. So now was the moment. Herb entered the room and exchanged pleasantries then took a seat.

Eini nodded and said, "Anything to report?"

He shook his head and said, "Nothing you don't already know, things are going well. So, I have an idea and I need you three to support me on it as well."

Carrie said, "What would that be?"

Herb said, "Let me lead the Mars discovery team we are all are thinking about sending out." He paused to let that sink in, then added, "In fact, I think we can use it to further encourage humanity. They need inspiration and lots of it to keep from sinking into the brine that leads to competition, wars, and plain old NIMBY. You know how humans, I mean people, can be."

Carrie looked confused and asked, "What the hell is NIMBY?"

"Ah. Old Earth saying I ran across. It means *Not in my back yard.*"

Eini shook her head in agreement and said, "He has a great point."

Celeste was still unconvinced. She said, "So, Herb, please, give us a few moments to confer with each other in private."

He stood, nodded, then stepped out into the hall.

He could not make out much of what was being said, but his telepathic link to Eini indicated she was working the other two and to let her focus. He replied. "I'll shut up for now." She answered, "I still hate to see you go so far away though I know it is needed."

Twenty minutes later, he was called back into the meeting.

Eini said, "Herb, we are good with you going, though one of us has to go with you. We agreed it should be Carrie. If you consent to those terms and promise to continue to function as President Coulick when in public, you can go to Mars."

Herb smiled and replied, "Very well. You won't regret this."

Eini said, "There's always some form of self-sacrifice to make this sort of thing happen for the many." The double meaning in her words did not escape Herb. Carrie stood and said, "Come on Herb. Let's go get a couple of those fancy Lattes and we can talk." She then hooked an arm around his and they headed to the breakroom.

Herb figured Carrie was the perfect choice for this mission. She was smart and had shown on Mars she could get things done. This might also be the Carrie exit strategy that he and Eini needed. Over the next ten days, Carrie and Herb met daily to work on the mission plan. During this same time, Herb also privately engaged with the brain liberated Dolphmaniens that had come up to speed on all the Kevorkian's technology and were working on some novel upgrades that only he, Eini, and their small team were aware of.

*

Flying around Mars a few days later, Jesmyn spotted a compound unlike any of the human settlements on the planet. She had Mimi join her to investigate. It was obvious once they scanned the location that it was Kevorkian designed and constructed. This was also when they located a lot of the aliens in some semi-dead state—what Jesmyn called "Suspended animation".

Mimi had asked, "So what the fuck is that?"

Jesmyn, tired of explaining her often off the top of her head thoughts, quipped, "They aren't moving?"

Later, they sat down at the Chateau to process what they had learned. Their best guess—the suspended condition of the aliens and their systems had somehow led to the two of them being returned

239

from their imprisonment. Jesmyn speculated, "It must have been some sort of failsafe in their tech that returned us?"

Mimi shrugged and said, "That's good enough for me, though it raises the question—what the hell is going on back on Earth?"

Jesmyn said, "Been wondering about that myself. And it's time to find out." In agreement for a change, the two began snooping for intel.

It turned out that Mimi, besides her musical background, had become adept at hacking into systems during her "activist terrorist" days and before long, they were looking through Solarspere systems back on Earth. From there they learned how the Kevorkians had subjugated the population and put the dolphmanien, Herb, in charge. But then the alien reign there collapsed. Reason unknown, though Jesmyn said, "This seems to line up with what we've seen here. I'm just not any clearer as to why this happened."

They then learned about "President Coulick" and the new planetary government. Jesmyn frowned as Mimi recalled her previous positive involvement with Herb. Then excitedly, Mimi said, "Whoa, look at this!" She had discovered "The Trio". Jesmyn growled, "Now this makes more sense." Mimi said nothing, though she suspected that what Jesmyn saw in the Trio were people that were greedy and powerful, reflecting her own behavior. However, as Mimi read further about the three women and Herb, she found nothing indicating a problem, in fact, it looked like Earth might finally be on a better track to the future.

As their efforts for the day wound down, they agreed their intelligence on the current situation on Earth was somewhat up to date but far from complete. Mimi then noted, "They don't know about us being back in the world."

Jesmyn nodded and said, "And they are headed here to survey the planet with a scouting mission. We should prepare a warm welcome. Also, we need to understand more about how they are using Kevorkian technology. That is an advantage we don't have at the moment." Mimi offered to keep going through the data.

Jesmyn said, "Let's pull in some analystbots as well to help. They can read through data far faster than we can if you properly program them. I will get some of the critters back online that I saw dumped in a room off the lobby."

Chapter 33

Carrie was keeping the Trio up to date on engineering and production progress as well as thinking she was keeping Herb distracted with sex and compliments, while at the same time, Herb was keeping Eini briefed on Carrie activities. At the moment, to her, Herb appeared to be occupied while supervising LoadBots that were storing provisions aboard their recently completed ship, the Solar Voyager. The sleek craft was loaded with upgraded Kevorkian technology that included a much more powerful drive system that would keep their travel time to Mars down to just two weeks. Human engineers now worked under the supervision of the same dolphmaniens that Herb had been mentoring over the last few weeks.

Located in a new production plant in San Diego, California, the team of dolphmanien engineers, all technically reporting to Carrie, (but in reality to Herb), were able to reproduce and upgrade Kevorkian technologies that drove the continued tech revolution racing over the Earth, gradually changing it back to its more habitable state of a pre-industrial climate.

Two larger versions of the Solar Voyager were being completed as well, the beginning of a new fleet of spacecraft. The plan was if they found other Kevorkian tech of interest on Mars, they could dispatch the new ships and begin carting off whatever they needed. Along with that, came the assessment of what else could be done to the red planet itself to make it support more life. Carrie hoped they would resume terraforming it. She secretly wanted her own planetary empire and as the Trio's plan appeared to be moving along quite well, she sensed opportunity to step away when the right moment presented itself.

Curious about Herb's progress, she strolled over to check in on him. He had his back to her and from a distance as she approached, she could see him pointing here and there to the LoadBots. She giggled to herself—the man never changed. The LoadBots were programmed to know where everything needed to go.

When she walked up behind him, she reached out and tickled him on both sides, making him jump away and he began laughing. When he settled down, she said, "How's it going?"

Herb, acting clueless, replied, "On schedule my dear. This direction pad I have here was a great idea. I've got this crew loading the ship at a premium pace." She nodded and smiled and said, "Wow! Hey, let's get some lunch." Herb said, "You read my mind," as he read hers—the woman still believed she was managing him.

They strolled off, her arm around his waist, as he called back to the LoadBots, "Take a break. We'll be back in an hour or so." He was well aware that the bots would stop where they were until the two were out of sight, then resume their activities as he had programmed them to do.

They climbed in his stump-ray and headed for Earl's. The place was an old fashioned Googie designed grill that had been moved from Los Angeles down to San Diego. Once they were seated in one of the booths along a row of windows, Herb asked, "You excited about this trip? I sure am."

Carrie nodded and said, "Yeah, actually I am. Looking forward to doing something on our own for a change."

As Herb nodded, she decided it might be a good time to work on furthering her own ambition. She said, "What if we could get a place there? On Mars? We could make it like a vacation home."

Herb nodded, and added, "I kind of like that idea. We could also resume some of the work we were doing on Cape Cod II."

Carrie replied, "I like this idea!"

"Great! Can I ask you a question?"

"Sure."

"You happy with your situation?"

"Pretty much, but I have ambitions."

"So, what if you took over the Mars projects. You could work with a lot of autonomy."

Carrie grinned and said, "You kind of read my mind."

Herb was smiling back as he said, "What do you think about some after lunch sexanigans?" She raised an eyebrow, grinned, and said, "I like this idea even more!", again thinking to herself, *Good thing the guy is insatiable. It keeps him distracted.* Herb was really smart, but she had believed if she kept his mind where she wanted it to be, like focused on her body, he could be easily manipulated, and she did enjoy her time with him—he had become a skillful lover.

Carrie said, "I just found out some actual shenanigans is going on. I discovered that data about our activities was being reviewed by unauthorized users. Somebody is gathering intel, and that it is most likely from Mars."

Herb asked, "Jesmyn?"

She said, "Probably."

Herb said, "How about we begin feeding new disinformation into that data stream. I have a few ideas in that regard."

Carrie giggled and replied, "This should be fun!"

*

The alliance between Mimi and Jesmyn had rapidly degraded. Disagreements started when Jesmyn had mentioned, almost in passing, that Mars was still her property, part of the original deal she made when Angela Koutouki departed decades ago to set up shop with the creation of TGIF on Earth. The comment reminded Mimi why she had originally despised Jesmyn for the way the woman had destroyed her career as a musician. All those negative feelings came rushing back. She now wondered how she could even have forgotten how awful Jesmyn was and vowed to herself that it was finally time to relegate AIGS to history.

For her part, Jesmyn had recently moved back into her mansion by the sea. She had taken the analystbots with her and programmed them to provide only her with intelligence data. This

244

morning, she was in a meeting with these bots to discuss the latest intel. She nodded to the appointed lead analyst bot and said, "Update. When are we predicting they will arrive?" The one she had cynically nicknamed "LeadAnalBot" replied, "We believe that it will take approximately four weeks."

"Why so long? I thought they had alien drive tech now."

"We don't believe the humans have it is as fully integrated into the ships systems as it needs to be. It may even take them longer. The data appears sound and we can provide that detail if you require it."

Jesmyn nodded and said, "No, I'm fine. So, we have plenty of time to prepare for their arrival. Good. Listen, LeadAnalBot, have your underlings leave, we need to talk in private."

LeadAnalBot rotated its artificial "eyes" around the round sphere that comprised an approximation of a head and nodded to the other analystbots. They immediately departed.

She stood after the bot's departure and looked out the window towards CC2. It was a beautiful, if artificial view, still part of her grand vision for the planet. She decided she needed to go for a swim, to spend a day with her creation. She advised LeadAnalBot, "Get my yacht out of storage mister! I am going out on the water for an afternoon of fun in the sun!"

*

Xeon had been enroute to Mars when Tachymus invoked the complete stasis shutdown of the starship and Mars based Kevorkians. He was the sole exception as he was no longer infected and on a mission.

At that time, he lost contact with the Mars colony, the Kevorkian Starship as well as his old friend. He suspected what had happened throughout the Alliance based on his own time in stasis, so his voyage took on a new urgency as he continued on to Mars to locate Chaos. He needed an ally, and time was of the utmost priority at this point.

As he approached the planet, he detected two life signs on the surface, one located by the lodgings and shopping area the humans had built by CCII. He recognized their bio signatures—these were the two human females that had been placed in Kevorkian lockup. One human was at the Chateau, the other located at the private mansion of the female known as Jesmyn.

To ensure he avoided detection, Xeon maneuvered his ship around to the far side of CCII and entered unobserved into the sea near the repair facility where Chaos had previously been undergoing repairs.

Chapter 34

It was time for the survey trip to Mars to begin though the event was very low key, since it was essentially a secret mission. Still, they had all gotten together for brunch. At the moment, Celeste, Jamie and Eini were all waving to Herb and Carrie as they boarded. Herb and Carrie gave a departing wave back, then disappeared into the ship. The hatch slid shut behind them and moments later, the spacecraft lifted off and accelerated into space.

After changing into their "space uniforms" that Herb had designed for everyone on board, Carrie headed to the bridge, which was suspiciously laid out to resemble an old sci-fi TV series configuration. When Herb showed up a few minutes later, he plunked himself down in the raised center chair, and said, "Sorry, was having a last minute meeting with the engineers", which were the same Dolphmaniens crew he had been working with on the ship buildout as well as other projects and were now coming along to Mars. Herb's excuse for bringing them along had been if they needed someone who could easily dive into the Kevorkian underwater city and that it made good sense to have these crew members along.

Carrie walked over to what Herb referred to as the "science station", though one could perform the same functions from just about anywhere on the ship since multiple levels of redundancy was a requirement for a vessel that could be millions of kilometers from any repair center.

In front of Herb was Harper Leventhal, whose job officially was to be the new helmsman. Herb smiled at Carrie and said, "Helmsman Leventhal! Prepare to leave orbit and lay in a course for Mars!"

Harper nodded and said, "Sure Captain. But can't we just go by first names? I mean, it is a long trip." She and Carrie giggled.

Herb joked, "Wow, is this a mutiny? We just got into orbit!"

Carrie walked over to him and said, "Calm down El Capitaine!"

Herb grinned, nodded and said, "Well, okay, if I must!"

With that, Harper laid in a course for Mars. Herb watched the two women in front of him, remembering how Harper had suddenly bubbled up for this mission, via a reference from Carrie. He had then asked Eini to do a bit of research on this candidate. As it turned out, it didn't take long to figure out the connection. Per her usual modus operandi, Carrie had not bothered to mention why she had selected Harper—the two were former comrades from her TGIF operative days prior to her disastrous Mars mission. It had been a few years since they had last worked together, but when Harper had applied for the position posted simply as "pilot" on the TGIF Solarspere, Carrie had already primed the woman to be on the lookout for the position. Then, Carrie had told Herb she had somehow spotted Harper amongst the thousands of applicants, (interesting jobs off the planet were still a rare commodity on Earth), and recommended her to Herb. He and Eini decided to go along with the recommendation as they knew Harper needed watching just as much as Carrie to see what the two were scheming.

*

Mimi was on her way to her destination with an asteroid trader's vessel, having liberated one of the many stump-rays sitting abandoned down on the surface. She was quite pleased with herself on the deal she had made to get back to Earth by providing musical entertainment for an asteroid freighter crew. Being around Jesmyn had become too big a burden and this trip sure beat the hell out of the purgatory she had been in. Once she met up and boarded the freighter, one of the crew members, a self-declared fan, recognized Mimi. As she settled into her quarters, the old ship lurched into motion as it resumed its course to Earth.

*

248

Jesmyn was in an upbeat mood with the departure of McCartney. When Jesmyn realized the woman's objective was to leave Mars for Earth, she assisted by bribing the freighter captain to accept the music performance deal. She laughed to herself, thinking this was surely one of the better trips this asteroid belt crew would ever be on. With Mimi now out of the way, it was a matter of waiting on the arrival of the Earth ship that was headed to Mars so she could capture the crew and perform some advanced interrogation work. She had LeadAnalBot working on that angle—plus it was time for another briefing on the Earth vessel that was coming.

Jesmyn queried, "What are you working on?"

LeadAnalBot replied, "I was calculating the course, speed and arrival time of the approaching ship, based on intel."

Jesmyn nodded and then asked, "Who's on board? How well armed are they?", along with other questions she felt were pertinent to the preparations. LeadAnalBot seemed to be lacking some vital information as no crew had been identified as well as any other vital data. She sighed and decided to arm up for the worst and left him further instructions to "get your ass ready!" then departed.

LeadAnalBot turned to the other robots and said, "I have no ass to get ready. Opinions?" A highly technical discussion broke out between the bots on how to acquire a fully prepared ass.

*

Carrie was sitting at her station on the bridge when a low priority alert appeared. An elderly spacecraft was moving at a fraction of their speed but in their general direction. After a short scan and breaking into the ship's logs, she saw it had been in earlier communication with Mars. She flagged Herb over to her station and said, "Whoa. This is interesting!"

Herb leaned forward in his seat and said, "I'm all ears, proceed commander."

Carrie gave him an amused expression though he apparently was ignoring her as he was watching the view screen in front of him.

She responded, "The approaching ship appears to have a well-known celebrity on it."

Herb now swung his attention to Carrie and said, "And that is?"

"Mimi McCartney. On course for Earth."

Herb nodded, "Battle stations!"

"What for? The ship is so far away, they don't even know we are here. We just have way better scanning ability than that ancient freighter."

Herb frowned and said, "Where's your sense of humor? I'm just kidding!"

Carrie sighed as she said to Harper, "Wanna grab some coffee?" Harper nodded and the two exited the bridge together. Herb leaned back and smiled to himself as he had earlier been notified by one of the Dolphmanien engineers about what was going on with the freighter well before Carrie made her announcement.

*

Once the two women were seated in the breakroom that had a nice forward viewport, Harper said, "What are we going to do about this McCartney woman?"

"Nothing. She's a nobody. I know from Herb that Mimi was on Mars and the Kevorkians made her disappear like they did Jesmyn. All of this stuff was just before the great exodus was ordered by the Kevorkians. We need to be ready for just about anything when we arrive because if Mimi is out and about, so is Jesmyn. I'm going to let Celeste and Eini know the woman is headed to Earth. Probably be at least five more weeks before that old ship gets there, so plenty of time to prepare."

Harper nodded, then said, "We should be on Mars in about two more days."

Carrie said, "Now that will be when we need to go to battle stations."

250

Harper chuckled and said, "Herb is smart and cute, but he says a lot of silly stuff."

Carrie nodded then added, "But he's good in the sack." The two women laughed and continued discussing their eminent arrival on the red planet.

*

Herb leaned back in his chair after the women left the bridge and activated an ear pod he had inserted in his left ear. The device was tied into the comms systems and allowed him to listen to discussions anywhere on the ship. The latest was the Carrie and Harper conversation. He immediately transmitted an encrypted update to Eini.

*

Back on Earth, Celeste and Eini were reviewing the information Carrie had provided on Mimi. Eini was also carefully comparing the information to what Herb had sent her. Celeste said, "Well, Carrie thinks Jesmyn is back in action on Mars. We'll let her handle that end of it."

Eini noticed how, once again, Herb never came up in any of Celeste's recommendations of who did what. She asked, "I see. So, what about Mimi?"

"Small potatoes, though she can be a pain in the ass. I am thinking of offering her old job and a new band to get her out of the terrorist/activist crap she formerly pontificated about on the Solarspere."

Eini cynically grinned then said, "Loses her profession and gets all upset. Wow! Humans are kind of fucked up, aren't they? No offense intended."

Distracted, Celeste nodded absently, "None taken. Yep, we can be pretty weird. So, if she accepts that, one less thing to deal with."

251

Chapter 35

Jesmyn was surprised when she learned from LeadAnalBot that the Earth survey ship had arrived ahead of schedule and she was forced to scramble preparations to deal with the situation just as Herb and Carrie were going into orbit around Mars. Taking a deep breath, she figured she would disable the thing, interrogate the crew, then she would make sure she fully hacked back into all the AIGS systems which would get her empire back under her total control. She was a moment away from giving the go order that would kick off the fireworks by her bot-based force she now had in place. She could really use some groupies to bolster her, but that would have to wait until she was fully back in control.

*

Back on Earth, Celeste and Jamie were having dinner at Scarpetta's. Ben, Alex and Josh had just arrived as well, taking some time off from their various projects. Eini had not yet arrived, having said she would be late. It had been a long but satisfying day as Celeste had sent a ship to intercept the asteroid freighter way before it got to Earth and they now had Mimi accommodated in a nice studio they had set up as well as secretly under guard in the Empire State Building HQ.

*

The recently replicated Tachymus and Xeon were considering their options. Tachymus was back up to speed after having his memories uploaded by his old friend. A hologram of Chaos was on their screen as well. Tachymus said, "This has been quite a journey for all of us. Chaos are we set?"

Chaos nodded and replied, "We are. Shall we begin?"

Tachymus replied, "Certainly!"

With a look of concentration on his AI generated features, Chaos began transmitting through the Solarspere infrastructure. His face appeared simultaneously in front of Jesmyn, Herb and Carrie, and finally the now somewhat tipsy Scarpetta's dinner party.

He began with "Ah, my old adversaries. How are all of you doing?' His volume level was so loud that he shattered the elegant wine glasses at Scarpetta's making the dinner party scatter away from their table and out onto the street. The volume level left Jesmyn with a stunned expression on her face. On their ship, Harper and Carrie were having a similar reaction. Herb, however, remained expressionless. He nodded to one of the dolphmanien engineers to crank the volume down.

Chaos continued, "I am happy to announce you will be finding your Kevorkian superiors are back, and you are all about to lose any positions of importance in your respective worlds. Hope you enjoy the fruits of your labors!"

With that, the Earth orbiting Kevorkian ship partially came back online, though it was highly compromised in functionality, (there were a lot of missing components that had been removed to help the restoration of Earth) just as Xeon docked with the starship. Tachymus rapidly boarded, immediately surrounded by resurrected alien associates, their chaotic thoughts gone. He swam onto his bridge and was now tied into Chaos's video feed. He said, "Hey there President Coulick! Thanks for sorta halfass, okay, not really, trying to help. You stopped well short of a real effort and left us hanging when I died the first time. I foolishly figured you would try to do more, but you didn't. In fact, it seems our ship is a mess with all the missing parts! Thankfully, Chaos came through for us after humans had attempted to destroy him. And yes, Chaos remembers that."

Herb now smiled, and said, "How are you Tachymus? Should I call you junior, the second, or…and inferior replacement?"

Tachymus appeared briefly confused at Herb's barbed comment but continued, "Better intelligence through wiser algorithms Herb. Bitwa!"

Jesmyn angrily interjected, "That's AIGS patented!"

Tachymus said, "Oh, right! Enjoy your trailer park dear!" Jesmyn was again standing nude outside her old trailer she had grown up in. She screamed, "Fuck no, not again!"

At the same moment, Eini arrived at Scarpettas as Tachymus continued, "Oh, and Herb, nothing beats a good backup of one's brain. The rest was just growing the new body, which Xeon managed while he brought our alliance back online."

Eini said, "Tachymus. You should carefully consider your next actions. And quit treating us like slaves, you know intelligent species are more deserving than that!"

Tachymus went silent for a moment, then continued with, "Hmm, you have a point Eini, though are humans intelligent? We will send you two out to your Pacific island with your Distainien and half breed Dolphmanien kind until I can review what should be done about your traitorous species. And yes, we figured out what you really are, thanks to Xeon!"

He then nodded to Chaos, but nothing happened to either Eini or Herb. Not aware his last order had failed, Tachymus said, "Now, for the rest of you, on your way back to Slab city! Much work to be done by your team cleaning up that mess you humans specialize in making. You know, manual labor sort of stuff. Then back to Miami for the ultimate shit detail! We'll be in touch!" Again, nobody went anywhere. Chaos stuttered "I...am deactivating?" Suddenly, the gravity of the situation settled in on the Kevorkians as Chaos's hologram began vibrating violently then disappeared.

Eini then said, "Herb, shall we now proceed?

Herb nodded grimly and said, "Tachymus, a change of plans. We will be in contact soon with *your* new assignments." With that, the Kevorkian ship unceremoniously shut back down, Chaos was totally deactivated and Eini was now on the bridge of Herb's ship pulling on a uniform that Herb had thoughtfully brough with him. Tachymus was there as well, in a confinement chamber that had appeared around him.

Herb walked over and said, "So, here we are. While you were away, Eini uncovered a lot more facts about how your alliance treated our Distainien ancestors as serfs and an inferior species. She educated me in your misdeeds. It seems we were smarter, in the end, than either yourselves or that AI monstrosity buddy of yours. So now, we begin a new era."

Tachymus shook his head, while flapping his tentacles in obvious confused frustration as he declared, "Distainiens! I detest you all! We will…"

"Fahgetaboutit Tachy! You work for us now. Plus, Xeon is back in stasis on your old starship along with the rest of the Kevorkians. Anyway, we'll talk later." Tachymus instantly went into stasis and Herb turned to Eini. They hugged and he said, "I really missed you woman."

*

Eini and Herb were back in the Dolphmanien enclave where they brought Tachymus out of stasis inside a large swimming pool at one of the condos. Both were in the water with the Kevorkian as he regained consciousness. Eini said, "Welcome Tachymus." The Kevorkian spun around to face her. Herb was several meters away to her left and added, "Morning dude."

Tachymus said, "What am I doing here? Where is my ship? And what makes you think I want to talk with you?" The Kevorkian was visibly trembling with anger and to some extent, fear, as his tentacles and eyestalks thrashed about in agitation.

Eini said, "I suggest we all remain calm and discuss the new paradigm that all of us are in."

Tachymus exclaimed, "We will defeat you! Just wait until we are all back online!"

255

Herb laughed and said, "Dude, that is not going to happen. We defeated *you* without firing a shot. We have reversed engineered all your technology and have already upgraded your old tech with features and functionality you simply don't have. Our Distainien and Dolphmanien allies have been working on this for months while your alliance took a nap! You need to be reasonable."

Tachymus finally shuddered himself to a stop, now sounding subdued. He said, "So, you defeated us. Then why am I even here? Why not be done with us and send the whole Alliance off to oblivion and death?"

Eini said, "We considered that option. But we are civilized."

"A weakness of Distainien character, apparently that made it into you… half breeds."

Herb said, "And with that comment, therein lies the problem with your so-called *alliance*. You take a choice and assign it as a trait of the species that lives by that choice. We know that our ancestors did much to get your original coalition of species underway, but the worst of your members wanted power. People like you apparently. And look where you wound up? In a swimming pool!"

Tachymus, quite agitated, said, "I see no further reason to talk."

Eini nodded and said, "You know Herb, I agree with Tachymus, this is a total waste of time." She blinked and Tachymus was back in stasis in his containment field.

The next day, with Celeste tagging along in an envirosuit, Eini and Herb brought Tachymus out of stasis on the bridge of his own starship. Herb said, "The vote is in dude. Kevorkians will shortly be on the way to another viable star system that you will be able to develop as you wish. It has all the elements needed for life but no active lifeforms. Should be perfect for your purposes."

Tachymus said, "How could you possibly know that?"

Eini said, "As we said in our earlier conversation, our Distainien/Dolphmanien alliance has used our expertise to implement and upgrade your technology for ourselves and the rest of this solar system. We obviously won't share any of this technology with you. However, your alliance of species will be fine. Just don't think about turning around and coming back."

Tachymus tentacles drooped as he replied, "Start over? Once again?"

Herb nodded and said, "Yeah, and we loaded the ship with all your people from out on Mars as well. We would love to have you as civilized neighbors… someday. Something for you Kevorkians to think about on your journey."

"Kiss my ass, Herb Coulick!"

"Do you have one?" Herb mocked as he glanced sidelong at Celeste, who had a repulsed look on her face. Eini said, "Just remember our warning. If you attempt to return with your current attitude, you will not like what happens next. And we'll be tracking you."

Tachymus waggled his tentacles to respond but before he could, he was back in stasis. Celeste giggled and said, "The way you all can turn him off and on again like a light switch, you would think Tachymus would realize it's time to behave." Moments later they departed the Kevorkian vessel. Now back on one of their own recently completed starships, they watched as the autopiloted Kevorkian vessel accelerated out of sight. Celeste declared, "Good riddance!"

Eini nodded in agreement. Herb then said, "How about dinner tonight at Scarpetta's? Celeste, have Jamie join us!" Celeste nodded, "Will do. And as Mimi McCartney now likes to sing, beats the hell out of purgatory!"